God Help Ye, Merry Gentleman

and Other Stories from the Family and Friends of
Toad Abersham and Sally Grenford and the Books of

Jude Knight and Mariana Gabrielle

God Help Ye, Merry Gentleman and Other Stories from the Family and Friends of Toad Abersham and Sally Grenford

Copyright 2017 Jude Knight and Mariana Gabrielle; published by Titchfield Press.

Print ISBN: 978-0-9951049-8-3

Graphics are public domain or used under Creative Commons licences, as noted.
God Help Ye, Merry Gentleman: Louise of Prussia, Grand Duchess of Baden, by Joseph Spelter
I: An Early Victorian, by William Logsdail
II: Portrait of a Man (possibly Alexander Boyd), 1845, Margaret Sarah Carpenter.
III: Reflection, by Jerry Barrett
IV: Contemplation, by Isaac Snowman
Prologue: Never Kiss a Toad: The Two Central Figures in 'Derby Day' by William Powell Frith; and Leinster House in Dublin, now the Irish Houses of Parliament, art print by James Malton
More Stories from the Childhoods of Toad Abersham and Sally Grenford: Untitled 2, by Erik Henningsen
A Toadstone for the King: Portrait of a Young Boy, by Therese Schwartze
Sally Falls Out of a Tree, and Toad Falls in Love: Dolly's Portrait, by Edith Scannell
A Ducal Daughter Demands a Liberal Education: Young Woman with Lace Shawl, by Adelaide Salles-Wagner
A Ducal Heir Follows in his Father's Rakish Footsteps: Portrait of Dominika Ieronima Radzivilla, by an unknown artist
Toad in France: Victorian Postcard
The Inception of Delphinus Shipping: Stockholm Fashion Journal: Magazine for the elegant world, 1847
The Christmas Letters: Lavacourt under Snow, by Claude Monet
Christmas 1841: Sally's letter to Toad: The Lady of the Snows, by George Henry Boughton
Christmas 1841: Toad's letter to Sally: Early Victorian Gentlemen, source unknown
Christmas 1842: Sally's letter to Toad: 1818 Regency Fashion Plate — Winter Carriage Dress (La Belle Assemblee Magazine)
Christmas 1842: Toad's letter to Sally: Early Victorian Gentlemen, source unknown
The Dukes and Duchesses: Silver-gilt coronet of the Duke of Portland, dated about 1820. Photographer unknown
The Infamous Rakes of Fickleton Wells: detail of James Grant of Grant, John Mytton, the Hon. Thomas Robinson, and Thomas Wynne, by Nathaniel Dance-Holland
The First Dance of the Duke and Duchess of Wellbridge: Victorian Couple Dancing, source unknown
The Duchess of Wellbridge's Start in Diplomacy: Portrait of a Young Woman with Roses in her Hair, by Friedrich Krepp
The Son of Privilege Meets the Son of Shame: A Noted Oyster Room near the Theatres, by Samuel Alken
A Gentleman is Never at a Loss: Naked Man Sleeping, by Jacques Dumont le Romain
Three Names in a Day: The Dressing of the Bride, by Carl Herpfer
Haverford's Courtship of His Cherry Followed a Bumpy Road: Edward Archer by Andrew Plimer and Portrait of Mrs. Allnutt by Sir Thomas Lawrence
Stories about Other Characters: A Garden Party at Holland House, by A. Hunt, published in the Illustrated London News, 1872
A Mother is Always Right: Still Life: Tea Set, by Jean-Étienne Liotard
Old Scandal Comes Home to Roost—and Inherit the Firthley Marquisate: William Spence, by William Thomas Fry
The first meeting between Firthley and Toad's Aunt Charlotte: Sophia Magdalena Cantzler, by Fredric Westin
The Scandal Keeping Gills Unmarriageable: Baron Schwiter, by Eugene Delacroix
Lord Coventon is provided a second son: Alexander Brullov (self-portrait)
Can Money and Wealthy Connections Buy a Respectable Groom? The Letter, by Vittorio Reggianini
Lady Athol Soddenfeld was Once a Darling Child: Portrait of Mariya Arkadyevna Bek with her Daughter, by Karl Bryullov
The Parents of Longford and Stocke Meet: September, by Edmund Blair Leighton
The Birth of Twins Brings Joy During a Difficult Time: Regency Couple at Tea, by Edmund Blair Leighton

Table of Contents

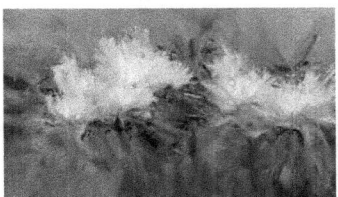

Non sum qualis eram bonae sub regno Cynarae
by Ernest Dowson

Last night, ah, yesternight, betwixt her lips and mine
There fell thy shadow, Cynara! thy breath was shed
Upon my soul between the kisses and the wine;
And I was desolate and sick of an old passion,
Yea, I was desolate and bowed my head:
I have been faithful to thee, Cynara! in my fashion.

All night upon mine heart I felt her warm heart beat,
Night-long within mine arms in love and sleep she lay;
Surely the kisses of her bought red mouth were sweet;
But I was desolate and sick of an old passion,
When I awoke and found the dawn was grey:
I have been faithful to thee, Cynara! in my fashion.

I have forgot much, Cynara! gone with the wind,
Flung roses, roses riotously with the throng,
Dancing, to put thy pale, lost lilies out of mind,
But I was desolate and sick of an old passion,
Yea, all the time, because the dance was long:
I have been faithful to thee, Cynara! in my fashion.

I cried for madder music and for stronger wine,
But when the feast is finished and the lamps expire,
Then falls thy shadow, Cynara! the night is thine;
And I am desolate and sick of an old passion,
Yea, hungry for the lips of my desire:
I have been faithful to thee, Cynara! in my fashion.

God Help Ye, Merry Gentleman

A Story from the Childhood of
Toad Abersham and Sally Grenford

I.

"Toad!" Sally Grenford jumped up and down in place as her friend, David Abersham, walked down the platform from the luggage car.

Her mother placed a hand on her arm. "Lady Sarah Grenford, restrain yourself. You are making a spectacle. You will not throw yourself at Wellbridge's heir. And must I again remind you to use proper address in social settings? His name is Lord Abersham; you are too old to be so familiar with a young man."

"But I haven't seen him for nine months!" Sally protested, then subsided at her mother's raised eyebrows. His parents were both inveterate travellers who owned, and frequently used, a frigate designed specifically for family journeys, but this trip to Europe after Toad's expulsion from Eton was the longest the two friends had ever been separated.

And Mama was not setting a good example, because as her godson walked up, doffing his hat to them, she smiled. "David, dear boy, it is good to have you home."

"Your Grace, my lady." He made his bow.

Sally took Toad's hand in both of hers and held it to her cheek. "Toad, I am so glad you are home. I missed you so dreadfully."

Toad gave her fingers a bit of a squeeze, but blushed as he murmured in her ear, "You aren't in short dresses anymore, Monkey, and this is a train station. You mustn't stand so close."

Ignoring his annoying lecture, she let his hand fall and made her curtsy, but when she tried to sidle closer to him again, Sally caught her mother's glare, and he admonished her: "Your presents are in my trunks with Meath, so you need not try to pick my pockets now."

Sally clapped her hands as she moved only a few inches away. "Presents!"

With a sideways glance at her mother, she added, "Only I am so pleased to have you home, Toad! I have so much to tell you You remember I wrote that

Papa had found a mathematics scholar to give me lessons now that I have so far outstripped my governess? Lady Lovelace recommended him, and told Papa I have an excellent understanding. Mr Galbraith has been teaching me quadratic equations. They are so fascinating, Toad! Did you know that—"

With a deep sigh, Mama chided, "He has barely stepped onto the platform. Do allow Lord Abersham to remove to the carriage before you inundate him with mathematical formulae."

Mama did not understand how wonderful numbers were, and how they could explain the whole world, if only one placed them in the right position and context. No one understood, except perhaps Lady Lovelace, who also saw their beauty, but had little time for a girl still in the schoolroom. Sally was certain Lady Lovelace was only humouring Sally because Papa had tried to help her mother mitigate the horrific scandal that fell upon anyone and anything Lady Lovelace's father ever touched. Even Sally had heard about Lord Byron, and no one ever told her anything she didn't ferret out herself.

"A better plan," Toad said, tweaking her nose, "do not force me to pretend I understand your equations, and so expose my intellectual deficiencies."

Once Toad had directed the porter to follow with his carpet bags, Sally tucked one hand under Toad's elbow, and wrapped the other around his forearm, pressing her chest to his arm and hoping he would notice how the shape had changed while he was away. His breath hitched, and he subtly shifted his body away, but he caressed her fingers with his other hand and gave her a soft smile. Then he held his other arm out for her mother. Sally stifled a scowl.

Pasting on a smile—boys like girls who smile—she danced about a bit, turning to show off her dress. "It is my first long dress, Toad. Mama let me wear it just to show you, even though Papa is still grumbling that I am too young and will not let me put my hair up yet. Is it not beautiful?"

With a smirk, he said, "It will make climbing trees difficult."

Sally hadn't thought of that, so she stopped walking for a second to consider it, yanking Toad and her mother to an abrupt stop a step ahead.

"I will thank you not to encourage her in things like tree-climbing, Abersham." Mama tugged at Toad and he tugged at Sally until they were three abreast again. "Our Sally is finding the road to ladyhood trying, I'm afraid."

With an older-and-wiser look on his smug face, Toad nodded gravely at Mama's pronouncement, as though he were any example of perfect company manners. A bit less smug when Mama added, with a deep sigh and a stern look, "Although you, Abersham, would undoubtedly be better off climbing trees and fishing in the river than the activities your father encourages."

And Sally's Papa, too, but Sally wasn't supposed to know that.

Chastened, but not quite contrite, Toad offered weakly, "Your dress is beautiful and so are you, Monkey Face. You have finally grown into your nose and ears. You shall be the terror of the *ton* in a few years' time."

With a glare exactly like her mother's, Sally said, "Just as you are the terror of the *demimonde*, having grown into your enormous co—?"

"Lady Sarah Grenford! Be silent," her mother commanded.

"Conceit, Mama. I was only going to say his enormous conceit. My nose and ears, indeed."

"Be nice, Monkey, or I will not give you your presents," Toad teased. "Ah, there is your coach. Excellent. Meath will come along with the luggage and the servants from Wellstone sent to open the house. Dalrymple House will have sent carriages for them." Toad greeted the Haverfords' driver by name, and helped the ladies into the carriage while the footmen secured his hand luggage. "Do you know if Etcetera is in London for his school break?"

Sally's cousin, Niko, whom Toad had nicknamed Etcetera, was his best friend from Eton, and they probably hadn't seen each other since Toad had been unceremoniously removed from school.

"He has not yet called at Haverford House, but yes, he is supposed to be staying with his brother in London for the holidays."

"Would you mind terribly if we stopped momentarily so I can leave my card? I wish to see him as soon as he is back in Town."

Sally stifled a sigh. Assuredly, he wished to see Niko so they could go out and cause trouble together.

"Of course, David. It is not at all an imposition, and Haverford will appreciate knowing if the boy has made it here safely."

As soon as they were settled and on their way, Toad said, "Thank you for meeting me. My parents and Almyra will come back to Town in a week or so, in time for the Yuletide season; my father has a touch of *la grippe*. But I haven't seen my friends in months. I wanted to spend at least a bit of time in London before I am packed off to school."

"I am so glad you have, Toad," Sally repeated. "It is so lovely to have you home."

"Yes, Lady Sarah, you have made your point," her mother admonished.

"Father told Mother I was a college man now," Toad straightened his shoulders, "so I should be allowed to come up to Town on my own if I wished." He seemingly couldn't help himself from preening, the self-centred nodcock. And was handsome even when he thought too much of himself.

"Has your travel remained uneventful since last you wrote, David?" Mama asked. "Nothing untoward occurred on the last of your sojourn?"

"Nothing eventful since we docked in Bristol. A sennight at Wellstone, and then here by carriage and train. But, Aunt Cherry, how can you imply no danger lurks for a ducal heir in the Courts of the Crowned Heads of Europe?" Toad said with a wink at Sally.

Mama chuckled, but Sally kept her lips tightly knit. It would not do to put forth her opinion that Toad was more dangerous to the noblewomen of Europe than they would ever be to him.

"Haverford is anticipating tales of your time as a courtier," Mama said. "It was he who pushed your parents to introduce you around the aristocracy now, while you are still young enough to be properly intimidated."

"Uncle Haverford seems to forget how many hours I spent dandling on Prinny's knee; I did not acquit myself poorly in Europe. But yes, I am a proper courtier now. I have made my bow to kings and queens and flirted with princesses in five different countries. Today, I am a man."

Toad laughed with an ironic twist to his lips, the only thing keeping him from looking and sounding like a pompous fool. Sally had to physically stop herself from snorting, and his quickly narrowed eyes showed he had noticed, even if her mother hadn't. When Mama turned away for a moment, he stuck his tongue out at her.

To disguise her giggle, ignoring her mother's sharp glances, Sally coughed and asked, "When must you go off to school, Toad?"

"I will leave after Twelfth Night, so about four weeks."

"That long? How wonderful!" Perhaps by then, he will have forgotten all the women he must have met on his travels.

Sally had guessed his expulsion from Eton had something to do with women, for otherwise he would have told her when she asked, and their parents wouldn't have stopped speaking about it every time she came in the room. And she had heard enough sharp asides from her mother and Aunt Bella to know his father and hers encouraged him in his pursuits, and neither duchess was pleased about it.

Nor was Sally. How could a girl like her compete with adult women? Beautiful women, who knew all the carnal mysteries from which she was excluded, and were prepared to share them?

The carriage hit a bump and Sally flew forward, grasping the strap on the wall for balance. Toad leaned forward to steady her, and his hand grazed her thigh. They both gasped and caught each other's eyes for an instant before they looked away.

Sally recovered first, settling back into her seat. "Papa and Mama and Grandmama and Grandpapa Winshire and most of my cousins are staying in London for the Little Season and for Christmas, so we can go skating and sledding and carolling and for sleigh rides and have chocolate in the Conservatory, and we still must pack poor baskets and toys for the orphans, and Mama and Papa are throwing a party with the whole family on Christmas Eve, and Mama is planning a ball for New Year's Eve, but she says I am too young to come to anything with dancing and gentlemen."

"And so you are, Monkey. You don't even put your hair up yet."

"And you have yet to learn to restrain your unruly tongue, Lady Sarah. You will swoon if you do not take a breath." With another pointed look at Sally, Mama offered to Toad, "David, of course, you are welcome to come to any of the parties you wish. I daresay, if you are old enough for throne rooms, you are old enough for adult *soirées*."

"He is only a year older than me!" Though she could hardly believe it herself. He had come home so much taller and broader, and his voice was deeper, and the way he was acting—why, he might have grown three years in the nine months he had been away.

"A year older and six royal courts wiser, Lady Sarah Grenford, and has been received by three British monarchs, which you have not and will not for at least three more years. You will cease with the petulant tone immediately. David, I hope you will have dinner with us this evening while your servants ready the house, but I cannot warrant Sally will not do something between now and then to see herself served supper in the nursery."

"I will not!"

"You say you will not, dear. Until you do."

The carriage slowed and came to a stop. "Only a moment, Your Grace, my lady."

While he stepped down and went to make his return known to Etcetera, or at least leave his card, Sally prodded her mother again, for the hundredth time this week. Once Toad returned, confirming, "Niko is in London, but he's gone riding," and the carriage was underway, Mama finally capitulated to Sally's incessant request:

"Of course, David, you may stay with us if you'd prefer company to the empty halls of Dalrymple House."

"Yes, do, Toad!" Sally bounced on the carriage seat.

"I will be delighted to have dinner; thank you for the invitation, Aunt Cherry. But I would not think of imposing myself as a houseguest. I haven't seen my rooms in so long, and I've just left word for Etcetera to meet me at home when he returns from his ride. In fact, will you mind very much dropping me at home, so I can make myself presentable and settle in, perhaps go for a ride in the park to blow the dust off? I can walk to Haverford House before dinner."

"Certainly," Aunt Cherry said. He had taken the backward-facing seat, so she pointed at the driver's window. "You may so order."

Toad slid the window open and established the new destination.

Sally did her best not to pout. She had been hinting to her mother for days, ever since the letter came saying Toad would be returning to Town without his parents, to ask him to stay with them. She had thought Toad would undoubtedly choose to stay at Haverford House with Sally instead of being all alone.

But perhaps he wasn't planning to be alone. What if he wanted the house to himself so he could dally with opera singers and actresses? Or invite his unsavoury bachelor friends over to play cards and dice and drink and debauch ladies of the night, and do other things Sally was supposed to be too young to know about, with whatever horrible lightskirts he could seduce or pay to do them.

Sally had to consciously smooth her forehead again.

'Aunt Cherry, may I take Sally skating tomorrow? And to Gunter's for chocolate?"

Oh. Now that was much better. "Oh, yes! Please say yes, Mama!"

Mama dithered a moment, her brow wrinkled, but finally said, "If Miss Thorne goes with you, and only if your lessons are entirely complete." After a brief pause, she invoked Sally's wrath for all eternity: "In fact, it would be nice if you took your brother. Jonny was just speaking of going skating the other day."

II.

Thank heavens Aunt Cherry suggested they bring Sally's little brother. How unfortunate Almyra is still at Wellstone, for an additional little sister between them could not hurt.

Toad had intended to ask if he could stay at Haverford House, but that plan went out the window as soon as he caught his first sight of Sally. Nine months had, at least in his opinion, made a man of him. But time had not left Sally the child he remembered. He was not certain he could keep himself from touching her, were they living under the same roof, which made him a perfect lecher, entirely unworthy to take a virtuous girl for an innocent outing. Aunt Cherry should be banning him from her house, not letting him take her little girl skating.

He said his farewells at Dalrymple House, thankful for the greatcoat that kept Aunt Cherry from knowing exactly what he had been thinking about Sal, and made his way up the front stairs, promising to be on time for dinner.

"Don't forget my presents," Sally called from the window of the carriage as he reached the door, only to subside at her mother's glare.

When she rubbed her breast against his arm...!

No. He couldn't think about that.

He was saved from his own illicit thoughts by the housekeeper, who met him in the front hall to say he had a visitor in the receiving room. "His Serene Highness Prince—"

"Etcetera," Toad said, his mood lightening on the spot. His Serene Highness Prince Johannes Wilhelm Nikolaus Victor von und zu Elchenberg. Toad had shortened it to "Your Serene Etcetera" when they met at Eton, and they had been fast friends since. "Excellent. I wish to change my clothes, but please show him into my sitting room and send up some brandy."

"Your Lordship?" The housekeeper wrung her hands, her brow furrowed.

Toad sighed. "Tea, then. And something sweet for His Highness." He would have to purloin some of his father's brandy later.

It didn't take long for Toad and his valet to accomplish a change from his sooty, dusty traveling suit into riding attire, and he joined his friend. "Etcetera! It is so good to clap eyes on you. I see they brought tea."

Niko rose from the sofa and set down his tea cup. "Toad Abersham. The only man I know who can turn expulsion from school into an extended European vacation."

The two embraced, and Toad took his seat, pouring himself tea and accepting a dash of whatever Etcetera had brought in his flask. He pushed the plate of cakes to the other side of the table; Toad's stomach was still a bit unsettled from the train ride.

"Before you ask, Jenny received your father's bank draft, plus ten gold sovereigns I gave her after you left. She said she would move to London, but I do not know what became of her after that."

Toad nodded. "Thank you."

Toad had known his father was sending money to the unfortunate girl for whom Toad was sent down from Eton, since Toad had been on a train to London before his valet could even pack his trunks. The duke had railed about the money for hours while he was screaming at Toad for being so stupid as to be caught, then had deducted the amount from his next allowance. And then Toad's mother had found out, which made everything worse. But Toad hadn't known Etcetera would shoulder the responsibility without being asked. "It was kind of you to take care of her when I couldn't. I'll reimburse you, of course."

Etcetera waved away the idea of payment. "It was nothing. You would have done the same for me."

That was, in fact, true. Though Toad doubted Eton would expel royalty, even if he had been caught one too many times with one too many of the maids, by exactly the wrong person on the wrong day at the wrong time. Besides, Niko had been smart enough to keep himself to only one of the maids, and had an allowance large enough to rent her rooms when she expressed dissatisfaction with her lot.

"It's brilliant you've come home in time for the holidays, Abersham. Everyone in the family is indulging the Duchess of Winshire's desire to stay in London for Christmas, and the sheer number of older, wiser, sanctimonious male relatives is staggering. Every cousin I have ever known must be in Town this year, and they all have an opinion on how I should be living my life. Brothers and uncles and cousins are intolerable."

"Do not leave fathers off the list. Though, I must say, I am quite in charity with the duke at present. He was a beast about the expulsion, but you couldn't ask for a better tour, or tour guide."

"Where did you stop?"

"France, Austria, Hanover, Sardinia, and the Two Sicilies. Five royal courts with their incumbent ladies, any number of brothels fit for royalty, introductions among the artists near my mother's apartment in Paris, and a veritable map of the back hallways of the opera houses in Paris and Austria."

"The Duke of Wellbridge attended brothels?" Niko's voice rose, expressing the same scepticism the entirety of the British aristocracy would, at the idea the duke was less than fully enamoured of the duchess. And conversely, that she might allow it without using a sword to make her point about marital fidelity. "Your mother has not beheaded him?"

"No, the duke did not indulge his base instincts, just performed introductions and paid bills. But he covered for me with my mother at every turn. In nine months, she never caught me once, and I assure you, she had many, many opportunities, and is no less dogged than ever. He even convinced her to leave me in Paris with only Meath for the last fortnight we were there, while they travelled to assess her shipyard in Marseilles, and my tutor visited family. And he is going to increase my allowance at Cambridge, so I can afford to keep a mistress."

"And I thought my brothers had been indulgent last time I went home to Erzherzog. Your father is a prince among men."

"Assuredly."

"My brother is not so bad, either, at least today. When I got home from Eton last night, he'd left word he will be in Kent until next week, and he left me this." Etcetera took a small, flimsy book from his pocket and waved it at Toad. "A Guide to the Ladies of London."

"Outstanding!" Toad took the book and flipped through it without reading it.

Now that Toad could envision the future of priapism before him as Sally Grenford's best chum, he would have to do something to keep from debauching her. Uncle Haverford and his father had both told him, when he came back from his travels, he should set up a mistress in Cambridge instead of spreading his seed indiscriminately across England. But in the meanwhile, he had to make it through a full month in London with Sally.

"This is excellent timing, Niko. I can't tell you how I need to be distracted from—" Toad stopped short. Etcetera was one of Sally's cousins, and Sally's cousins stood up like a stone wall to protect their "Little Princess." Toad was his best mate, to be sure, but Niko was second in line to be the Duke of Haverford, and so, however remote the possibility, could conceivably end up as Sally's guardian. She was Niko's family.

Etcetera shoved Toad's shoulder. "Distract you from what? Or should I say, from whom? Did you fall madly in love with an entirely inappropriate woman on your travels?"

"No, nothing like that. I—" Toad cleared his throat and handed back the book. "I just—" He couldn't tell Etcetera he was nursing an obsession with his cousin. "I met a lot of women for sport. And I flirted with enough ladies in royal courts, but I still don't know how one goes about courting a woman one wishes to marry. An innocent, I mean. A lady you can't touch, no matter how much you want to."

Niko's mouth fell open. "You met a woman you wish to *marry?*"

"No!" *Yes!* "Not..." *Not yet. It's too early. We are too young.* "I just... one doesn't want to look like an idiot before young ladies with whom one might end up sharing one's life."

Raising one brow in a manner that recalled every royal whom Toad had ever met, Etcetera asked, "Any particular young lady?"

"No! It's only… some of them are so pretty, are they not?" He could feel heat rising in his cheeks. "I mean… I know better than to defile a nobleman's daughter without planning to be married. But some men are rakes, are they not? Some men have carnal relations with anyone they want, damn the consequence. Girls are ruined, which means men must be willing to ruin them, but surely some indiscretions go unnoticed."

"Abersham! What are you suggesting?" Etcetera waved the book at Toad, with a superior smirk he had clearly borrowed from one of his older brothers. "That is what the Ladies of London are for, you randy, immoral fool. Leave titled young women alone until you are ready to be married." For good measure, Etcetera smacked Toad in the back of the head with the book before sliding it back into his pocket.

"Ow! I don't mean to hurt anyone," Toad said, rubbing the back of his head. "I just can't stop thinking about… about a girl I know. I know I can't touch her, but she comes near me and I can't stop myself imagining the most degenerate… I'm depraved, Niko. She's like a madness. And she is only ever going to see me as a chum. She thinks I am 'safe.' I might as well be her brother, and all I want to do is throw up her skirts and—" Toad stop short, glancing over and seeing Niko as Sally's cousin once more. He repeated, rubbing a hand across his face, "It's perverted, Niko. I'm vile."

Now raising both brows and straightening in a way Toad only associated with grown men, Niko asked, gravely, "Are you speaking of my cousin, Sally?"

Toad stared in utter horror, all the blood draining from his face—indeed, from his brain. "No! I—She's not—" Finally choked by everything he was trying not to say, and stymied by a suddenly non-functional mind, he stopped short and just stared. Niko tilted his head and waited.

"Yes, it's Sally."

Dropping his head into his hands, Toad groaned. "Go ahead. Hit me. I am done for anyway, Niko. The rest of her cousins are going to kill me if you don't. And then my mother will take aim, and then my father. And finally, when there is literally nothing left of me but bone, Haverford will dig up my grave to kill me again." Toad let his head remain in his hands, visualising the horrific end he would come to by following the logical course of his thoughts. Finally, after some time passed with no word from his friend, Toad looked up.

Etcetera's face was serious, but not angry. "I will not even speak of Haverford, but to say you cannot have imagined anything as horrible as it will be if he catches you corrupting our Princess. Longford will beat you bloody, Stocke will run you through, and any one of the Wakefields—male or female—will slit your throat and drop you in the Thames. Elfingham will tell his grandfather, who will speak to your father and then tell Grandmama Winshire, who will speak to your mother, just in case your father hasn't."

Toad moaned and rose to pace. "I'd rather be boiled in oil than hear what my mother would say. Aunt Cherry asked me to stay with them at Haverford House until my parents come to Town! Stay with them?! What was she thinking inviting a man like me under the same roof as her innocent daughter? If she knew what I did on the Continent? If she had any idea what I am thinking about Sall— Lady Sarah—she would emasculate me with the nearest sharp object. And my mother would hold me down."

"This is a serious matter, Abersham. Do not mistake me. I am Haverford's spare, so she is more than a cousin to me, not someone to trifle with. But it is common knowledge you two were all but betrothed in the cradle. If that is so, why not make an offer? You are a ducal heir. She can be in your marriage bed in a matter of weeks."

Toad gulped. "Are we not too young for that? I've not even finished school yet."

Etcetera shrugged. "Nobles have married far younger for less salient reasons."

He could do it. He could have his ring on her finger and her body in his bed. Their parents might kick up a bit of a fuss about their age, but it was what they had always wanted. They would come around. For a moment, he imagined it: Sally Grenford spread out across his bedcovers for feasting, and then sunk his head back into his hands and groaned. Gentlemen didn't do such things to proper ladies, did they? He was an unprincipled, lascivious, wicked deviant to even imagine it. He could marry her when they were older, when he'd worn out his lusts a bit on lesser females, so he wouldn't offend her. Then it would be safe.

But Niko was waiting for his answer.

"I do not think she even wants to marry me, Niko. I truly believe she sees me as the older counterpart to Jonny. In a few years, I will ask Haverford to allow me to court her properly, as she deserves." He sighed. "But how am I to go on now? Everything I am thinking is… it's forbidden. Sally Grenford is forbidden. I cannot be alone with her. You must see that. You have to help me. I cannot make it through a month in London with Sally always at my side; I will disgrace myself and dishonour her and disappoint our parents irreparably."

"No, I can see you must do something to calm yourself, or you will be unable to function. I can help you keep your distance. And as long as you do, I will not tell any of our cousins of your shame, for you have never told them any of the things I got up to at school. To begin my mission of mercy…" He tugged the book from his pocket again. "Let us go meet the Ladies of London tonight."

With a deep sigh, Toad demurred. "I cannot. I've said I will have dinner at Haverford House, and told Sal I would bring her presents." He hastened to add, "All her presents are entirely appropriate." Heaven help him if even Etcetera knew about the items for her Scrapbook that he would hide in the secret compartments of the jewellery cabinet he'd brought back.

With a sceptical glance, Etcetera said, "I should hope you would not insult my cousin by doing otherwise." Toad turned his head away on the off chance his guilt was as visible as it felt. "I'll show you," he said.

Meath had unpacked some of his trunks already, including the presents in question. They were laid out on a table in his bedchamber, so Toad ushered Niko in from the sitting room. The cunningly made cabinet took pride of place; the most beautiful item Toad had ever bought in his life—with enough obvious and hidden compartments for the piles of jewels any wealthy duchess might hold in her keeping. About half the size of one of his traveling trunks, it was contrived of and inlaid with ten different types of wood and three different precious metals. It was empty now, but Toad was planning to secret any number of items in the cabinet that he hoped no one but Sally would ever see.

Etcetera whistled his appreciation. "For the Wellbridge jewels, is it?" He pulled out various drawers and opened doors, with Toad hovering at his elbow hoping he wouldn't puzzle out the hidden compartments or find their latches.

Toad couldn't help expelling a breath of relief when Etcetera turned his attention to the other items. The fortune-telling cards met with his approval, but he frowned at the beaded, beribboned evening bag, the bolt of silk, and the dozen patterns of hand-tatted lace. He gave Toad a shove. "You can't give her anything she will wear on her person, you idiot."

Toad pushed back. "No one would say a thing if Jonny gave her a bolt of silk. It is the exact colour of her eyes."

Etcetera's jaw fell open. "Her *eyes*, Abersham? *Her eyes?* If we had not already established that you are not Jonny, that would do it. He doesn't even know his sister has eyes, much less their colour. You'd better save the fabric and the bag for when you are courting her in earnest, and were I you, I would ask Aunt Cherry beforehand, even then. The cabinet and the cards will be enough for now."

Toad ran a hand over the silk, soft as the skin of the girl who had sold it to him but not, he imagined, as soft as Sally's. Perhaps Etcetera was right. He had already decided not to give her the finest silk stockings he had ever seen, and the garters of French lace tatted with silver thread and trimmed with pearls. Not yet. Not until he had won the privilege of removing them with his teeth.

To divert his thoughts, he commented on the pretty gypsy girl who had sold him the fortune-telling cards, and Etcetera laughed. "You are not so far gone as all that. Did you only buy things from pretty girls? You'll have to tell me all about them."

Toad smiled, remembering the model who sold him the bag at the Parisian fashion house and the friendly lacemaker in Burano. "Something like that."

"Well, don't tell my cousin that. Go to dinner and give Sally her presents, then explain the two of us have made firm plans at half-nine. I will meet you at Haverford House with regards for my uncle to ensure you can make your escape."

"That's an excellent plan," Toad said absently. "So, I should leave here at half-seven."

"No. Quarter to eight," Niko said, "or you will have to sit with her in the drawing room before supper."

"Good point."

"And I suggest, every time you find yourself thinking anything less than holy about the angel who is my very young, very innocent cousin, you consider, rather, what your mother would do if she were to hear what you just told me."

Toad hung his head. "It is disgraceful, isn't it?"

Etcetera clapped him on the shoulder again. "Not disgraceful, no. But not wholesome, either. Never fear. I shall save you from your worst inclinations by distracting you with the finest fleshpots in the kingdom. And when our other cousins wake up and realize our Sal is growing up to be a very pretty, very wealthy heiress, I shall direct their attentions elsewhere while you gird yourself to do what's right and marry her."

"You do not think your cousins would really..."

Niko just laughed.

Toad felt suddenly threatened by the greater portion of his male extended family, over a relationship he hadn't known was quite so important a few days ago. "Will you vow not to court her for yourself?"

"Sally?" Etcetera's tone of horror deserved a punch to defend Sal's honour, if Toad had not been so grateful for it.

"I prefer my girls less brainy and more tractable. Sally Grenford can be some other man's shrewish wife, thank you kindly." Etcetera sighed at Toad's raised eyebrows. "Oh, very well. I promise. And I will never again refer to her as a shrew, so you will not be forced to challenge me. Now, we are both dressed for riding, it is almost five o'clock, and having just come from the park, I assure you, it is filled with the most exotic birds of paradise showing off their fine feathers. We shall soon find *something* to distract you."

III.

Five days later…

In the first hint something odd was happening, Sally answered the front door of Haverford House herself. Toad's heart stuttered and he reached up to steady himself against the door jamb. Even in her schoolgirl dress, with her hair in two braids tied with ribbon, she looked unutterably grown up and lovely.

The second clue: no servant was anywhere in sight. It was early, to be sure, at eight o'clock, but the servants should have been about for hours now.

"Er… Sal? Where is everyone?"

Sally grasped his hand and pulled him through the house. They passed the receiving room, the music room, the study, the dining room, and the breakfast room on the path to the Conservatory.

"I thought I was coming for breakfast?"

"You are."

As she pulled him through the door to the Conservatory, he stopped short. "I thought your parents and brother would be here."

Apparently not. She'd had a table for four set for two in one of the nooks on the side wall, screened by pots of ferns and overhung with flowering plants. She beckoned him into the room, but he stood close to the door, glancing over to make sure it didn't accidentally close.

"What is wrong? Have you already eaten?"

He looked around. "Where are your parents?"

"Mama took Jonny to buy some sort of scientific instrument he was promised for high marks, and Papa had an early meeting with his solicitor."

"But… they knew I was coming?" No, of course they didn't. Sally's feigned innocence told him that.

"Where are the servants? Do you not have your governess or a maid with you?"

Sally wrinkled her nose. "Miss Thorne was called away three days ago for a family emergency, so of course I have a maid. I sent her to the kitchens with strict orders to leave me alone, and Papa does not insist on me being attended when only family are in the house. Now, come in and sit down. You may not be hungry, but I am."

"Monkey, I am not sitting down to breakfast alone with you."

"Oh, don't be silly. What do you think I will do, bite you?"

He nearly groaned at the thought of her lovely little teeth buried in his shoulder while she—

"I do not think you will do anything, but your father will unman me, should he find us alone."

Sally sighed and took a roll from the silver basket that had been set on the table, *a la française*. "Papa has found us alone hundreds of times, you blockhead. We have grown up together, roaming each other's houses and estates. We are two friends having a meal. For Heaven's sake, you are almost like my brother, are you not?"

Toad's heart slowed just slightly. If she thought of him as her brother, he could, too. Though he couldn't imagine she would go to such lengths to be alone with Jonny.

"Will you not sit?"

Slowly, cautiously, as though she might bite him and he might like it, he moved around her, his back to the wall, to sit across the table from her, not at her elbow, moving the place setting to do it. She eyed him and pressed her lips together, but only said, "I wished to speak to you alone. You have been here five whole days, and while you are everything polite and kind, you avoid me at every turn. I demand to know why you have started acting like an utter nincompoop."

He slunk into his chair, looking anywhere but at her. She dropped the hand holding the toast she'd half buttered. "What in cinders is wrong with you?"

She shoved the basket of bread and rolls at him.

"Nothing is wrong… exactly," he mumbled.

With a huff, she snapped. "You are the most infuriating boy I have ever known. It's because you've spent months and months bouncing from one woman's bed to another like an absolute dog, and you are afraid I will scold you like our mothers."

"No… not…"

"And now that you have flirted with princesses, you've suddenly realized you are eligible and I will come out in three years, and our wretched fathers have told you every noblewoman in the world wants to trap you into marriage any way she can."

"I don't…"

"Do not be such a bufflebrain. I do not need to trap you into marriage; I only have to wait until our parents can no longer contain their will to meddle, and hope you are not trapped by some other girl in the meanwhile."

"Beauty, I—"

Sally tipped her head.

Had he just said that out loud?

"Did you just call me *Beauty*? Goodness. That's new." She gave him a coy smile. "Do you truly think me beautiful, David?"

"Sally, I… Monkey Face, you know I don't…"

With narrowed eyes, she pronounced, "You are an utter idiot, Abersham. I am not like all those other silly women. I. Am. Your. Friend. You ridiculous boy."

"Ridiculous *man*, Monkey."

Sally took a bite of her pastry, then set it down and drummed her fingertips against the table. "And since I am your friend, I expect you to answer me honestly. I have some questions for you, Toad Abersham, and I will not hear your evasive, noncommittal responses. You will answer me fully and completely. Do you understand me?" She poked her finger at him the same way her mother did, just for good measure.

Toad groaned. "You are going to scold, aren't you?"

"I am not going to scold. You are the flawed boy our fathers have made you, and sooner or later, you will grow out of it and be ready to be a duke and a husband. Until then, I expect you will keep doing stupid, exasperating things I will hold over your head for the rest of our lives, once we are married."

"You needn't imagine I will marry a shrew, Sally Grenford. You won't get anyone in the noose till you learn to bridle your tongue."

She stuck out her tongue at him, and he returned the gesture, with the addition of crossed eyes. Stifling a chuckle, Sally turned up her nose and continued as though he hadn't spoken. "I do not care to hear your amorous adventures or excuses for your unseemly behavior. I wish to ask you questions about The Scrapbook. I have been studying the pictures, and I can't understand exactly how it works, and since you are now clearly an expert, you must tell me."

"Sally!" His protest came out in a squeak.

"Do not 'Sally' me. I never agreed not to ask you *any* questions."

"But surely the poems… the papers. Didn't the novels give you the general idea of things?"

"David Abersham, do not shirk your bargain with me. Have you finished eating?"

"I cannot keep anything down until we have ended this conversation."

"Very good, then. Come here." She stood and took his reluctant hand, leading him to the half-hidden niche with the sofa, where they had spent so many rainy afternoons. He sat at the very end of the sofa, hoping she would take the other end. But no, she collected the blasted Scrapbook from a hiding place beneath the flagstone, and sat right in the middle, not close enough for her skirts to touch him, but still leaving him quite crowded. Toad tugged at his cravat.

She opened it to the first page and pulled out a full page of notes she had taken, which meant she would be tormenting him with this for hours if he allowed it.

He stood up. "I will not do it, Monkey. I will not corrupt you so thoroughly.

It is not right, and not fair to you. I never should have let you talk me into any of this."

She turned the first page before she answered. "Are you certain?"

"I am. I'll not do it, Sally Grenford."

Closing the book slowly, she shrugged and sighed. "Very well. I will have to wait until Etcetera comes to call. Or perhaps Elf or Longford. They will all be here for Christmas, so I shan't have to wait long, but I did hope for answers before then."

"Sally!" That was better. More of a manly growl.

"You may cease snapping at me in that tone of voice. I hear it quite enough from our parents, and I know you do not wish to sound like them."

"I wish to sound any way that will convince you to stop this nonsense."

"Will you stop cavorting with random young women?"

"Sally!" An innocent like her shouldn't even know what he did with women, random or otherwise. And that she did was all his fault.

"Exactly. Why should you be the only one who learns anything?"

"You cannot ask gentlemen questions about marital relations. Not even your cousins." Heaven help Toad if any of her cousins found out what he had been teaching her. "Especially not your cousins." Though, anything they did to him would be like a warm hug compared to what Uncle Haverford would do.

"Well, they are not technically *marital* relations, are they? I mean, you have not married, but you are performing lewd acts with opera singers and prostitutes anyway, are you not?"

Another round of 'Sally!' was clearly not going to make her to stop this inappropriate line of questioning, but he didn't know what would, barring telling her parents, for which he would see the worst punishment of his entire life.

Rubbing a hand over his face and rising to pace the floor, he capitulated. "What do you wish to know?"

She patted the seat next to her. "Sit down."

"I will not. Just ask me what you wish to know."

"Very well. The first thing I have been wondering is how long it takes. I can see the pictures, of course, and read passages in books, but I get no sense of whether lovemaking lasts five minutes or five hours."

Toad's mouth fell open and stayed there for long moments before he snapped it shut. "It's... it... depends." He blushed, but persisted. She would make good on her threats if she had to. Before she asked the follow-on question, he answered it: "It depends on the people and the situation. It can last five minutes or five hours. Or five days." Toad's face flamed with a whole new level of heat, for he had proved this thesis not a month past, before he left Paris.

Sally nodded.

Thank the gods and goddesses.

"Then, how many times can a person do it in a row? Some of the literature you sent seems awfully improbable, just applying simple logic."

"It… it depends. There is no hard-and-fast rule."

"I shall accept 'it depends' as an answer only once more, Toad Abersham, so choose the question carefully." She held up the Scrapbook, open to a page on which she had pasted some of the French boudoir postcards he had concealed in the jewellery cabinet. He had thought them more artistic and less revealing than those used by the madam his father had hired to train him, but under Sally's hands he suddenly saw them as obscenities, and the knowledge horrified him. She pointed at the top picture. "In this one, it looks like she has put his… well, we shall get to what it is one should call it…" He groaned. "It appears she has his… man-part in her mouth. Is that right?"

Toad choked on even the possibility of a response, finally nodding just slightly.

"Do you think she enjoys that? It seems like it would be unsatisfying. It can't be comfortable. I mean, just judging from the pictures of man parts. Like trying to swallow a cucumber whole."

He coughed so hard he thought he might bring up a lung. She waited patiently for him to pull himself back together. "Well?"

"I… I… Monkey, I…"

Sally sighed. "I am certain you are not so tongue-tied when you flirt with princesses."

"No. No, I am never so tongue-tied with anyone as I am with you. I do not know if she enjoys it." Before he thought, he blurted out, "I enjoy it."

"You do? What does it feel like?"

Oh, god, what have I done?

"Monkey, I cannot possibly answer that. And I am not evading your questions; it simply defies description. And you've exposed a deficiency in my honour. I had never considered whether the woman might or might not enjoy it." With a brief cough, he added: "Which is not to say I hadn't considered her pleasure at all."

"I'm certain you are ever so considerate of your paramours, Toad. Is the… mouth thing something gentlemen can do to ladies, too?"

"To women, at any rate," he muttered, before clearing his throat and answering, "There is very little in the fleshly arena that is not in some way reciprocal, Monkey. Once you are married, your husband will show you."

"Yes, that is what Mama says: 'Your husband will tell you anything you need to know.' But you will be my husband, will you not, Toad? When we are grown?"

"I… er… Monkey, I…" He tugged at his jacket. "Bit stuffy in here. Would you mind if I open a window?"

"There. There it is. You are doing it again."

"Doing what?" he asked, crossing to loosen the casement and breathe in the fetid London air.

"Acting like a nincompoop."

"I am not a nincompoop. And I am not answering any more of your questions. Whomever you wed, you can jolly well wait until you are married to find out how the mechanics work, like well-bred young ladies do."

Sally pursed her lips and she turned a page in the Scrapbook to Füssli's erotic drawings, another present he had concealed in the cabinet. "I suppose Grandmama would answer my questions." If Aunt Eleanor saw those pictures she would flay him alive.

"Aunt Eleanor?! You cannot ask Aunt Eleanor about... marital... carnal relations. You especially cannot show her anything I have ever given you, nor even imply I have procured it on your behalf!"

"If you will not tell me what I wish to know, and you do not wish me to involve my cousins, Grandmama makes the most sense. She does not believe in girls being left ignorant."

"Sally!"

"Have you not learned saying my name in that tone of voice will accomplish nothing? Grandmama says girls should be informed, so they are not taken in by the lies of rogues and scoundrels. She might not even mind so much that you gave me the pictures. Papa is the one who would take poorly to that."

"We are not going to find out!"

She clapped her hands and turned a page. "Excellent. Then you will answer my questions?"

The choking gurgle in his throat could not possibly have denoted consent, but, of course, she took it as such.

"In this picture, the gentleman appears to be entertaining two ladies—I mean, assuming he is entertaining; he might be boring them to tears, I suppose. Does this lady not look as though she is in pain, like Mama being kind to the vicar's wife even when she's waspish?"

Toad barely turned his head to look at the picture in question, continuing to let gurgling stand as communication as long as Sally would permit it.

"What I truly wish to know about this picture is, do ladies ever entertain two gentlemen? And could a person entertain more than two others?"

Toad whimpered.

IV.

Christmas Eve...

Sally was not putting up with Toad's behaviour a minute longer.

He had been avoiding her since their conversation in the Conservatory. Oh, she had seen him most days, but always in company. Her parents. Her brother. His sister. His parents. Cousins and friends. They had been shopping, and skating, and for rides in the park. Several times, they had made up a party for the theatre, and once they had taken a barge ride down the Thames.

Toad was polite and friendly, even affectionate. But he went to extraordinary lengths not to be alone with her, not to stand close to her, not even to touch her. And she was fairly certain Niko was abetting him, always turning up as soon as Sally's schemes to get Toad alone showed the least prospect of success.

For the first week, she had been so overwhelmed by his revelations about the materials he had sent her, and the new items he had secreted in the jewellery cabinet, that she barely noticed his withdrawal, but by Christmas Eve she had had enough. This was all her own fault, pushing when she should have left him alone, and talking about marriage when the whole world knew boys of Toad's age, especially noble ones, were frightened of the word.

But that didn't mean she had to put up with it.

She needed to let Toad know she had no expectations of him, so that they could go back to being friends again. Hopes, but no expectations. For at night alone in her bed, she imagined doing the things in the pictures, and her imaginary partner in that enterprise always wore Toad's face. If he did not wish to become her husband, what would become of her?

He had arrived with his parents Christmas Eve morning, when Haverford House opened its doors to family and friends for a long day of decorating and charitable endeavours, which would end with an evening party, and continue the next morning with services and gift giving.

Now, he was standing there—no, slouching—chatting with Etcetera and Stocke, pretending to pack the boxes they would take to the poorhouses before dinner, sipping brandy Stocke had poured for them, after quietly gaining approval from Uncle Wellbridge and Etcetera's older brother. Poured for them after he watered it, Sally knew, as she had seen him adulterating a carafe in Papa's study; he had told Papa and Longford he would make sure none of the adult men were forced to the sacrilege of diluted liquor, and no growing boy made too much a fool of himself.

It was too late for that. Standing there with Etcetera, the two of them mimicking Stocke's pose: the casual way the glass hung from his relaxed fingers, the half-slump to the left, the smirk lifting the opposite corner of his mouth. Sally could barely keep from snickering and rolling her eyes, watching Etcetera and Toad trying to outdo each other in manliness.

Toad glanced over at her twice, as though he were keeping track of her movements, presumably to see if she was taken in by his foolish act. Or to keep himself on the other side of the room.

She. Would. Not. Have it.

Hoping to overhear something before they noticed her, Sally sidled along the wall while he was turned away, as gracefully and sedately as she could manage. On the other side of the potted plants that screened her from her cousins and her friend, Baron Nincompoop, the Moronic Marquess, she stopped to listen to the conversation.

"First time drinking brandy, Abersham?" Stocke asked.

Toad shrugged one shoulder and answered as though he were an old hand. "Of course not. I've travelled the world, you know." Taking another sip, he pronounced, "But this is better than most."

Etcetera nodded solemnly. "Haverford has excellent cellars."

"Indeed," Stocke agreed easily, though Sally imagined he wanted to laugh at them as much as she did.

"I'm not a little boy, you know, Stocke. I'm a college man, now. I've drunk and wenched my way through Europe this year," he boasted. Sally rolled her eyes. A college man because Eton would not have him.

"The last holiday I spent in Erzherzog, I barely left the whorehouse," Etcetera bragged. "And I will not be spending my nights in London chaste."

"I'll be in Cambridge in a fortnight, or I would have a mistress even now."

"My brother gave me a Guide to the Ladies of London," Etcetera enthused to Stocke. "Abersham and I are going to explore some of the finer offerings before we go back to school."

"A man has to have some entertainment to tide him over between mistresses, does he not?" Toad asked rhetorically. Sally's lips twitched when she saw Stocke's quiver.

She nearly laughed aloud when Stocke said, "I'm sure there are plenty of women in the world for both of you, boys. You needn't run through all of them this week."

With eyes narrowed and a flush rising in his cheeks at Stocke's bland set-down, Toad insisted, "I will arrange something more regular upon arrival in Cambridge."

"A willing widow?" Stocke asked knowingly. "University towns are filled with them."

"Toad prefers actresses and opera dancers." Etcetera said with a lewd chuckle. "True patron of the arts, is Abersham."

With an airy wave, Toad said, "I shall assess my alternatives once I am there."

Sally suppressed a huff that would alert them she was on the other side of the potted plants, instead stepping out from behind the leafy screen, making them wonder how much she might have heard. The sheepish shock and guilt from all three of them was quite gratifying. It served Toad right, and Stocke and Etcetera were no better. *Actresses and willing widows, indeed.*

"If you do not want Mama to come over here and scold, gentlemen, you'd better put down your brandy glasses and pay attention to packing boxes. This is the time of year when we should reflect on our charitable duty by providing more of our time and attention to those who need our Savior's mercy. We have all been so blessed, how can you waste the chance to bring comfort to someone less fortunate during this season of giving?"

"Who needs your mother to scold, Princess," Stocke teased, "when you do so perfect an impression of her?"

But all three men put down their glasses and made a more concerted effort to fill the boxes with the correct number of the right items, in the order Aunt Cherry demanded, Sally making corrections until she was called away to adjudicate the disposition of ten extra crocks of mincemeat. When she left them to their sure-to-be-unseemly bachelor chatter, Toad most likely had a satisfying bruise forming from an "accidental" foot on his toe.

Opera dancers. Harumph.

Later, after the house had been decorated completely for the Yuletide season, after boxes had been delivered to the workhouse and the orphanage and the various charitable enterprises of the Duchesses of Haverford, Winshire, and Wellbridge, and after supper had been eaten, port and sherry imbibed, servants released to their own celebrations, and carolling around the pianoforte exhausted, the Wellbridges and others who were not guests in the house went home, and Sally had still not had her private moment with Toad.

Surely Christmas Day would give her that one gift?

It was no better the next day, family and friends in one cheerful crowd through the church service and breakfast, until they all sat down in the double drawing room to exchange presents and toast one another and the season.

Sally couldn't imagine how Toad could give her any gift as stunning as the jewellery cabinet that would one day hold the gemstones she inherited from her parents or was given by her future husband—the Wellbridge jewels, if Sally could figure out how to bring this new, grown-up Toad up to scratch. For now, though, it was a superlative hiding place for the items Toad gave her that wouldn't fit in the Scrapbook and, in fact, the Scrapbook itself, for a latch behind the back-right foot released a false bottom, just large enough for the book she had started two years ago, with a tiny bit of room to grow.

And she didn't have to hide the cabinet in the priest hole, because it looked, to all appearances, like an innocent piece of fine furniture, designed to fit into the décor of her sitting room. Her parents' significant glances when he gave it to her, the first night he was back in London, could only mean they had immediately considered the Wellbridge jewels, too, but Toad's raised brow when he presented it had alerted her to greater magnitude. It hadn't taken her ten seconds to find the first latch, but a brief shake of his head warned her not to open it near her parents.

He'd whispered in her ear when no one was looking that she could expect to find eight hidden compartments, and she'd found six thus far, containing pictures she had pasted into the Scrapbook, and a few larger items. She had giggled over the novel about a Turkish harem, while jingling the bells on the silver chain around her ankle, attached to a jeweled toe ring, like a heathen dancing girl might wear; the book had been bound in leather and stamped as *The Collected Sermons and Moral Teachings of Reverend Calvin Whitehead*. She was shocked almost to speechlessness at the price list for an unholy number of mysterious services at a French brothel, but she'd found it after the discussion in the Conservatory. She intended to make Toad explain every item, eventually.

Two more secret gifts remained to be found, so she still ran her fingers over the edges and corners and cracks at least once a day, before bed, to find the last hidden clasps opening a concealed drawer or shelf. She was ever hopeful a drawer would pop open, exactly the right size for an engagement ring. Papa would say she was too young, but if it were Toad asking for Sally's hand, he would give his blessing, surely.

While Sally was musing by the fire, Toad's sister, Almyra, had made it her business to run presents back and forth from the tables and under the Christmas tree to each addressed recipient. For the moment, inadvertently, Sally was left alone with her thoughts in a crowded room.

Interrupted suddenly when a shadow fell over her. Toad.

"So, you have come to speak to me at last?"

Toad tugged at the curl Sally's lady's maid had left to dangle at her shoulder when she put up Sal's hair for the first time in public—the Christmas gift she had told Papa she wanted more than anything else in the world. Except Toad, of course, but it wouldn't do to say that to Papa. But now Toad was actually touching her hair and hadn't even noticed her neck and shoulders. The dunderhead.

"Do not be churlish, Lady Sarah. The pout does not complement your new chignon, which, by the by, is beautiful on you, as is your new gown, though I am aggrieved to think I must be the last man in the house to say so."

Sally offered him a slight smile.

"You must forgive me, Monkey, for I've brought you a present—no, *two presents*—even after the copious number I brought you from the Continent. May I sit with you a moment while my sister wreaks havoc in someone else's home and my father indulges her?"

"Your sister is like my sister, Abersham. We are all family, are we not?" That was the right note. He was, of course, nothing like a brother to her, but he mustn't think she had serious expectations. Sally scooted over on the loveseat and patted the cushion. "It is as though she is wreaking havoc in your own home, as I did at Dalrymple House when I was twelve, though, admittedly, you are better at leading me into mischief than Jonny is at leading Almyra. Jonny is hopeless at mischief. Please sit, Abersham."

Toad sat pleasingly close, which might have been due to the size of the sofa, but Sally would take the warmth of his thigh however it was offered up. He handed her two shallow wrapped boxes, one stacked atop the other, both wrapped in printed fabric and tied with ribbon.

"I'm afraid you will have to wait for your gift until Almyra delivers it, for I put it with all the others," Sally said, hoping hers would be vaguely equivalent to whatever was in these boxes. Unless they contained the Wellbridge parure and were meant to announce their engagement in one grand gesture… there was nothing Sally could give Toad that was equivalent to that, but for her hand in marriage.

As she began unwrapping the first box, he murmured a bit closer to her ear, "Have you found all eight, then?"

Blushing, and with a quick glance at her parents, completely immersed in discussion with the Wellbridges, she whispered, "No, not yet. But I will."

"I will give you the key if you promise to never ask me another question about any of it."

"I do not need to give up my questions, for I shall find the latches without your help."

Toad rubbed his right hand over his face and groaned. "Of course you will." He brightened, though, as he added, "But I am afraid your questions must wait, for Etcetera and I ride out this afternoon to my cousin Smythe's place." Another of their set at Eton. "We will return next week for your mother's ball, but I'd like to see my aunt and uncle and cousins before I go off to school."

Sally sighed. "Of course, you must go, and I hope you will remember me to Lord and Lady Ostelbrooke. But we only have such a short time left before you go away to school." She stopped herself a second too late. She mustn't whine. She mustn't impose herself on his time, or annoy him.

"I'll not neglect you, Monkey. I promise. On my return, you shall have first pick of every moment of every day before I leave. And you'll hardly know I am gone, with all the activities your mother has planned." She hardly wished to consider what sorts of activities he, Smythe, and Etcetera had planned, once outside their parents' purview.

"You are right, but I will miss you, Toad."

"I will be back in no time."

She opened the top box, a finely wrought wooden case with brass latches, that opened on three hinged tiers of mathematical instruments, a full set of more than two dozen items also wrought of brass, each piece engraved with her initials and set snugly in its own velvet-covered place.

"I found them in Germany." Running his finger along the side of the box in a way that made Sally shiver, Toad offered, "They are Swiss, so of course, they are as precise as can be."

Sally couldn't explain why she had to suddenly blink away tears. It was such a functional gift. Not something frilly or girlish or decadent, like practically every other gift she'd ever been given in fifteen years. But something that acknowledged her intellect; acknowledged and applauded the love of numbers that others, even Papa, found inexplicable and unfeminine. That Toad should give her such a gift moved her, soul-deep.

"Toad, I… thank you. I think I shall surpass Mr Galbraith's knowledge of mathematics with these at hand."

"Then the other box will see you the first woman admitted to Oxford."

Something in her chest was shifting with every word he said, and she couldn't explain it. It was seismic—and perfectly right in every respect. And completely foreign. Before she had to force words out, Almyra came up with a small box. "This is for you, Toad, from Sally. And here is another from Papa. There are more, I'm sure, but I haven't found them yet."

"You mustn't keep the others waiting," Sally said, selfishly, recklessly, hoping to keep Toad to herself a bit longer.

Almyra scurried off, and Sally blushed when she thought of the gift he was to open.

"What is it, Sal? Should I not open this here?"

"No. No, I wouldn't give you something in front of our parents that they can't see. I am not a dunce."

With a broad grin, Toad said, "Then I shall open it without delay. You have a talent for giving exactly the right things to the right people, Sally Grenford, which I expect you learned from your mother."

"That is probably so, and it would please her to hear it."

She carefully unwrapped her second box, while he tore the paper from his.

"Sally," he said in a voice that was at once a caress, a wistful glance, and a throaty plea for something Sally could not discern. She turned and he was rubbing the talisman between his finger and thumb, smiling at it, then her, then back at the gold watch fob she'd had made in the shape of a monkey's face. He attached it to his watch chain immediately. "So I won't ever forget my Monkey Face. I will take you everywhere with me, Beauty." He reached out as though to touch her cheek, but pulled his hand back at the sound of Papa clearing his throat in a suddenly quiet room.

"Do open the next box, Sally," Toad said in an overly loud voice. "You've dawdled long enough, and I've something from Father."

At the same time Toad opened a matched set of duelling pistols, Italian-made, Sally opened a second wooden box to match the first, but for size and shape. Before it was even completely open, her heart did another flip. It was a slide rule. But as she looked closer, more detailed than either of the two in her schoolroom.

"It has some sort of new calculations on it, the man said, and more functions than I've ever seen. It can be used for trigonometrical computations, or even navigation somehow, but I can barely understand the great mysteries of mathematics in English, much less in Swiss German. My mother may be of help with the navigation, or your Mr Galbraith."

Sally ran her fingers across the numbers, sliding the mechanism back and forth. "I will ask them and puzzle it out in short order. Toad, this is…" She was, again, close to tears with no explanation whatsoever, but now all of their parents and most of her cousins were watching. Longford broke the tension, calling across the room, "You've given her protractors, Abersham, not feathers and furbelows? Who taught you how to buy gifts for women?"

The room laughed, but Sally's mother and Toad's traded speaking glances, and their fathers both stifled smug smiles. "Buy gifts to appeal to your lady's interests, not her vanities," the two dukes had advised. "And if you have not spoken to her long enough to discern her interests, it is not yet time to purchase a gift."

Beneath her voice, trying to keep the conversation nominally private, Sally murmured to Toad, "This is the nicest gift I've ever been given, Toad. It is… I cannot explain it. It is the nicest thing anyone has ever done for me."

With a glance around the room, now a bit less focused on the two of them, Toad chucked her under the chin and chided, "You needn't be satisfied with feathers and furbelows, Sally, when you are so much more than that. Longford is an idiot. You are twice as smart as he is."

As Longford called out, "I heard that, Abersham," Sally leaned over and gave Toad a kiss on his cheek and made him blush. Papa cleared his throat again.

This was the reason she would marry Toad Abersham, future Duke of Wellbridge. He would never wish his wife to be naught but ornamental, and he was the one person in her entire life who had never treated her like she was silly.

The basic facts of the matter—that he was her best friend and closest confidant, and easily the most handsome man of her acquaintance, and had a smile that grew more captivating with every glance, and they had been all but promised before Sally had even been born—were hardly relevant at all.

While everyone was distracted by a puppy Papa's nephew Tony had brought for his sister's children, Sally reached out a hand and squeezed Toad's fingers, and for the first time since he arrived back in London, he didn't tug his back. He rubbed his thumb across her knuckles, then without looking away from the canine scene across the room, lifted her hand to his lips and kissed her fingertips.

"Happy Christmas, Beauty."

"Happy Christmas, David."

He startled at the use of his Christian name, but didn't comment or rebuke her. "You are a wondrous young woman, Lady Sarah, and I beg you not forget me while I am away at school."

Forget Toad? Was he daft? He was the other half of her soul. And he thought her *wondrous*.

"How can I forget you when you still owe me answers to the rest of my questions?"

With a tortured sound somewhere between groaning and keening, Toad buried his face in one hand, squeezing Sally's fingers ever tighter with the other, until, finally, Stocke said, "Has she at last scandalized you to actual death, Abersham? Are you having apoplexy? Princess has been trying to get one or another of us for years. I thought it would be Elf."

"Or her poor, beleaguered Papa," Haverford opined with a smirk.

Sally stuck her tongue out at Stocke and pulled her hand away from Abersham, who was laughing at her now, albeit with a sheepish smile.

"She's not killed me yet, gentlemen, but I think there are better than even odds Sally Grenford's curiosity will play a part in my demise when I go."

Keep reading for more stories
from the childhoods of Toad Abersham and Sally Grenford
and the books of Jude Knight and Mariana Gabrielle

Prologue: Never Kiss a Toad

The Genesis of the Ongoing Serial Historical Romance,
Available at Wattpad

October 1823
Haverford House
London, England

Nick Northope, Duke of Wellbridge, paced the floor in a receiving room of Haverford House, waiting nervously for his oldest friend. He and his wife had been shown to the Duke of Haverford's family wing, where the rooms were as opulent and gargantuan as the public spaces, but a few touches showed that this space was for living rather than show. A workbasket stood by one chair, angled toward the fire, and a small stack of well-thumbed books sat within easy reach of another.

On a couch that favored comfort without sacrificing elegance, Wellbridge's duchess, Bella, clucked over little Davey, the new Marquess of Abersham, not just nine months old, ensconced in Nurse's lap. It had been more than two years since the Wellbridges had married and left England to live on her frigate in his Venetian lagoon. In two days' time Davey would be christened, with King George IV for a godfather. After all they had been through with His Majesty, the dinner he was throwing in their honor on the morrow might prove the most trying of all their joint experiences thus far—even considering their previous ordeals had included kidnap, murder, penury, and exile.

"Do light somewhere, my love," Bella said. "You are wearing a hole through the Aubusson. Surely your friend will be along shortly." She distracted the baby with a silver rattle.

"It's not that.... it's... good God, Bella, it has been five years since I have seen my oldest friend, and so much has changed." Not least, Wellbridge had followed Haverford into matrimony, a state both men had sworn to always avoid, and between them, the two couples had logged an enormous amount of time in various ports abroad, adventures they had only shared in occasional letters. "I cannot believe he has yet to meet you, even after all this time. And though I have met his duchess, I cannot say we took to one another. But she makes him happy, or so his letters say. It is like I am to be introduced to a man I have never known, not one who knows me nearly as well as you do." With a half-smirk, he added, "Better, on a few topics."

Bella crossed to the decanter of brandy and poured for her husband, pressing it into his hand, gently pushing him to a seat in her inexorable way, her smile the only license she needed to manhandle him. "Calm yourself; you are vexing Davey. Haverford has invited us, so you need no longer fret he will bar the door to you, and after tomorrow, you not be able to fuss about having dinner with the king. And Haverford shall be there for that, too, so you are assured more friendly faces than just mine, so that fear may also be laid to rest."

Nick scowled slightly at Bella, even as he did her bidding. "I do not *fret* or *fuss*, and I am not afraid."

"No?" Bella gestured for him to drink. "I shall wager ten guineas the next thing you say will be in the very language of fussing."

"I do not a *fuss*, Your Grace." His eyes narrowed, but his lips turned up. "You must be cautious of Haverford. He is quite charming, and the greatest rakehell in all the British Empire, to hear the tabbies tell it."

"And here I believed you to be the greatest rakehell in all the British Empire," she teased, reaching into his purse for a guinea, transferring the coin to her reticule with a brow that begged him to suggest his comment was not the purview of a worrywart.

With a sardonic chuckle, he explained, "It is not that I do not trust him. I do. With my very life."

"Just not with your wife."

"Just so."

"Is he not reformed? I heard in Paris that he has been tamed these eight years."

"Haverford will never be entirely tamed, though given I can be so ensorcelled by you, I must believe it is possible for Haverford, too. I did not understand that when last I met Her Grace, and so she did not regard me with favor. Damn and blast!" Nick snapped. "I wish to Heaven he would hurry!"

Nick jumped up at the sound of the door opening, and set down his glass on the table. Bella looked up from calming Davey, who had become momentarily fussy at his father's outburst. The Duke of Haverford bore a slight resemblance to Wellbridge, if only in the greying blond hair, noble bearing, and perfectly tailored suits that needed no padding. The way he stooped and shortened his stride to give his lady his elbow was also reminiscent of Nick while Bella had been increasing.

The Duchess of Haverford was unremarkable in looks, brown-haired and brown-eyed, and shorter, by far, than her husband. She would be slender under other circumstances, but now moved with the cautious gait of the very pregnant. When they entered the room, she narrowed her eyes at her husband, and gestured for him to greet his friend. "Go on, dearest. You know you want to see your old friend. I have stood on my own two feet nearly forty years. I assure you, I will not fall without your arm."

Without a word, the two men rushed at each other and embraced. They had been the closest of friends for more than twenty years, two wealthy dukes' sons with an eye for the ladies and more money than sense. When Haverford had still been the Marquis of Aldridge, before he inherited his father's title and just down from university, Wellbridge had, at the marquis' father's request, escorted the boy to the appropriate clubs and gaming hells and brothels, setting up his accounts with Weston and Hoby and Tattersall's and making sure he got the right sort of town bronze.

Eventually, their exploits had expanded past London, and they had spent a full year traversing the byways of England before a spot of trouble led their fathers—and the Prince of Wales—to banish them for a time. After that, though, they racketed about England—and indeed, the rest of the world—as though they had no cares, until each had, finally, been given a noble title he could not avoid, and discovered a love and a woman they had both insisted for years just did not exist.

"Cherry, my love," Haverford said, drawing the woman forward to his side, "you remember my dear friend, His Grace, the Duke of Wellbridge? Nick, my duchess, Charlotte."

Nick made the politest bow he could muster, which was quite deferential indeed. "Your Grace, I am delighted to meet you again and to make known to you my wife, Bella, the Duchess of Wellbridge." Bella tried to give Davey to the nurse to rise and make her curtsey, but the little boy raised a fuss and grabbed on to her hair. "And, as it seems he has need of his mother, my heir, David George Northope, the Marquess of Abersham." He gently disentangled the tiny fingers from Bella's hair, caressing the nape of Bella's neck as he did so, and dropping a kiss on the little boy's curls.

"Normally, we would not have brought Davey, but your note did say..." Bella blushed a bit, settling Davey into her arms again, once he was satisfied he was not being handed away.

Cherry disengaged herself from her over-protective husband and sank onto the couch beside Bella. "Oh," she breathed, "he is beautiful, Your Grace."

Bella's smoldering look beneath lowered lashes set Nick's mind tripping off into directions better not explored in mixed company, but his libido was set aside in a wave of paternal pride when she said, "He looks exactly like his father." Nick stood a bit straighter, and Bella continued, "Call me Bella, please, and the duke always prefers Nick."

Cherry rested her hand on her belly and blushed herself. "Normally, I would not be entertaining guests to dinner—I've no more than two months before I am called to childbed, but I could not wait all that time to meet you, and I could not bear you to think I will miss the dinner tomorrow out of malice or ill intent. It is only that I am unfit for broader company at present. Anthony insisted that Wellbridge is like family, and so it shall be. You must call me Cherry, and Haverford will be hurt should you call him Your Grace. We will dine *en famille* tonight and speak deeply, from our souls, of ghosts long forgotten."

Bella spoke softly, so as not to awaken Davey, who seemed to be nodding off as she rocked him. "I am grateful Haverford will be there when we make our return to court, for Nicky especially, though I am sorry the timing is such that you cannot attend. Nick is more nervous than he will say, which is still only half as anxious as I."

"Prinny is excited about Wellbridge's return and proud to be asked to stand as godfather," Haverford said. "He has missed Nick, though he would never say so and will pretend otherwise. You hurt his feelings when you wouldn't let him arrange your lives for you, but a little flattery and a purse dropped in a card game will mend all. Let him poke his fun and take his pound of flesh, and all shall be as it should."

Cherry dimpled at Bella. "Largely because the king admires Wellbridge's wife, it is said."

"At which, one cannot wonder," said Haverford, with a courtly bow, earning himself a scornful glare from both women and an assessing glare from his old friend.

Bella frowned. "I am not flattered by the king's interest. I would rather avoid this entire debacle. His Majesty is quite the worst part of marrying Nick. He has kicked us both in the teeth, and now the duke will crawl back and act as though all is well again. I am not so pleased to put on my Court smile. Especially not when the newspapers have finally, obligingly, forgotten our existence. There is no chance that will continue with His Majesty making much of us in all quarters. We shall be back in the gossip columns again in no time."

"My sovereign has decreed that all is well, my dear," Nick chided, "and so it must be."

"Wellbridge has the right of it," Haverford agreed. "If one has the opportunity to smooth rough patches with one's monarch before one loses one's lands—or one's head—it behooves one to do so. And not the gossip columns, surely. Wellbridge will star, along with his bride, in the Society news."

"I leave the gossip columns to you, Haverford."

"No more, Nick. Not for many years. The papers are not interested in one's personal life when one lives it in domestic harmony with a veritable angel." Haverford possessed himself of his wife's hand, and kissed it, a smug smile at his old friend, who they all knew would garner Fleet Street's unwelcome attentions once again in a matter of moments.

Under her breath, Bella muttered, "Just because one speaks in the ducal register, does not mean one's pronouncements have been sent from on high."

Cherry's lips twitched, but Nick and Haverford both laughed aloud. "My wife finds the ducal disposition more trying than the papers, Haverford."

"I daresay I have never met a duchess who does not, from time to time," Cherry offered.

"Time to time?" Bella asked archly.

"Minute to minute," Cherry conceded. "But, if we can forgive our esteemed husbands their innate arrogance, then surely, you can forgive Prinny, when a king's self-worth must be exponentially larger than a mere duke." She shrugged. "And while it is true, he is the king and so holds much sway over all of us, he is not the whole of England. I hope you will find some compensations in raising this lovely little boy in his own land, among his family and your friends. We are honored, by the by, to stand as godparents to him. Anthony was so pleased to get your letter."

"I am pleased my husband is so happy to be back in England," Bella said, without any conspicuous happiness reaching her eyes from her wan smile. "And for the chance to meet his dear friends, though Nick has promised we will return to Italy before the winter."

"Before the winter?" Haverford asked, leaning forward in his seat. "Nick? I say, London is a dead bore without you here. Stay through the Season, at least. It cannot be so bad without enduring the marriage mart, surely?"

"I hope you will consent to remain at least until..." Cherry rested her hand on her distended abdomen again, and her mouth curved in a soft smile. "I know Haverford wishes you and Wellbridge to stand up for our baby, as we will for little Lord Abersham."

"Oh!" Bella exclaimed, her hand covering her mouth, blinking away the beginnings of tears. "I... well..." She looked over at Wellbridge.

"Of course," he said immediately, slapping his old friend's shoulder. "Of course we will. I am so pleased to think our families will be so joined. If I must commandeer the ship wherever we are and sail back to England myself, I will return to stand up for your heir."

"No need to ask if you wish a boy or a girl," Bella said to Cherry, "with a dukedom in the balance."

Cherry's eyes clouded. "Haverford says he will be delighted with a daughter, but I have had so much trouble... We have been wed eight years, Your Grace. I have only once before carried so close to term and—" she stops short at the admission, and to blink back a tear, then looks from Bella to Nick. "Nick, Anthony will have told you, I suppose, of our sorrowful loss. I can only hope this is a boy, and healthy."

Haverford cut in, with a sharp edge to his pronouncement, "My brother Jon's eldest will be Archduke of Erzherzog after his mother, but Jon has four more sons. If this is a girl, I will petition the king to name one my heir presumptive and foster him here in England. I will not risk my lady's present-day health in pursuit of posterity."

"Davey is a miracle, truly, after many similar losses with my first husband," Bella said, "but I admit to being much relieved I provided the requisite heir when we hadn't thought to be blessed at all."

"I am overjoyed to have an heir," Wellbridge said, "but were Davey a girl, I could be no less pleased."

Haverford adjusted the curtains to keep the late afternoon sun from shining in his wife's eyes, then pushed a cushion behind her back and draped a blanket over her knees. He stroked a hand across the crown of her head as she bent over his friend's baby, tucking a curl behind his tiny ear. He grinned, leaning over them to drop a kiss on her shoulder. "I am quite decided. Cherry, my love, you shall give me a daughter, and we will marry her to little Lord Abersham here."

Cherry smiled at his whimsy. "Really, dearest? They may have something to say to that, themselves." She turns to Bella, and said, "But I do hope they will have the opportunity to grow up as friends. My little one will be so much younger than my sister's children, or the children of our other friends. And a duke's eldest son—to have a friend his own age, in the same circumstances, would be a treasure to our little boy, I think."

"Or girl," Haverford insisted.

"I make no promises to stay in England," Bella said, "but I am in complete agreement that our children should, at the very least, be friends."

"As to that," Cherry smiled up into her husband's warm hazel eyes, "they may be friends in Venice or Paris or Alexandria as easily as in Margate or Cornwall or London, can they not? We shall simply have to make an effort that our children should know each other, wherever life might take us all. Should that lead to shared grandchildren, we will rejoice, but I think, my lord dukes…" Her glance took in both Haverford and Wellbridge and caressed them with a loving scold, "the two of you must cease your meddling before it begins, lest you have your hearts broken when your children do not bow to the ducal will as easily as the rest of the world."

Follow @JudeKnight and @MarianaGabrielle on Wattpad to read more of the free serial romance, _Never Kiss a Toad_

More Stories from the Childhoods of
Toad Abersham and Sally Grenford

A Toadstone for the King

(The origin of Toad's detested nickname.)

The latest peerage to be created by our beloved monarch is a Toad. Yes, my dears, you heard correctly. A Toad, or so says the King, and who is this correspondent to gainsay such an esteemed prince? His Majesty has seen fit to bestow a barony on the infant son of none other than the Duke of W— (once a regular source of scandal, but now—so we are told—reformed). A source close to the palace has given your faithful correspondent the true tale of the amphibious appellation our newest baron shall undoubtedly bear from this day forth. I trust he will be suitably grateful to His Majesty upon reaching his majority.

Prinny dandled his godson, the young Marquess of Abersham, on his knee with a bit more abandon than comfortable for the boy's father, the Duke of Wellbridge. The duke's hands seemed to try to hold the four-year-old boy aloft, even from across the card table. There was no chance of removing him from the king's lap, however, as Prinny had won three rounds easily with his "Lucky Piece" at hand.

"Draw a card, Abersham, my boy," the king said, offering the deck.

Davey took a card from the top and threw it on the table, face-down. A slight grin on the king's face showed that his good-luck charm had proven effective once again, and the duke let out an almost imperceptible sigh of relief. If anyone knew the limits of royal regard, it was the Duke of Wellbridge, who had fought his way back into Prinny's good graces only by the skin of his teeth. In part, because he was highly skilled at purposefully losing money to the king, a game made more difficult with his heir in the middle of things. He wished Davey's sniffles had remained, so he would have had an excuse to keep the boy from his royal godfather's presence. He wished he had gone along with the duchess's suggestion that they remove to the countryside, rather than remaining in London.

Thankfully, once more, Prinny held winning cards. Wellbridge was another thousand guineas down, but he was in need of the magnanimous side of his sovereign's nature. And it seemed he was on the right track. When Davey began wiggling and climbing on the king's lap, he was indulged, even as he crawled halfway onto the table to grab at the royal plate of foodstuffs.

"Davey! That is not yours!" Nick snapped, but Prinny corrected the duke, not the child.

"Let him have it. I am not hungry."

Prinny seated Davey on the edge of the table, and the boy grabbed handfuls of whatever was on the plate, but none of it found favor, and to his father's horror, he threw it on the floor, where one of His Majesty's pugs rid the world of excess mushroom tart. Rubbing his hand over his face, Nick said, "Truly, it is time for Master David to be in bed. To say nothing of his mother's opinion of him being engaged in gambling."

Prinny chuckled, "I do not envy you the sharp tongue of your wife, Wellbridge, through her sharp mind holds great appeal."

"I cannot say I disagree with your assessment, Sire."

Davey continued to throw mushroom tart at the dog, with the king offering up commentary on his aim, and the dog continued to make a meal of his master's supper. Until, suddenly, it began choking, frothing at the mouth, and fell to its tiny knees.

At a glance, Nick swept around the table to pick up his son and shield him from the sight he had already seen and clean his hands and face of any trace of poison. Prinny sat staring in shock at the dog, dead not three minutes after eating from the king's plate, while Nick tried to keep Davey from wiggling his way out of his father's arms. With one word from Nick at the door, guards came in and removed Prinny and the dead animal, and began detaining everyone else currently in the castle. At the top of the list, the two gentlemen who had been closeted with His Majesty for two hours before the attempted poisoning: the Duke of Wellbridge and his heir.

It was the next morning, and many hours of questioning by men who should know better, before they were allowed to leave the palace. First, though, Wellbridge and his tired, cranky, frightened son were escorted to the king's chambers, where Prinny made much of Davey, calling him, "my own toadstone," feeding him from his tray, and casually giving him the Barony of Harburn, which included a manor house Prinny renamed Toadstone Hall, in recognition of the service Davey had unknowingly provided by virtue of poor manners.

His father's courtesy title was rendered unnecessary, he now a peer in his own right, as well as heir to all of his father's titles. But the whispers through Court didn't now call him Harburn, but rather, they called the little boy "the king's toadstone." Within a week, Davey was called "The Toadstone" in his father's presence; in a month, he was "Toad" to anyone who knew, or knew of, him. Within a half-year, it was obvious: he would remain "Toad Abersham, Wellbridge's boy," the rest of his days.

His mother has sworn never to forgive His Majesty.

<u>Sally Falls Out of a Tree, and Toad Falls in Love</u>

(The first time Toad knew he would marry Sal.)

Someone was calling her name. Someone beloved. Sally woke with a smile, and then frowned as she looked up into the canopy of an oak tree instead of her own bed hangings.

Still mazed with sleep, she examined her surroundings. Here, twenty or more feet above the ground, great branches sprang from the giant trunk, forming a safe bowl that she had filled with blankets and pillows for her evening's escapade.

At least, it was meant to be evening. But the sun had risen, and below her she could hear David Abersham shouting for her to come out and get back to the house before she got them both into trouble.

He sounded cross, and come to think of it, she was cross with him. For four months, she had been looking forward to his return to English shores, when he and his parents would stay with the Haverfords for a whole four weeks, taking in both Sally's tenth birthday at the beginning and Toad's eleventh at the end.

She had made all sorts of plans; had even intended to include him in last night's adventure. But all he could talk about was his mother's plaguey ship, and how to sail it, and the places he had been. He didn't even talk to her, but to the Chirbury and Wakefield boy cousins of his own age. And when she tried to find out how to use a sextant, he brushed her off, and told her girls didn't need to know that sort of thing.

"Aunt Bella knows. So there," she said, and didn't speak to him for the rest of the day. Not that he noticed.

She thawed a little after supper when he came to find her in the nursery and apologised, and cried *pax*. But when she began to tell him about the transit of Mercury across the sun, which could be seen from England only a few times a century, he told her she was the most unaccountable girl, and he had promised to play Spillikins with Henry Redepenning.

Sally lay back against the pillows with a contented sigh. Despite the stupidity and selfishness of boys, she had seen the transit.

She had not found the planet during its approach, but once it touched the sun's corona, two arms of solar light surrounded it, making a disk against which the dark planet appeared to be travelling in a halo. She watched through the telescope Aunt Bella had given her for her tenth birthday a week ago, the glass smoked over a candle to protect her eyes. She never moved, barely even breathed, until clouds covered the sky.

What a pity that she could not afford to have her escape from the nursery discovered. If Mama and Papa found that she had been out all night, she would not be able to sit for a week. But how she would love to tell them of the ruddy glow around the planet, of the calculations she had been able to do that should give her Mercury's diameter, if she had correctly followed the method recorded in the Journal of the Royal Astronomical Society.

Not that the astronomers would care. They did not allow woman members, Papa said. Stupid, selfish boys, even if they were old men.

David was still shouting, right under her tree now. If he continued, he would attract just the kind of attention she had climbed up here to avoid. She crept to the edge of her nest and looked down. There he was, just below her, looking around.

"Drat the girl. Where can she have gone?" he asked the air, and Sally stifled a giggle. Perhaps if she was very quiet, he would go away. Or perhaps she should drop on him like the Indians did in Uncle Rede's stories. He had been a logger in the Canadian forests, and knew all about ambushes from trees.

Yes. That's what she would do. She would drop on David—no, Toad. He hated the nickname, and she seldom used it, but he was being a toad, so she would call him one. She would drop on Toad and knock him out. And then sneak back into the nursery and her bed, before her maid came to wake her.

The ploy was more successful that she expected, the height turning her and her book on planets and stars into a dangerous missile. Indeed, if Toad had not been below to break her fall, she might have been hurt. She leapt to her feet and dashed away towards the house, leaving Toad stunned on the ground.

But before she rounded the hedge that screened this coppice of oaks from the house, she stopped. She couldn't abandon him. Even if the injured boy wasn't her dear friend, it would be wrong to leave him hurt. And he was her best friend in the whole world, despite his behaviour this past sennight.

She trudged back up the hill to where he was beginning to sit up, where his first words melted the last of her anger. "Are you all right, Sally? That was a champion ambush."

It wouldn't do to let him know he was forgiven. She lifted her chin and flared her nostrils, ready for battle. "I told you I was going to watch the transit of Mercury."

"I know. That's what I thought when your cousin Hermione told me you were missing. I thought I'd better come and help you sneak back into the nursery. Was it worth it, Sal?"

He accepted the hand she held out to him, and used it to pull himself to his feet, dusting off his knickerbockers and listening with every sign of attention as she described the wonderful heavenly sights for which she would risk a thousand parents' anger. Yes, and girls could do astronomy, for she had calculated the diameter of Mercury, and what did Toad think of that?

A Ducal Daughter Demands a Liberal Education

(Sally reacts to Toad's first expulsion.)

Sally Grenford managed to slip away from her governess at the book emporium. Miss Robinson was deep in conversation with some other governesses, their heads close together over their cups in the tea room, books spread across the table as they argued about where in the world they would like to travel.

Miss Robinson thought Sally was with the charges of the other governesses, which went to show how foolish the woman was. The girls were universally silly, without a thought in their heads beyond fashion and court news, and terrified of doing anything fun, in case it might be considered improper. However, it suited Sally well to have a naïve and trusting governess. Miss Robinson's assumption that Sally was like the others, and could be safely left unsupervised, meant Sally was often left to her own devices on outings such as this.

Sally would have preferred a governess who was a half-decent mathematician, but rather suspected such a paragon would be clever enough to limit Sally's freedom, which would never do. Sally, therefore, kept the secret of Miss Robinson's incompetence, and spent visits to the bookshop seeking out texts to advance her own knowledge.

So, there she was, deep in the recesses of the bookshelves, when someone came up behind her and placed his hands over her eyes. "Guess who, Monkey?"

Sally jumped, but then felt a smile spread from her middle all the way out to her fingertips. "Toad!" She spun under his hands and gave him a big hug.

He grasped her shoulders and held her apart to look at her. "You are so tall! And so... female! When did you stop looking like a beanpole?"

Sally blushed a little. She was quite unused to her new shape, and the jumps that seemed to be a necessary adjunct. "Do you like it?" she asked, a little anxiously.

Toad caressed her cheek with his thumb. "You are turning into a veritable diamond, and will soon be a threat to the liberty of every unattached gentleman in England."

Sally stuck her nose in the air. "They can keep their liberty. I value my own, Toad, and have no intention of giving it up to become somebody's property." Except Toad's, because she was that already. But she wouldn't tell him so for the world. He was already puffed up in his own consequence; thinking she would come running at a snap of his fingers would make him that much worse.

He laughed. "Your father will have something to say about that."

"Papa says I have years before I need to think about making a choice, and he will not make it for me."

Toad shook his head. "Not too many years now. You will make you come-out in, what, two years? Three? And surely every gentleman in the ton will be banging down your father's study door making offers."

"Mama was twenty-one when she married Papa. I will not be twenty-one for six more years. And she married for love. I will accept nothing less. I would rather be single all my life than marry where I am not loved."

Toad put an arm around her shoulder and gave her a quick hug, then looked around to make sure no one saw him touching her. "I should hope not. I should hate to have to challenge your future husband before you even wed, and anyone who would marry you with less than the noblest of purpose will meet the wrong end of my fists, I promise you."

This, while not quite the declaration of undying affection she was looking for, was very satisfying. Likewise looking around, she gave him a quick peck on the cheek. "Whomever I marry, you will always be my dear friend, Toad."

He touched the spot where her lips touched his cheek, then reached out to smooth down her hair. "The dearest of friends, my sweet."

Sally shot him a mischievous smile. "I rather think my husband might object if you are my dearest of friends, Toad. If I have one. If I marry for love, as I plan." Though not, of course, if she married Toad. "But why are you here? How long do we have?

"I expect to be locked in my room at Dalrymple House directly," her friend said, gloomily, "but my father is still at Wellstone and my mother does not yet know I've been sent do—er... that I'm back home. I may yet be able to spend the afternoon at liberty, if I avoid Grosvenor Square. Can you spend the day with me?"

Sally could feel herself glowing from within. A whole day with Toad? No. Miss Robinson would never agree. She frowned. "I will need an excuse to give my governess."

"Can you not bring her? I have no ill intent, and you must have a chaperone. As long as your parents don't talk to my parents before suppertime, we will have the whole day to play."

"She says we are going home after this so I can work on my history," Sally said, mournfully, but a thought raises her spirits again. "Perhaps we could go to the Tower to see the Line of Kings, and I could be doing my history and spending time with you, all at the same time! But she will want to know why you are not at school. What were you sent down for, anyway? Was it a famous jape? Tell me all about it."

"The Tower is an excellent plan!" he said. "And it is not your governess's concern why I am not in school. I am the Marquess of Abersham, not a little boy she is supervising." He straightened and threw back his shoulders.

"Very good," Sally says approvingly. "You sound almost grown up when you do that."

He did not, she noted, answer her question. Which meant the answer was something to do with a female. Sally's habit of lurking in quiet corners had allowed her to garner a wealth of overhead conversations about Toad and females, little of which she understood and none of which she approved. Though she wouldn't let him know that for the world.

In the tea room, they found Miss Robinson looking around somewhat anxiously. Sally didn't wait for her to remonstrate. "Miss Robinson, such luck! Here we have been wanting to go to the Tower this age to help me with my history, and here is Lord Abersham willing to escort us."

Toad made a most elegant bow, several inches deeper than the governess's dignity. "Miss Robinson, it has been quite some time, but of course I recall the lady whose fear of frogs resulted in the most spectacular hiding of my life. How could I possibly forget?" He smiled his charming smile, the one that made Sally feel like slapping him. Miss Robinson, Sally noted with some derision, melted at the attention. "Why, Lord Abersham, how kind of you to remember me. If you are sure we are not imposing, my lord...? Lady Sarah has not been importunate, I trust?" She frowned at her charge. Sally smiled back, beatifically, her conscience clear.

"No, nothing of the sort. I would merely hate to keep her from her studies, when she has been so anxious to see the Tower. Since I have a free afternoon, it is not an imposition at all to join you on a tour."

Sally had an inspiration. This afternoon would be no fun at all if Miss Robinson spent it flirting with Toad. "Perhaps your friend Miss Westlake might be free to join us?" she asks. "Miss Westlake is somewhat at a loose end, since her children have been sent away to the country to recover from chicken pox."

Toad was such a champion, reassuring a flattered Miss Westlake that he would like nothing better than to have her join them, and soothing all of Miss Robinson's worries, until he at last managed to get them all out of the shop and into the carriage.

Toad took a place on the seat next to Miss Robinson, opposite Sally, on whom his performance with the governesses was having an unpleasant effect. *Was she jealous? She was jealous!* Papa and Uncle Wellbridge chuckled together when they thought they could not be overheard—they said that Toad would be even more of a success with the ladies than they were as young men. And Sally was not meant to know—barely did know—what that meant, except that it involved Toad and females who were not Sally. And she had once overheard Mama, in a rare temper, claiming that her marriage was haunted by all the women Papa had 'been involved with' before he met Mama, and the children he had fathered on them. Sally didn't want a haunted marriage.

"Why so glum, my dear?" the object of her ruminations asked.

She could hardly tell him in front of Miss Robinson and her friend. "Glum? No, not at all. I am just thinking."

"A dangerous occupation, to be sure. I am sure I will not want to know what you are planning."

Sally's smile felt stiff. She sat up straighter and concentrated on looking happy. She was happy. She had a whole afternoon with Toad, and the future would just have to take care of itself, a decision Toad made easier when he proposed stopping at Gunter's for an ice.

"Yes, thank you." Sally rewarded him with a beaming smile. It was not his fault he was male and, therefore, imperfect.

At Gunter's, the two governesses sat in the carriage. Sally was not permitted to follow Toad to the counter, but she was allowed to stand beside the carriage in full sight of Miss Robinson and the coachman. She was watching the carriages go by when she felt ice on her neck, and then slithering down her back inside her dress. With a wriggle and a squirm, she twisted to glare at Toad, who had crept up behind her. The ice was making its way further down, thankfully outside her corset.

Stupid boy. If she had screamed, they both would have been in deep trouble, and their time together would be spoiled. Sally checked the carriage, where Miss Robinson and her friend were enjoying their ices, oblivious to their charges. Good. She would get her revenge later, when she could avoid being sent to her room for a week.

Toad grinned. "Here's your ice, Sal. The other was a bonus."

It was so unfair that girls had to be well behaved and always careful not to give any appearance of personality or intelligence, when boys could behave disgracefully and still be praised and welcome in society. Without considering, she blurted what was in her mind. "If men have to sow their wild oats, Toad, surely women do too? Do you not think?"

"Sal! I should say not! Who is putting such thoughts into your head?"

"Papa and Uncle Wellbridge say that men have to sow their wild oats. But I do not see why. I am expected to be chaste and respectable until I marry. Should I not expect the same of any man worthy of me?"

She could always read Toad's face. He had no idea how to answer her, and took another bite of his ice instead. As she thought. It was just a silly rule, probably made up by men.

"Or perhaps a man might expect me to find out..." she was at a loss to finish the sentence, since she had little idea what sowing ones wild oats might comprise. Except it had to do with touching, and she was certainly not interested in touching or being touched by any of the silly boys she knew. Except Toad.

Toad's voice sounded strained. "Once you marry, you will be glad of a husband who knows what women find pleasing."

Sal licked her spoon slowly, meditating on Toad's words. "And will my husband be glad of a wife who knows what men find pleasing?" she asked.

He choked on his spoon. "He will be delighted to show you *what he finds pleasing*. You mustn't experiment, Beauty. You will be ruined and forced to marry, and you cannot want that. Trust me when I say you will be a much happier bride if you go to your marriage bed pure."

Sally was not at all convinced. "I think I would be a much happier bride if my husband does not have a string of lovers and by-blows scattered through society to haunt our marriage."

Toad blushed. "I say, you haven't met anyone trying to... do things with which you are not comfortable, have you? For I must insist you tell your father, if you have."

Sally gave an inelegant snort. "When do you imagine I might meet anyone? I cannot move without a maid, a governess, a groom, and half a dozen other unnecessary people falling over one another to make sure that Lady Sarah Grenford is never allowed to have any fun."

Toad was still spluttering. "If that is the sort of fun they keep you from, then

I cannot say I disagree with the constraints." He took a deep breath, and his voice vibrated with sincerity as he pleaded. "Please, Sally—Lady Sarah—please take my counsel in this matter. Please do not be tempted. I cannot say how it would pain me to see you forced to wed to a man who was unworthy of you. I do not think I could bear it."

Sally shot a glance at the governesses, and sure enough, they were deep in their own discussion.

Toad's reaction was satisfactory, on the whole. Though all it meant was that he was fond of her, and she already knew that. She decided to twist the knife a little. "I daresay I should not like to be compromised, Toad. Though perhaps it would not be so bad, if the man were handsome and rich."

Lowering his voice, Toad took her hand, hiding the physical connection from the chaperones by virtue of his stance.

"You know... do you not... that I mean to be your husband? One day, I mean. Not until we are older, but when I do marry... I cannot imagine being wed to any other woman. I cannot stand it if you are wed to another before my eyes. Please promise me you will be careful, Beauty."

Yes. Very satisfactory. Not quite a declaration of love, but still. On the other hand, "Do you intend it, Toad? I know our fathers spoke of it, but Papa will not require it of me if I give my heart elsewhere."

If Toad does not know he has held her heart since she was in her cradle, then he deserves to worry a little. 'I mean to be your husband,' indeed! As if she has no choice in the matter.

Making his own check on the governesses first, he ran his hand over her cheek and into her hair. "Do you not know you have held my heart since I was in knickerbockers? You silly thing. How could I ever love another?"

Sally melted, all her reservations evaporating in the warmth of his regard. She blurted the truth, not pausing to measure her words. "It frightens me, a little, how much I love you. You are the keeper of my heart, David. And if you are careless with it, I shall die."

"I shall be as careful as you are yourself," Toad chided.

Sally retorted, "I shall be as careful as you are, David," and turned her nose up.

Sally was already afraid Toad was not being at all careful. Men seem to think their hearts and bodies are disconnected, Mama said, though she did not know that Sally was listening. Sally thought about this while eating the last of her ice.

"You will grow up and keep opera dancers and fall in love with fascinating widows, and break my heart into a million pieces," she concluded, sadly. "And I will wait for you to come back, and I will forgive you. But don't take too long,

Toad. For I will not wait forever."

She sucked down the last of her ice and licked the bowl of the spoon. Miss Robinson would growl, but she was engrossed in gossip.

Toad leaned closer and whispered low in her ear, "I do love you, Monkey. No other will ever hold my heart, no matter what else I do. You are right. It is not fair to ask you to be chaste when I am not, and I would never judge you as the rest of Society might, were you not. But how I long to be the only man to bring you the sort of pleasures to be had between a man and wife. It is only... Monkey, we are both still so young... You make me feel a perfect lecher, just in the presence of your innocence. How can I despoil you, or wish to see any other man do the same?"

"I do not know what half of that means, Toad. But I know you are less than a year older than me. Papa was thirty-four when he married. Your father was older still." Sally looked to see if her governess was still occupied. "I am only fifteen. You say 'innocent.' 'Ignorant' is a better word, I think. I do not like being ignorant, Toad."

"Will you make me a bargain?"

"What bargain?"

He looked over his shoulder. Thank goodness for gossipy chaperones. "I shall find you the finest examples of literature and art and scientific treatise on the subject, and send you back such items as your father would castrate me for providing, so you shall have your every curiosity sated."

"Yes. I would like that. But what do you want from me in return?"

"In return, you leave the trying of the techniques in question for your marital bed."

Sally thought about that. She had no intention of experimenting at all, yet. And certainly, no intention of discovering what he was talking about with anyone except Toad. But her pride would not let her say so; not when he had every intention of continuing to try said techniques, whatever they may be, with women who were not her.

Toad hadn't finished with his bargain, though. "I will promise to not be a cad like our fathers, and not be indiscriminate. And not to make conquests among women you will ever encounter."

As if that made it better. She thought about that. *Actually, it does make it a bit better.*

"I will promise to wait for... five years. Is that fair? Yes. I shall refuse everyone else for five years, Toad, and then we shall see where we are. I promise I will not try..." She blushes. "I will not try 'anything'..." *Whatever that means.* "... Except with you, Toad. For five years."

And for another five after that, and five after that, for her whole life. But it wouldn't do at all to say that to Toad.

"We are pressing our luck with your guard dogs, my lady, and I am certain your father would have already thrice torn my limbs from my body, had he been privy to this conversation. Likewise, my father and both of our mothers. You must never let anyone gain access to my letters."

"It shall be our secret, Toad. I don't wish to be locked up in the tower at Margate Castle until I am sixty, and that is what Papa would do, I am certain."

Toad pulled her hand to his lips and kissed the palm, folding her fingers over the kiss.

No one else will ever make Sally feel the way Toad does. If he does not come home to marry her, she will just die. She will just curl up into a ball and fade away. And then she will find him wherever he is and haunt him for the rest of his days. Him and his opera dancers and chambermaids, and anyone else he is defiling when he should be defiling her.

"Children?" Miss Robinson called. "What are you up to?" Then, the governess straightened to attention, her eyes panicked. Without looking, Sally could tell who was approaching.

Toad looked around, colour draining from his face. He leaned in and whispered, "I'm done for now, Monkey. I shall write soon. I promise."

It was, indeed, the Duke of Haverford, checking his stride as he realised with whom Sally was speaking.

Toad bravely made his bow. "Uncle Haverford."

Haverford frowned, but ignored Toad and leaned over to kiss Sarah's cheek. "Hello, princess. I saw the carriage and thought I'd stop and say hello. A field trip, is it, Miss Robinson? And who is this?" Miss Robinson introduced Miss Westlake, who managed to squeak a greeting as she curtsied. "And Abersham, too. What a surprise."

"Lord Abersham is escorting us to see the Line of Kings, Papa," Sally said, looking anxiously from one man to the other.

"Lady Sarah needed to go to the Tower to gain insight for her History lesson, Uncle Haverford. I offered to escort her. I know how you concern yourself with her safety."

"How fortunate for Lady Sarah that you happened to be London, Abersham." Haverford raised one eyebrow in question.

"Yes, isn't it?" Toad asked brightly.

Oh, dear, Sally thought. That is not all the way to handle Papa. Toad should just come right out with the truth.

"During term time." Papa's voice was almost a purr, now. Very dangerous.

Toad tugged at his cravat. "Er... yes...?"

Haverford looked at the two governesses, their eyes round and their ears pricked. "I think we will not hold the ladies up on their educational mission. I will deprive you of your escort for the moment, ladies, but you have Lady Sarah's footmen and grooms to ensure your safety. Have you money for the tickets? Yes? Then allow me to hand you up, princess, and be on your way."

"But Papa, Toad…"

"Your playmate and I have some matters to discuss, dearest. Undoubtedly, his father will release him from prison some time before Christmas, and you shall see him again."

"Soon, Toad," Sally said, evading her father's hand to take Toad's and give it a squeeze.

Papa did that imperious thing with his eyebrows, but nothing more, so he wasn't too angry. With luck, Toad would be allowed to come to see them later today, perhaps even to have tea. She kissed Papa's cheek and let him help her up into the carriage, and Miss Robinson gave the order for the groom.

Looking behind, Sally could see Toad hanging his head as he faced his godfather. But Papa wouldn't hurt him. In fact, when Toad confessed whatever disgraceful thing he wouldn't share with her, Papa would probably laugh.

A Ducal Heir Follows in his Father's Rakish Footsteps

(The first time Toad was sent down.)

Gentle reader, today's column concerns a personage no less august than Toad, the Marquess of Abersham, heir to that regular denizen of our newspaper, the Duke of Wellbridge, and his esteemed duchess, Bella, former envoy for the Crown and majority owner of Seventh Sea Shipping, one of England's largest such concerns.

April 1838

Spotted, not two hours past in front of Gunter's Tea Shop: Toad Northope, Marquess of Abersham, now sixteen, in London during Eton term time. He was seen in close quarters with the daughter of the Duke of Haverford, Lady Sarah Grenford, who is still in the schoolroom, but has, seemingly, already caught this rogue's eye. And not only his eye, as he was caressing her face and kissing the back of her neck while two oblivious chaperones overlooked the entire episode.

Will we yet see the joining of these noble houses? Perhaps sooner than later, lest young Abersham find himself on the wrong end of Haverford's pistol. It might be counted a shame that such a young girl–barely fifteen herself–could be forced to wed a known rake over such a small incident, were the groom not heir to the immense wealth and privilege of the Wellbridge duchy. However, Haverford may yet wish to think twice about joining his daughter to Wellbridge's spawn.

Upon investigation, it has become plain Abersham has been asked to leave Eton for such crimes as this newssheet is loath to print, though one wonders if the ducal name (and purse) will mitigate such a sentence. Certainly, few at Eton expect Toad Northope to remain *persona non grata* permanently. His father is a wealthy duke and intimate of the House of Hanover, and the girl not unwilling. In fact, to his credit, Abersham left her well seated to face the loss of her position and reputation. The girl herself is quite keen for the marquess to return to Berkshire.

Clearly, the Abersham apple falls not far from the Wellbridge tree, as anyone who knew the duke before his marriage can attest. The Wellbridges' good friend, Haverford (Abersham's godfather, in point of fact), may do well to recall his own ignoble past, and Wellbridge's, and save his daughter's virtue from a man who follows the example of their early histories. Young Abersham bids fair to exceed the rakish exploits of his legendary father and godfather. Those who remember their scandalous youth may beg leave to doubt the possibility, but this correspondent would remind those souls that the two dukes were considerably older than Abersham when banished from England by their own fathers (and the Prince of Wales). Given a decade, we submit, Toad Northope will put his father's legend to rest.

Meanwhile, we are told the duke has made inquiries about entrance exams at Oxford, Trinity, and Cambridge. Perhaps a change of locale will solve the problem, but we caution His Grace that there are ladies strewn across England and the Continent, and anywhere else he might send the young marquess, and no shortage of ones willing to entertain a nobleman without benefit of clergy. It might be better to warn the boy of the dangers of the pox and the dignity due a noble title, admonish him not to follow his father's poor example, and send him back to Eton to grow up.

Toad in France

The Inception of Delphinus Shipping

(How Toad met his school friends, Piero, Bey, and Zajac.)

David, Lord Abersham

David, Marquess of Abersham, leaned against the wall at the back of a small orchestra platform at the *soirée de présentation*, the evening before classes would begin at *L'école Supérieure de Commerce*, the ESCP. He wished he could bang the back of his head against the plaster until he was injured enough to be carted away. Monsieur Bechand, head of the new Practical Curriculum in Maritime Commerce, which David's mother had endowed with a shipyard in Marseilles, was droning on again, addressing the entire room filled with students from across the globe. Eleven different countries, Bechand had said.

David was displayed on the platform with two other men like animals in a zoo—*genus nobilus*—as it was the first time any member of the peerage had deigned to attend the business school, and now they had nobles from three nations. The infernal Frenchman kept blathering about the excellent opportunity David's mother had provided and the fact they had three—count them, three— members of the nobility attending for the first time in history. Being concussed would be preferable to listening to more of this.

The others had the same pasted-on public-school smile, and both looked like they also wanted to do something to liven up the proceedings. David wished he had a set of sleigh bells, so he could drown the man out every time he opened his mouth.

"And it is due entirely to the largesse of the Duchess of Wellbridge that we can begin such a comprehensive…" Yes, yes, David's mother was a bloody saint. Willing to pay thousands of pounds to destroy all of her son's future happiness;

but otherwise, quite perfect.

Lord Piero d'Alvieri, as Bechand had introduced one of the others on display, was slightly shorter than David, but stockier, with an olive cast to his skin and eyes dark enough to call black. He was at least David's sartorial equal, though David was not wearing his best, and had the aura of a courtier who had learned the art from childhood; in that, he reminded David a bit of his Eton chum, Niko, otherwise known as Etcetera, a literal prince from Erzherzog. Lord Piero's heavy-lidded eyes betrayed nothing, but his half-smirk might be one of recognition. Unless David missed his guess, d'Alvieri had just identified David as his peer, but he wasn't sure in what. Most likely wildness, if the spark in his eyes was any indication.

David would have to see if Lord Piero had made his bow at the French Court yet. David had been putting it off, but he couldn't get away with that much longer, and without his parents to present him, it would be less daunting to greet a monarch he'd only met once before if he weren't on his own.

He suspected he knew the other man being exhibited for the entertainment of Monsieur Bechand, but he couldn't be certain by the name alone. A shipping heir from the Levant, who was also grandson to a duke? There was a better than even chance this was one of the younger generation of Kopet Dag, His Grace of Winshire's shipping operation, though David had never been made privy to all their names. That meant this man represented Seventh Sea Shipping's primary competition in some parts of the world, so was more than an annoyance to the duchess. David would have to encourage an acquaintance.

"While we are fortunate to have these sons of the nobility in our midst, nevertheless…" *Would the man never cease?* "…we are an egalitarian institution, and do not wish to raise one student above another for any reason but academic and business achievements. As such, we will all address the gentlemen as Monsieur Abersham, Monsieur Muhadow, and Monsieur d'Alvieri."

What on Earth? Oh, the duke would be livid if he heard this. The duchess was never fussy about such things; she had been 'Missus Bella' on board ship for fifteen years while she was a baroness, but the Duke of High Dudgeon? He would not stand for such blatant disrespect from anyone, especially not a Frenchman. Come to think of it, if Wellbridge heard, perhaps he would bring David back to England, where he could tie up his unfinished business with Sally Grenford… No, still too much dudgeon directed toward David for that to work. He would just be carted off to some ungodly place not half as interesting as Paris.

So, before the sun rose tomorrow, he would have a plan to make sure his father never found out. To start, he had to keep it from the ducal spy living in the servants' quarters, and his mother's man, Captain Hawley, sailing back and forth to check up on him.

"I trust you will not object?" Bechand trailed off without turning his head toward the men to whom he professed to speak.

David was not stupid enough to make a public objection to the head in plain view of the entire class, before they had even been assigned any coursework. But his jaw ached from holding back his father's ducal rejoinders.

He was sure he must have some ducal stationery in his father's study at the apartment. A letter explaining the duchess was having second thoughts about the shipyard, having heard of Bechand's republican sentiments and the disrespect paid her son, would change Bechand's tune fast enough. David stifled a sigh and rested the back of his head against the wall. It couldn't be accomplished fast enough to end the current torment. And the results would be truly horrible if his parents found out.

He squinted for a moment and straightened. He saw someone he thought he knew. Yes, there. That blond man near the back, towering over everyone else, the width of one-and-a-half of the men next to him. David could not recall his name, but he was sure it was one of Sally's uncle's wards. It must have been ten years ago now, during the traveling years of his childhood, before he had been sent to Eton. They had both been rather scrawny then.

On one of their stops in Erzherzog to make obeisance at the Court where Sally's uncle, Gren, was consort, David had been housed in the nursery and included in the schoolroom at the palace. There had been more than a dozen noble sons and a few boys of more limited means, whose parents had some connection to the palace, whom Sally's uncle educated and provided a start in the world. David was sure that man was one of them.

Nartay Muhadow Bey

Nartay Muhadow was contemplating the rhetorical talents of the Persians he had observed in the Shah's court. They could weave an insult into a compliment so skilfully you were halfway over the Kopet Dag Mountains and nearly home before the remark drew blood. Even his own people could give offence with more dignity than the old windbag who had him trapped on this stage—and they did not stand on much ceremony unless there was trade to be won. His tribe were mongrel refugees from other kingdoms, a composite of Persians, Kurds, Turkomen, Britons, and the strays of dozens of races who travelled the Silk Roads. Nartay himself had a large admixture of English blood from his mother's side, though she had chosen to stay with Nartay's Turkomen father, rather than travel to England, when her own father ascended to a dukedom there.

Bechand, head of the school to which his family had condemned him for the next two years, was both praising the school for attracting three nobles and explaining why they would be treated like commoners. Intolerable cretin.

Nartay Muhadow, whose title, 'Bey,' was ubiquitous in his own lands, didn't give a lump of camel dung for unearned honours. Or anyone else's dignity, either. Behind the mask of polite interest perfected in a dozen Eastern courts and scores of horse fairs, he eyed the other two victims, wondering what they thought of this odd mix of republican sentiment and conventional arse-licking.

He knew one of them was the Englishman, David, Marquess of Abersham, heir to Seventh Sea Shipping. Accord to Nartay's cousins in London, he was known far and wide as Toad. He was a family connection in a way, and a rival in another. His mother was a close friend of the Duchess of Wingate, second wife to Nartay's grandfather, and Toad was said to be courting a granddaughter of the duchess's first marriage. Toad's mother, also, was the primary competitor to Kopet Dag, as owner of Seventh Sea Shipping.

The other man, the one with the sardonic curl to his lip, was a stranger who might yet become a friend. D'Alvieri, Bechand called him, so Italian, heir to one of the noble families scattered about the countryside.

Bechand droned on. Nartay let his mind drift to his activities the previous night. The cherished only son of a widowed mother, nephew to a *kagan* known for his piety and regard for domestic virtues, Nartay had long dreamt of the freedoms of a corrupt European city. Last night had certainly lived up to expectations. He would return to the *Palace de Plaisir* as soon as he could, after he had sampled any of dozens of similar offerings, in between—or while—exploring the gaming hells of Paris. It was a remarkable thing, to be young and free and provided double the quarterly income one is accustomed to receiving.

He would pay any amount if he had two or three of the lovely ladies right now. He imagined them sashaying through the door and sweeping up to the stage: the tall dark-haired one in the red silk corset, and the fair treasure whose assets were only partially obscured by feathers. Yes, and the one with hair like fire, whose white shift would have been innocent, if it were not translucent. Nartay would pay them extra to surround Bechand with caresses, avowals of devotion, and reminders of a fictitious time together. Let him be humiliated before the whole class, instead of Nartay and the other noble gentlemen. Bechand would void his bladder.

Lord Piero d'Alvieri

Piero d'Alvieri, heir to *il conte d'Alvieri*, and a skilled courtier in the Court of Grand Duke Leopold in Florence, thought it almost a certainty he had the same look of polite half-interest on his face as the other two gentlemen on the platform. All three were standing behind the head of the new programme at the ESCP, an hour into the *soirée de présentation*, being introduced to everyone else accepted into the inaugural class of the Practical Curriculum in Maritime Commerce at the most elite business school in Europe.

Yes, there it was again, for the twelfth time, Bechand making much of this Abersham bloke, whose mother had provided the school a shipyard. His mother? What woman owned a shipyard? He must have misheard, or misunderstood the

French. And what had Abersham done in England, that a shipyard was required to secure his attendance at a school in France?

Something amusing, Piero was sure, given the subtle smirk on Abersham's face, his shoulder leaned against the wall behind him, implying the same boredom as Piero, possibly also imagining a plan he would never execute, to disrupt the proceedings for his own enjoyment. The third gentleman appeared to be plotting something, too. Bechand had said he was a son of Persian royalty and grandson of an English duke.

In truth, Piero had been kicking himself for not having made his bow at French Court, as Arturo had insisted upon. If he had, he might have borrowed one of the king's trumpeters to drown out this fool, Bechand, every time he began to speak. Sadly, in the absence of horns, he would have to listen to more of this poppycock.

He glanced over at the two others again, who had to be more interesting than Bechand. By attire alone, Piero could tell they were noblemen; he didn't need Bechand to drone on about it all night, especially not in front of the other students among whom the three of them would have to live. Abersham looked like a cheerful sort, who might not stand on much ceremony, and the Persian fellow seemed jolly enough, not at all a prig, entertaining a small group into gales of laughter before Bechand had forced them all up onto the stage to be fawned over.

Piero's head snapped up at Bechand's next words: "While we are fortunate to have these sons of the nobility in our midst..." He said *nobility* as through the word smelled bad. "...nevertheless, we are an egalitarian institution, and do not wish to raise one student above another for any reason but academic and business achievements...."

What an utter arse this man was. Two years of this? Piero was fairly certain he could not stand it. He didn't care much about people calling him Lord Piero, but he would like to make the distinction himself, at his own discretion, not have it announced as policy to every other student at the school. Arturo, his brother and guardian and the count, would be furious if he heard this drivel. Which meant he would bring Piero back to Italy, so Piero would be sure never to tell him.

"We will be expecting great things from our aristocrats, will we not?" Bechand asked the room rhetorically. "Now, before I release you all to the refreshments, I wish to, once more, offer up the ESCP's deepest and heartfelt appreciation to Mr Abersham's mother, the Duchess of Wellbridge..."

Perhaps the catch-fart should try honouring the duchess by using her son's proper title.

"Her Grace is, herself, a noted diplomat at the French Court, and owner of one of the largest shipping concerns in Europe."

Well, that was interesting. He had never even considered a woman could run a business. Or be a diplomat. Piero's eldest sister, Maddalena, would be angling for a trip to England and an introduction if she heard, and Arturo would make

Piero's life miserable if he encouraged their sisters to rebellion before they were even old enough to marry. "It is our job to make certain they are marriageable," Arturo would say. "No man wishes to marry a girl who acts unwomanly."

Ridiculous. Arturo just didn't want to be overrun alone in the *castello* with five sisters and their mother, so he acted like a tyrant to maintain strict order. Thank God, Piero had been deemed too indolent as the second son and sent to learn to advance the family fortunes on water.

"Truly, we could not have undertaken such a comprehensive program without the support of the Duke and Duchess of…"

At least a few people in the crowd had the grace to look mortified for the three of them as Bechand kept on and on and on. A blond man near the back grimaced every time Bechand said *Abersham*, presumably made as nauseous as Piero by the sycophancy.

Mr Karl Zajac

From his corner, Karl Zajac observed the three nobles being alternately praised and demeaned by Monsieur Bechand, head of the new Practical Curriculum in Maritime Commerce. This *soirée de présentation* for the course had devolved into an embarrassing display of the first three aristocrats ever to attend *L'école Supérieure de Commerce*, and one could hardly help but feel sorry for them. They looked so tortured.

Zajac's father had sent him to Paris expressly because a scion of Kopet Dag Shipping would be attending; that would be the slim youth with the dark skin and eyes, and the secretive half smile. His father had also known the heir to Seventh Sea would be here, but he didn't know Zajac had met the young English marquess years ago. Though they were both considerably taller and broader than they were when they briefly shared a schoolroom with the Erzherzog royal princes during one of Abersham's visits with his parents.

Would the peer acknowledge the acquaintance? If he didn't, Zajac would have to carry out his father's distasteful plan to ingratiate himself with the aristocrats.

Zajac was a nobody; a merchant's son with a royal patron who made a point of educating middle-class sons far beyond their station, then using them to encourage commerce and secure influence beyond his own borders. Still, when they were children in the palace schoolroom, the marquess had been as casual and as friendly as his royal friends. Lord Abersham had said then, "Am I not just a merchant's son? A merchant and her husband, the duke."

Zajac would put it to the test as soon as Abersham and the other two victims managed to escape that old blowhard Bechand, who had been addressing the group for an age.

His father would, in any case, expect him to make friends with the heirs to such sizable enterprises, no matter how it must be accomplished. Two of the most powerful merchant fleets in the Atlantic and Mediterranean, both suppliers to Zajac's father, and both represented here at the school. It was an opportunity not to be missed. Zajac only wished he could meet these men without his father's expectations echoing in his head, as they all looked like quite nice fellows.

Zajac didn't know the other man at all. D'Alvieri, the head of the programme called him. An Italian, then. Well, one could always do with more friends, Batya would say, and if they hold power, so much the better. He kept his warehouses full and supplied half of Northern Europe on the strength of that wisdom. Zajac was here to learn, yes, but also to make influential friends for his father's company and his patron's Grand Duchy.

Thank all the saints. The old man on the stage was winding to a close. Now perhaps Zajac could have a drink and find a chance to reintroduce himself to the English milord. Who, Bechand decreed, was to be called Mr Abersham. Judging from the expressions on the three aristocratic faces, the edict was distasteful in the extreme, so he would avoid being so familiar unless they offered him such a courtesy. Zajac could imagine the reaction of Prince Nikolaus, the royal schoolmate closest to him in age. He insisted his friends call him Niko, and was as relaxed and approachable as could be—until some overfamiliar idiot trod on his tender noble prerogatives. Then out came the royal ice, fit to freeze the offender's balls right off.

Bechand had held Abersham back after releasing the others, but as soon as he was free, Abersham made straight for Zajac, hand held out, and greeted him in Russian.

There. *Step one accomplished, Batya,* and a pleasure it was, too. Abersham was as friendly as Zajac remembered.

David, Lord Abersham

Finally! The arse-licking toady, Bechand, was finished degrading the three of them. David did not get away without another dose, one-on-one, directly afterward, with more treacle about the duchess's legend and generosity. But eventually, after everyone else had drinks and had chosen their food from the insipid-looking buffet, Bechand allowed him to withdraw, and David made his way toward the one other person in the room whom he knew, and engaged him in competent, but not fluent, Russian.

"*Dobriy vyecher.* Please forgive the intrusion, but while I cannot remember your name, I am certain we met in Erzherzog, at the palace, when we were children. I am David Abersham. Did we not share a tutor for a time?"

The blond giant grinned. "Karl Zajac, my lord. Yes, I remember you, and the trick with the slugs."

With a hearty laugh, David said, "I had forgotten that. But did you not hear Monsieur Bechand? You need no longer address me as 'my lord.' Abersham is sufficient."

"Not Toad?" Zajac asked with a sly smile.

Groaning, David begged, "Please do not say that so loudly. I am trying to outrun that dratted moniker."

"Your secret is safe, my lord."

When David raised a brow at the honorific, Zajac shrugged, "I cannot think your parents will approve of Monsieur Bechand's rules."

"No, they will not, but they are not here, and if they were, it would only add to the long list of my unpardonable sins. How do you come to be here? Is your family in shipping? I am afraid I remember very little, but for your skill with a hoop and stick."

"My father is a merchant with dealings with the palace in Erzherzog, who thinks a son in shipping would be a good idea, and Pfalzgraf Grenford agreed. And in this instance..." Zajac winked. "...they both believe your Seven Seas connection is more interesting than your English peerage."

"I see," David chuckled. "I find it more interesting myself, until it is time to seduce a lady. There is no better technique than to attach a title to one's name."

"So says every nobleman I've ever known, but alas, I shall never know. Thankfully, sailors have a certain reputation of which I shall avail myself starting tomorrow."

Nartay Muhadow Bey

Bechand had finished, thank goodness. Time for Nartay to introduce himself to the family connection. When his uncle had insisted, Nartay's mother had fretted about rumours of Toad Abersham's exploits with women in England, which was endorsement enough for Nartay. He had intended to visit Toad the day before, but the pleasure house was on his way, so what was Nartay to do? He would not wish to invite his new noble friend to a whorehouse he hadn't tried out first himself.

He captured a drink from a passing waiter, took a sip, and returned it to the next tray that passed. Disgusting stuff.

Toad had made a straight course for a tall, blond man, built like the side of a mountain, but with the same gleam of humour Nartay had recognised in d'Alvieri. As he approached, he could hear the two speaking of women and conquest, a conversation to which Nartay could certainly contribute.

"We have youth, good looks, wealth, and charm," he said as he approached, hand held out in greeting. "The ladies of Paris will be at our feet. Nartay Muhadow. Lord Abersham, I believe your parents are acquainted with my grandmother, the Duchess of Winshire."

"Aunt Eleanor is your grandmother. I knew it! I knew you must be one of the Kopet Dag heirs."

Nartay bowed, one hand on his heart. "I carry that burden, yes." Being heir to anything had liabilities, to be sure, but carrying the weight of all the work done by prior generations was a special sort of load to bear.

"Burden, indeed," Toad agreed. "It is good to meet you. Please, let me introduce you to Karl Zajac. We met briefly as children and have just been renewing our acquaintance."

"Mr. Zajac, I am pleased to meet you. You must both call me Nartay."

"Abersham," Toad said.

"My friends call me Zajac." Or Bull, which was not a name he intended to share with these gentlemen. To distract them, he returned to the subject of Bechand's oration. "Abersham is carefully avoiding being called a marquess, as instructed by our esteemed head horse's arse. What title must we *avoid* calling you, son of Kopet Dag. Prince, is it?"

The man was clearly referring to the family shipping line, named after the home mountains, not Nartay's connections to the ruling family of the *kaganate* nestled in within that wild range.

"Nothing so grand. At home, those who wish to be polite call me Bey. Lord, the English would say. Bey can also mean prince, but I am not in the line of descent, being a daughter's son to the man who was *kagan* and is now a duke in England. It is a courtesy only."

Introductions accomplished, Toad turned to Nartay. "You are cousin to the girl I mean to marry, Sally—Lady Sarah—Grenford. You share the same grandmother in the Duchess of Winshire."

Nartay shrugged. "I have thus far managed to avoid meeting my esteemed grandfather and his undoubtedly gracious lady, and I am sorry to say, I have not met your Lady Sarah."

Lord Piero d'Alvieri

When Bechand finally released them from the interminable torture, Piero made his way to the nearest of the footmen who circulated with trays of red wine.

At least, that is what they were told it was. If it was actually wine, it was the worst he had ever drunk in France, or anywhere else. And it was watered, so it would not even relieve the agony of this event. Why in the name of Neptune had he agreed to this?

Abersham must know the blond man in the crowd, as he went right up to him when Bechand finally stopped licking his arse. It would be rude to interrupt a reunion, so he wandered over to the buffet tables and placed a few appetizers on a small plate. One bite, however, and he put the plate down on the table. He would have to repair to his club for supper after this.

Now, the Persian gentleman had joined Abersham and the other man. Surely, Piero would not be poorly received if they'd already been interrupted? He sidled up to the group of them, just as Muhadow said, "I ask you, my new friends, why travel so far from home, only to put myself under the eye of relatives once more? My father's family is spread across the Levant, and my mother's relations are in London. Long may that great distance continue."

"I will toast to that," Piero said in French, by way of entering the conversation. "May my brother evermore remain in *Italia*."

"Brothers, cousins, uncles, grandfathers. A plague on them all," the Persian prince agreed.

"Fathers and mothers, too," Abersham added, "especially when they are ducal."

They all raised their glasses, but no one drank very deeply of the supposed wine.

David, Lord Abersham

David barely wet his lips with the execrable wine. He had never drunk bad French wine in his life, and wasn't sure how they had managed to find such vile stuff.

He was drawn back into the conversation in time to be introduced in exactly the way he had been hoping to avoid: "D'Alvieri, was it? I am Nartay. This giant is Zajac. And the Englishman with the lofty chin is known as Toad. Something about saving the life of his king, I believe? A hero while still in frocks, or so my cousins tell me."

David groaned. "A hero while I was too young to even remember the incident." With a deep sigh, Abersham complained, "Now I shall be haunted by that awful moniker on both sides of the English Channel." Infusing a bit of sarcasm into his self-pity, he added, "Merci, *Bey Bey*, my Lord Prince."

Nartay groaned in turn.

"You've brought it upon yourself. I truly had hoped to avoid 'Toad' altogether, and I might have, but for you."

Piero snickered at 'Bey Bey,' but slapped David on the shoulder. "Toad it shall be, then. And you shall offer to kiss princesses until one curses you to marriage."

While Toad professed to be amenable to kissing princesses, he nevertheless declared his intention to marry Sally. When they appeared to be about to ask questions, however, he shifted the conversation to possible nicknames for d'Alvieri and Zajac.

The ensuing banter was necessary only because Bechand would not take his eyes off his pet nobles long enough for them all to leave early, but within a quarter-hour, Toad rather thought the four of them had discovered common ground, if only in the fact none of them lacked for wit.

"We shall toast your sorrows, Toad Abersham..." Bey raised his nearly full glass once more and raised it in salute.

Lord Piero d'Alvieri

The conversation was lively and witty and altogether more civilized than Piero had expected to find at a business school. And Piero was in a better position than the two other noblemen, because he had no nickname; Arturo would have beheaded anyone who suggested anything so frivolous and disrespectful. How Abersham became Toad, Piero could not wait to hear.

In part to encourage that particular confidence, Piero invited them all to his club for an edible supper and better drinks. The others agreed, and Abersham even asked for details of the club, as he had yet to join one and had been eating at food stalls and in cafes. He said his quarterly income only allowed for two servants in his eight-room *pied-a-terre*, which was one apartment and one servant more than the rest of them had. Piero was living in two rented rooms, with his valet in one across the hall; Nartay was in one room with a manservant he shared with three other students; and Zajac was in one room and did for himself. Arturo wished to instil "character" in his younger brother, and "compassion for the less fortunate." Or so he said. More likely, he was just being a parsimonious, sanctimonious horse's arse.

"I would have to go without brandy and wine to hire a cook," Abersham said, with another smirk sneaking across his face. "And that would be a travesty. As for attending a brothel, I will decline, though I would not be averse to a trip to the Opera or theatre to assess the available actresses or dancers. Why live in Paris if not to take in the cultural offerings?"

What Abersham said next, though, was surprising. What nobleman of their age wishes to be married? And what man in love wishes to dally with other women? His Sally must be a reluctant virgin. Or he hadn't wanted to be sacrificed to matrimony if they were caught.

Bey took a wine glass from a passing footman and raised it in salute. "Then we shall toast your sorrows, Toad Abersham, and the beauty and constancy of your fair maiden. And courage to our good selves and confusion on all parents and guardians who want to run our lives for us."

"I would toast with you," Piero drawled, "but this wine is worse than rat piss."

"Drink a lot of rat piss, do you?" Abersham joked.

"Not when I can avoid it, and tonight, I can. Shall we find the exit as soon as Bechand turns his back and make our way to a more palatable meal?"

No better case needed to be made. Everyone in the room was ready to leave, except Bechand, and as such, the entire inaugural class in Maritime Commerce was trapped here. Finally, the head of the programme slipped out of the room for some reason, and Toad remarked it with a gesture.

"Gather your things," Piero said at a whisper. "Let us take our leave. Zajac? Bey? Are you with us?"

Mr Karl Zajac

Zajac was delighted the three noblemen had gravitated to one another. Like attracts like, perhaps, and Zajac, having the advantage of a prior acquaintance, was along for the ride. He could be their token commoner, to placate Bechand, the horse's arse. And perhaps, if the past quarter-hour were any indication, he might find he had made actual friends. Zajac had known many different kinds of nobles in his youth, and all three of these men were the best sort.

Batya always said, "Listen ten times, ponder a hundred times, speak once." Zajac's new friends had clearly not had the advantage of that wisdom, as they chattered like a parliament of magpies. He listened as they sparred with one another, speaking of nicknames, and women, and drink, and pestilential relations.

"Vodka," he offered at one point. "Vodka is the only drink for a man."

Certainly not this rotgut the school claimed as red wine, so he was pleased on all accounts to be invited to join the others for supper at Piero d'Alviero's club. Connections for Batya and the Pfalzgraf, friends—maybe good friends—for Zajac, and vodka. What more could a man want?

The Christmas Letters

<u>Christmas 1841: Sally's letter to Toad</u>

(Sent through the Duchess of Winshire)

January 2nd, 1841
London

Dear Toad,

We are heading home to Margate, after spending Christmastide at Wellstone. How strange it was to be there without you. I kept expecting to see you around every corner, in every room I entered, in all of our favourite places. My usual letter, sent by Papa's hand, will be full of enthusiasm for the dinners we attended, the parties we held, the entertainments we enjoyed. My first grown-up holiday at Wellstone.

All of that is true, and none of it.

Here, where only you will see, I can tell the truth, my dearest friend. I wished myself anywhere but there. In London, even in Margate, I can pretend you are away at school or on some escapade with your friends, and will be back shortly. I have never been to Wellstone without you, and every moment of every day, I missed you.

Why did they not let you return home for Christmas, David? I cannot understand it. Papa would say only that Uncle Wellbridge thought it best, and Uncle Wellbridge would not answer at all, but kept arranging new activities for me, as though a sleigh ride or a game of charades would distract me, like a child in the nursery.

Enough of that. I do not mean to fill this letter with whinging, and give you a distaste for me. I hope all is well with you, and that you are studying hard, so you can excel in your examinations and come home at your next school break.

I feel I must tell you some of the guests at Wellstone met you in Paris, and they say you spend much of your time in gaming clubs and with women of dubious morality. I told them I did not believe them, and I did not wish to hear any more. Oh Toad, if it is true, I pray you will think of your dear mother, and others who miss you and would hate to see you demean yourself so.

I have no right to scold, and I know you have always done well at school despite your other activities. (About which I am supposed to know nothing, at least according to Papa and Uncle Wellbridge. As if I have no ears.) I can imagine you telling me it is none of my business, which is true. But even if I have no right to object to how you spend your time, I do not want you to come to harm, or to draw the kind of slanderous comment I heard this holiday at your mother's own dining table. Please be careful and circumspect.

Do not be cross with me for writing so. We have been the closest of confidants our whole lives, which I hope gives me some small license to opine. Write and tell me that you are still my friend, for I am yours.

Your faithful,
Sally

Christmas 1841: Toad's letter to Sally

(Sent through the Duchess of Wirshire)

December 16, 1841

Dear Sally,

As you may know by now, my parents have decreed I not return to England for the winter holiday. My mother blames travel times and shipyard scheduling, but of course, my father is behind it. I am so sorry I cannot be there to visit with you and enjoy the Yuletide season together, as we have every year of our lives. I beg you understand I have done all my parents have asked to be afforded the chance to come home, if only for a few days, and have been refused in any case. I cannot see what they hold so zealously against me; but equally, I cannot fight against what I cannot see.

I am writing from my cabin on the family frigate, docked in Marseilles, and will send this through Aunt Eleanor before we set sail. With luck and a fast wind, this will arrive in time for Christmas. I wish I had posted it earlier, but I had hoped so much to see you in person. We will be on our way to Livorno in the morning, then Florence, where I will spend the holiday with Lord Piero d'Alvieri and his family at the count's *castello*.

You will like Piero when you meet him, though he is even more a rogue than your David, so you must never be alone with him. He has five younger sisters, the eldest, Maddalena, a year younger than Almyra. Piero assures me we will be followed incessantly by pestilential girl children, which will remind me how much I miss my own pestilential shadow, Monkey. I've only just met his brother,

Arturo, il conte d'Alvieri, who is quite a good chap, though Piero will forever accuse him of meddling.

Fortunate am I that he meddles, for, ever your errant boy, I managed to find myself gaoled for fighting in a gaming hell, and Arturo used his influence to secure my release. (It truly was a minor incident, resolved in less than a day.) I would think this the reason I was denied the chance to come home, but it was my mother's letter refusing me that sent me off on the unfortunate drunken spree that resulted in my incarceration. If you can discover what I have done that is so awful as to keep me from your side, even for a visit, pray, write to me so I may rectify the error. I cannot think news of my imprisonment will help, but I have received the highest marks, and, on the whole, my life has been far less profligate than in the past.

My mother writes you will have Christmas at Wellstone, so you may be sure I hold you in my heart and my mind's eye as I remember all the winter months we have spent there. Please write, I beg, with an account of the holiday, for I cannot expect to enjoy any of our favourite Yuletide pastimes in Italy. From Piero's descriptions, one wonders if we will do anything but attend endless Catholic masses morning to night. (I pray you do not say so to my mother, lest she fear for my immortal Anglican soul.)

Since you are at Wellstone, and I cannot safely send a gift through all the ports of France and England, I have written to the bookshop in the village and placed ten pounds on account for you to spend as you like, and I have instructed they send to London for any book you request, without question, without bothering the dukes and duchesses about the subject matter. (I leave to you the damage to your reputation, should you choose unwisely.)

I will miss you sorely, Monkey, for there is no one else with whom I can always prevail at every parlour game. Happy Christmas and Joyous New Year, my dearest girl.

Ever Your,
David Abersham

Christmas 1842: Sally's letter to Toad

(Sent through the Duke of Haverford)

December 12, 1842
Wind's Gate

Dear Toad,

How odd that you will receive and be reading this letter sometime in the new year, and I am writing it in early December. Where are you at the moment, I wonder? And where will you be as this gigantic house fills with guests and then with all the festivities? I hope you are with congenial friends since you cannot be at home with us.

As I told you in my last, Grandmama has commandeered my services as her aide-de-camp, to organise the house party she was determined to hold, which is now but days away. Her role is to drop vague suggestions; mine, to scurry from attics to cellars, by way of every bedchamber and three separate kitchens, in order to carry them out.

Yes, Toad, I said <u>three kitchens</u>. I am sure, when we were six or seven and attempted to count all the rooms in Winds' Gate, we failed to notice at least one of these kitchens, without which, three separate cooks and their respective staffs would murder one another (or so I have come to believe) while preparing the food needed for all the dozens of guests Grandmama has invited. Or rather, I have invited, in the name of the Duchess of Winshire, who has had very little to do with the enterprise. Still, I am certain she would be distressed should dinner consist of braised kitchen boy and roast haunch of chef, so I shall endeavour to keep the peace between the three independent domains ruled by my three gustatory tyrants.

Grandmama says I must never forget that I rule them, and indeed, Toad, you would laugh to see how I give my orders to high and low, sending out lists and minions from the sitting room Etcetera has dubbed The Command Centre.

Did I mention Etcetera is here? He came to keep company with Grandmama, and when I first saw him, I was a little in awe. He must have been sixteen the last time we met, abetting you as you tried to avoid me the Christmas after you returned from touring Europe. He has, I can assure you, grown considerably; the giant who bent over my hand bore little resemblance, aside from his fair hair, to the lanky boy who supported you in vexing me so unmercifully that winter.

I have quickly lost my shyness, for the same Etcetera lurks behind the beard and broad shoulders. As ever, he is always ready with a joke and willing to turn his hand to anything. He is not my only helper, of course. I am also ably assisted by Jonny and Almyra and several of my other cousins. The stalwarts are Elf—I should say Sutton, but it does not come easily when I have called him Elf all my life—and his sister Anna, Michael St James and his sister Henry, who have come to spend the holidays with us.

I am determined everyone will have a wonderful time. The party will fill every one of those 103 bedchambers we counted, and every day, a succession of planned activities. And the food coming out of those three kitchens would make your eyes widen and your mouth water, I can assure you!

You would be proud of your Sal, were you here, my dear friend. I wish you were.

Your,
Sal

Christmas 1842: Toad's letter to Sally

(Sent by courier)

December 5, 1842
Marseilles

Sally, my dearest,

I'm sorry to send this in a manner that may alarm you, but the rough man who delivered it was the only Seventh Sea sailor willing to defy Hawley—only because he is soon leaving my mother's employ to join my new venture with Uncle Firthley, which is a great secret. I will ask Bey to explain in detail when he is in London for Sutton's nuptials in January.

I wish you to know I will return home after my graduation, before I go to Greece—with or without the duke's assent—and stay until the weather warms enough to easily make the passage. Yours is the first face I hope to see when I reach English shores again.

If, that is, you will have me.

I have been a damned fool, my love. With that dreadful comtesse, to start (for whom I cannot apologize abjectly enough), but every time I have behaved in a manner that might bring you shame, make you doubt my devotion, or keep me banished from England and apart from you. Until a few months ago, I was a terrible choice for a husband, and while I will never forgive your father, I begin to understand his reservations about placing you in my care. I swear to you, my sweet, I repent my wicked deeds, and beg you forgive me as I become a man upon whom you can depend for the rest of our lives.

It will be Christmastime by the time you receive this, and while I do not feel comfortable sending anything of excessive value with this particular courier, I wished you to have some token of my adoration, so I had these calling cards made when last I visited Florence with Piero. (His oldest two sisters are exceptionally talented with brush and quill, and they have adopted me as another older brother.) The cards are not the sort of thing you expect me to send for your Scrapbook, but I hope you will not mind if I bare my heart to you this once, and not more carnal assets, though both are yours in their entirety, my dear one.

I must go now, my darling, but pray, do not forsake me before I can come to you.

Your devoted slave,
David

The Dukes and Duchesses

The Infamous Rakes of Fickleton Wells

(A story of Wellbridge and Haverford, before either ascended to their titles, that plumbs the depths of their stunning hypocrisy.)

The year is 1801 in Fickleton Wells, Somerset.

The Marquis of Aldridge, heir to the Duke of Haverford, is 21, just down from Oxford. Lord Nicholas Northope, second son of the Duke of Wellbridge has been, at 27, racketing about England unchecked a fair few years without much purpose. And the trajectories of both young lives are about to change.

"I don't fancy hanging so much, myself," Lord Nicholas Northope observes, rubbing his fingertips along his throat, the iron chains at his wrist clanking as he considered the length of his neck. "I always thought if Prinny ordered it, I'd be drawn and quartered or boiled in oil. I seem to bring out his bloodlust."

Nick looks out the window. They have been imprisoned in an old Norman tower at the home of the local baron. Fortunately. With the entire town of Fickleton Wells on the rampage, the local gaol would not have been safe. Even from this place of relative safety, he can see angry townspeople keeping watch from beyond the gate.

The two young noblemen are sitting, cramped and freezing, in torn, grimy clothes, awaiting the Prince of Wales' pleasure after rather an uproar in one of his royal townships. Wrist and ankle shackles clank at each gesture, chains long enough to allow considered movement, but short enough to impede them if they run.

Back to the wall on the cold stone floor, Lord Aldridge, the Merry Marquis, tosses out, casually, "I don't qualify for silk myself, you know. I'm just using my father's second title. Hemp for me, same as you," Nick thinks Aldridge is taking rather a ghoulish interest in the possible mechanics of his death. "Though I did rather fancy *Madame La Guillotine* if I were ever put to death. There is something so divinely aristocratic about it."

"It seems one can only play so many pranks on a monarch," Nick opines, "before one's neck is stretched."

"It wasn't our fault. Those women..." Aldridge shudders. "I can't have swived more than three or four, surely? We only had them to ourselves for one evening, after all."

"I can't *possibly* have swived all of them. Though perhaps half... There were... how many? Fifteen? Surely not."

"I don't remember much after the dancing. They danced beautifully, didn't they? The rector's daughters?"

Both men fell into rather a trance for a few minutes, remembering the plump thighs and comely smiles of the rector's twelve lovely, lonely daughters.

"Nick, we didn't do anything... dishonorable... Did we? They won't really hang us? And the prince—he wouldn't... Hell, Nick, I played with his little brothers and sisters from the time I could toddle."

Nick shrugged, "And I might have married Sophia. You will do best not to remind him you might have touched his younger sisters with the same hands you used to defile the rector's daughters. In fact, Aldridge, speaking as a man six years older and wiser, you will not want to mention the princesses—or defiling—at all."

He can't keep his chained hands away from his neck.

"My head feels very fuzzy," Aldridge complains. "Nick, how many hands am I holding up? And what is that elephant doing in the corner?"

"Prinny won't be fooled by false deliria. I've tried it once already and he caught me out by calling a physician."

Aldridge subsides, grumbling. "Is it not worth trying? And how very like you to steal a man's alibi before he even has the chance to use it."

Perhaps Aldridge has a point. "The gin did have rather a sharp taste, to be sure, though. Did you not think?"

Aldridge straightens, clearly prepared to synchronize their stories. "Yes, of course. Assuredly. Quite sharp indeed."

Nick laughs and shakes his finger. "Do not lie to your sovereign, Aldridge, and if you must, never so poorly as that. The mayor, the rector, and the squire have truth on their side. There can be no doubt of our guilt. I did visit the squire's wife, and you did enjoy the mayor's younger sister, no matter what we might or might not remember about the rector's daughters. We both knew the town was on the prince's estate—is that not why we were there? To avoid our fathers' holdings? No, my friend, we've been well and truly served up for His Royal Highness's supper."

Aldridge utters an expletive, and sinks his head in his hands.

A sound outside the tower room brings them both to their feet. A key turns in the lock.

The Duke of Haverford brushes past the burly guard who opens the door. "Out!" he barks.

Lord Nicholas Northope is no stranger to the ducal disposition and backs into a corner first thing, a tactical error he started making in childhood and has never outgrown. Aldridge, the son of this particular angry duke, stays at rigid attention, which does not avert the ducal fire.

"You miserable, self-indulgent, beef-witted nodcocks! What on earth possessed you? What were you thinking? Don't answer that. You were not thinking!" Nick and Aldridge shrink, inch by inch, to the size of ten-year-olds. "Northope, I blame you for this mess. *Show the boy the town*, I said. *Give him a good time. Keep him out of trouble.* What the hell do you mean by it, eh?"

If Aldridge thinks Nick will step forward to do the honorable thing and admit his part, he has lost his bloody mind.

"Aldridge," the duke barks as his heir begins to edge to one side. "Stand, boy. I'll get to you." The last is uttered in a low steady monotone.

Nick sinks ever-deeper into the corner he should have abandoned when he had the chance.

"Listen to me, and listen well, you buffle-brained nincompoops. You have been banned from Fickleton Wells! Banned! The sons of two of the greatest men in the United Kingdoms *banned* from an English town. How on earth did this happen?"

Nick clears his throat and still manages to squeak, "Patent medicine, Sir, I swear it!" He shoulders his way out of the corner, determined to give his lies confidence. "In the... in the gin... we were... we were poisoned! The brandy, too, I'll wager. Lucky to be alive... Surely cannot be held responsible for..."

"Rubbish, Northope. Rubbish! I'll tell you how it happened. You let a pack of women lead you by your willies. Yes, you did. Your father and I have talked to them. And paid them off, the bitches. Because..." he walks right up and taps Nick's chest as he makes his point. "You. Let. Them. Fool. You."

Nick's hand runs around his neck again.

"Your Grace," Aldridge has suddenly realized that they wouldn't be banned if they were to be hanged. This has given him an altogether overly optimistic sense of confidence. "They say they are pregnant, Your Grace." Haverford's head swivels dangerously in Aldridge's direction. "It can't be us, Your Grace. It's only been a week since we arrived, and surely, virile as we are, we cannot each have impregnated a dozen women in a week? Surely, not even Your Grace could—"

Nick suddenly realizes the benefit of being six years wiser.

Haverford turns all his attention on his son and heir, and Aldridge's confidence shrinks to a needle point.

"They claim you have been visiting them for months," Haverford explains, his suddenly gentle tones a sure sign that Aldridge is about to be very, very sorry. And then even sorrier than that.

While Aldridge tries to duck out of sight, Nick moves to a position well away from any more corners. He is a grown man, for heaven's sake. And there are plenty of places to stand.

"I haven't finished with you, Northope."

"Months?" Nick responds, shaking his head, straightening his cuffs. "You've been coming here months, Aldridge?"

"Not I, Your Grace. It's a lie." Aldridge squeaks.

"I, on the other hand," Nick offers, "just came to Fickleton Wells for a prize fight. At least that is why your son *told me* he was bringing me here. If he had another purpose... well... I cannot speak to that..."

Haverford casts his eyes to heaven. "No honour among thieves or scoundrels. Did the Duke of Wellbridge's wife play him false with the village idiot? Aldridge, if your mother weren't a saint I would swear you couldn't be mine."

Aldridge is casting Nick a look of deep betrayal. "Nick, how could you?"

Nick relents. There is no need to leave all the blame on Aldridge. "Admittedly, Your Grace, we had a bit more gin than two gentlemen should... But I would swear Aldridge and I were both unknown to them. And the gin had quite a sharp taste, rather like... patent medicine. I can't help but think they are lying."

"Of course they are lying." Haverford throws up his hands in despair. "And of course they set out to trap you. And of course they drugged you. And of course you would drink anything put in front of you! Do you think I'm as big a fool as the two of you? But they have the whole town believing them, and the prince half believes them, too."

"The prince," Nick gulps. "What is Wales going to do to us?"

Haverford ignores him to continue his version of a fatherly sermon. "I have told you before, Aldridge. And you should listen, too, Northope. Never, ever, indulge yourself with the lower gentry or the middle sort. Servants, yes. Farmers' wives and such. But never with people who can embarrass me... you. Keep a mistress. Keep ten; your allowance is large enough. Just don't let your mother know, and stay away from the middle sort. One of our own, if you must, and if she has done her duty by her Lord. But never the middle sort. You have embarrassed me. You have embarrassed Wellbridge. And you have embarrassed the Prince of Wales."

"On the topic of, er... Wellbridge... Sir?" Nick's tentative voice demonstrated not an ounce of the Eton/Oxford poise he was so fond of displaying. "Did my, er... father... say what he would do? And Wales? What has he decided?"

"If it were up to me, and if Aldridge weren't—God help the Haverford name—my heir, you'd both hang. But Prinny is inclined to be generous. I have no idea why." He fixes Aldridge with another glare. "Your mother may have spoken to him."

That brought up a very good point.

"Sir, Your Grace," Nick asks, "might it be possible to bring this up with the Duchess of Wellbridge, not the duke?"

"There will be no discussion of anything with you, Northope. The king discussed it with Prinny, who discussed it with me and Wellbridge; we discussed it with your mothers, and the petty provincials in Fickleton Wells discussed it the length and breadth of England! You are asked not to find yourselves in the royal presence until such time as you are requested. You are further banned, until the general sense of noble fury is abated, from all of Prinny's estates, his father's, your father's, and mine."

"Which. Will. Not. Be. Difficult." Haverford's finger drives the point home, "as you are both leaving England. Northope, your father has booked passage and suggests your long-delayed Grand Tour commence immediately on conclusion of this interview. Aldridge will be going to my estate in Outer Strathclyde, to study the wool trade. It is time he took a hand in estate business."

"But Your Grace, isn't Outer Strathclyde... didn't you complain that you can't seem to keep anyone there under the age of sixty?"

"Outer Strathclyde," Nick snickers.

Aldridge looks hunted. "Outer Strathclyde," he whimpers.

"Live to a ripe old age, they do in those parts. Something to do with the fine crisp air. Of course, all the young people have long since gone. But you could learn a lot there, Aldridge."

"But Your Grace. You said you would never go there because you couldn't get a woman to..." Aldridge's voice trails off. Nick thinks he would have been better not to have opened his mouth.

Haverford, though, just smirks. "Precisely. And so the estate is neglected. But now I have no need to go. My ungrateful son—who could clearly do with fewer women—will represent me instead. And you, Northope…"

Nick knows exactly where he will be going, and if he can go without the ducal blessing, so much the better.

"Hanover, I presume?" he shrugs.

Nick has been recently considering a visit to his old friend, Adolphus, the viceroy, and Prinny will have no objection to Nick causing trouble in his brother's viceregal Court. Northope second sons have a tradition of travel; it is how the French and Italian titles were acquired, and Nick will be more than delighted to continue the custom. Unexpected, given his brother's infirmity, but not at all unwelcome. He does hope his father allows him a valet and enough money to eat well.

"Aldridge, you will not disappoint me," Haverford's mere tone of voice is a threat to both men… er, boys, who thus comply with the two burly servants come to escort the young lords to their respective transports.

"This is so unfair," Aldridge hisses to Nick as they are separated. "You are being given the freedom of the globe, while I am being sent into celibate exile in a community of geriatric woollen weavers."

Nick cannot help but grin. Aldridge is bearing the real punishment for their prank, and Nick is being rewarded with a merry jaunt across the Continent and no way for his father to object to it.

"I'll remember this day, Northope," Aldridge calls, as his keepers escort him away. "And I vow my exile will be a short one."

Nick vows his might last forever.

The First Dance of the Duke and Duchess of Wellbridge

(Excerpt from Royal Regard, *by Mariana Gabrielle, wherein the Duke of Wellbridge begins his seduction of Bella, the Countess of Huntleigh, the woman who will become his duchess and mother to his children.)*

Chapter 6

Opening night of *Il Barbiere di Siviglia* at the Italian Opera House, Nick saw Lady Holsworthy—no, Lady Huntleigh—the second time. She and her husband visited the boxes of Lord Huntleigh's more important investors, and Nick was the guest of Lord Pinnester, who had brought Seventh Sea Shipping to the attention of the last king thirty years earlier.

Nick was quite taken with her shocking tales of their travels, though he was the only one amused, aside from Lord and Lady Pinnester, whose entire fortune had been built on the back of Huntleigh's company. From the whispering behind hands, Nick knew Lady Huntleigh's stories were fanning gossip all over London, but within the Pinnesters' hearing, nothing but counterfeit cordiality and feigned fascination with their travels.

When Lady Huntleigh told the story of a tribe of Black Africans mistaking her for a goddess, he found himself considering the implications of worshiping at her feet. Her anecdotes about their frigate outrunning and outgunning pirates took him back twenty years, though he had learned the hard way not to discuss such adventures in company. He thought perhaps he should take Lord Huntleigh aside to discuss the ramifications of such public disclosure, but was far too intrigued by the lady's narrative to suggest she not continue.

Nick was chagrined Lady Huntleigh had seen him in the company of the widowed Lady Rowena Astewithe, who set his teeth on edge. Allison had arranged his escort, trying yet again to marry him to any fertile woman with a pulse. He hadn't expected to see the Huntleighs, or he might have—

Might have what, exactly? he wondered to himself a few days later, as he surreptitiously changed the place cards at a small supper given by Lord and Lady Carrick. *It isn't as though I can marry her,* he thought, as he gave a viscountess a place at the table far higher than her position warranted, just to seat himself directly across from Lady Huntleigh.

I don't even want to be married.

Lady Huntleigh barely uttered a word to him beyond, "It is an honor to make your acquaintance, Your Grace," and he was entirely circumspect: he might have used a protractor to gauge the degree of his bow and a ruler to measure the appropriate distance between her hand and his lips. But she couldn't keep from staring when she thought he wasn't looking.

Improving matters, her husband had declined to attend at the last minute, citing ill health, leaving her in the care of her cousin's inattentive husband. Lady Huntleigh was preoccupied all evening and left early, against Lady Firthley's objections, but it was the first time he was able to converse with her beyond a polite greeting.

When they spoke just before the exodus to the dining room, Lady Huntleigh was shy, glances slipping away toward the walls, but couldn't avoid him with everyone else in the room engaged in other conversations.

"I had not remembered London being so cold in the springtime."

"It is chilly this year, to be sure." When he added, "The shawl you are wearing is lovely," she seemed to lose her breath and looked as though she wished to hide behind it.

"So kind of you to say."

As he caught her eye with an impertinent grin, bewilderment stained her cheeks. She was prettier every time he saw her, especially in her emerald-green gown with primrose trim, better fitting and better suited to her coloring than any previous frocks, bringing out the bronze tones of her hair and the gold of her sun-kissed skin.

She couldn't stop the heat rising from her chest to her forehead with each syllable of the four innocuous sentences they shared while the guests were being seated, so he did his best to turn his attention elsewhere. Taking too much notice would give him away.

All he could do was quietly take in her features one glance at a time: her soft, plump mouth, the rounded tip of her nose, her genuine smile and real blushes. He didn't know the color of her eyes yet—maybe blue, maybe green. If he looked too closely, he might not be able to tear himself away.

She wasn't as striking as Nick's usual conquests, not jaded or restive or hostile, not resorting to paint on her face or suggestive banter or sending him signals with her fan. Still, he caught her looking often enough to warrant an impudent wink across the table while everyone else listened to a drunken baron rudely regale the entire table with a bizarre tale of minor municipal chicanery. When her eyes rounded with shock at Nick's shamelessness, he determined they were a crystal-clear *aqua marina*, the color of a Caribbean coastline.

From the corner of his eye, Nick watched Lady Huntleigh whisper to the woman next to her, who both ogled him just long enough for him to notice. Whatever she heard made her mouth fall open, but she quickly clamped her jaw shut against any semblance of interest. Only she didn't turn away from him as fast as she might.

A slow, wolfish smirk crossed his face as he inclined his head to Lady Huntleigh and the woman who was spreading rumors. They both gulped and looked down at their squab in port wine and cherries.

Unknowingly saving her from ignominy, the hostess turned the table and Lady Huntleigh opened a clumsy, self-conscious conversational gambit with the gentleman on her left. Given the beginnings of a polite dialogue with the woman next to him, Nick couldn't quite hear the *faux pas* written all over Lady Huntleigh's face, even only four feet away, but he could tell he unsettled her, and that was a good start. Her puzzlement at his small attentions shone like a gas light.

Heaven help him, he was nearly old enough to be her father—no, older brother—which, he rationalized, made him at least twenty years less a reprobate than her husband. Huntleigh was ancient as alphabets, but Nick guessed Lady Huntleigh was only three-and-thirty, maybe four, given the fifteen years since her debut. As some catty women might say, the bloom was off the rose, but she still had the improbable air of an untouched maiden, not cynical enough to be a world traveler, not staid enough to be a stodgy merchant's wife.

And Nick had never met anyone stodgier than the new Earl of Huntleigh. Even the king said so. A devout Anglican whose knowledge of the Bible rivaled any vicar; a staunch teetotaler who drank naught but small beer and gambled only enough to do business with men at the tables; a faithful spouse who made plain his disgust for the fleshpots of London. The only sailor Nick had ever met disdainful of dockside temptations. As a dubious testament to his own wit, Prinny had conferred an earldom named to fit the decades-old moniker first coined by the king's father—with all due pomp and ceremony, Humdrum Holsworthy had been elevated to Humdrum Huntleigh.

A little more than a week after the Carrick's supper, at a rout given by the Countess of Estermore, Nick came up behind the new earl and his wife as her wrap was being taken by a servant.

"Lord Huntleigh, I was hoping you would be here this evening."

"Your Grace," Lord Huntleigh bowed politely and Lady Huntleigh curtsied, studiously avoiding his eyes and only whispering a greeting.

"I hadn't expected to see you, Sir," Lord Huntleigh said, neck not half as stiff as his wife's shoulders. "From all accounts, you avoid the *beau monde*." The clear implication: Lord Huntleigh had heard about Nick's propensity for gambling in the rookeries. Nick neither admitted nor acknowledged the polite aspersion.

"I wished to congratulate you on your elevation, and I have a piece of business to discuss on the advice of Lord Pinnester. Begging the pardon of your lovely wife, of course." Nick bent over her hand and kissed the air above her knuckles, but held on a bit too tightly and a bit too long.

She tugged her hand away and improved on her mumbled salutation. "It is a pleasure to see you again, Sir."

"Humble servant, Lady Huntleigh."

Myron smiled with difficulty, the face of a man secure in his own position, but ready to defend it anyway. "With due respect, Sir, I've been warned to keep my wife close whilst in your company." Lady Huntleigh took her husband literally, scooting a step closer to his side and holding on to his arm with both hands. "I hate to credit rumors, but I am not in the habit of inviting scandal, especially not involving my wife."

Nick took a step back. Husbands normally didn't confront him with his intentions directly.

"No scandal intended. Although, with a wife so charming, it must be trying to keep the blackguards away." He grinned at Lady Huntleigh, but she looked at the floor. He couldn't tell if she were being coy or if he had truly caused a problem in her marriage, nor did he know Huntleigh well enough to gauge how he might treat his wife if he were incensed. Nick hadn't been trying to make trouble, but had spoken more to, and about, Lady Huntleigh in two weeks than he could possibly explain.

"It is not difficult to keep you away," Lord Huntleigh said, not quite joking, and turned to his wife. "My dear, if you will forgive, we can find the card room to discuss our business." He pinched her cheek. "And you must never entertain the Duke of Wellbridge outside my company. Any man with a wife will tell you so." He motioned to Nick. "Shall we attempt to avoid the ballroom entirely?"

About an hour later, Nick made his way back to her. "Lady Huntleigh, I had not meant to keep you from the dancing."

She looked up in surprise. "My goodness, Your Grace, you startled me. Are you finished with your business then?" She peered around him, twisting her hands together. "Is my husband behind you?"

"Any moment." He leaned in and lowered his voice. "You needn't call me 'Your Grace,' you know. You are an unquestioned countess now, not a country-mouse-come-to-Town."

She made a concerted effort to disengage her fidgety hands, but merely moved them from her waist to begin worrying the fabric of her skirt. "Hardly unquestioned, Your Grace." She conceded with a nod, almost in a whisper, "Duke." She couldn't stop the nervous twitching of a wallflower, which might explain her not dancing, if one discounted gossip as the more likely justification.

Before they had retired to play whist, Nick had noted her faintly injured glances toward Lord Huntleigh. They must have had a fight before the party, or Huntleigh said something thoughtless or hurtful. It wasn't so important she would feign a megrim to go home, but not so small she would forget by morning. Though most women would be flagrantly flirting with every man present to make known any upset with their husbands.

Huntleigh, Nick had discovered in the card room, saw nothing wrong at all, just a youthful, compliant, entirely respectable girl who did everything he asked. He had been nothing but generous in everything he said about her, though never as besotted as some old men become about their young wives. She was a veritable paragon, to hear her husband tell it—as hostess and nursemaid and housekeeper and opponent at backgammon. He probably didn't even realize she might be pleasing in the bedroom.

Nick would be doing this poor young lady a service, paying her a bit of attention, he told himself, liven things up a bit. Every woman deserves to know when a gentleman thinks she's pretty, and any husband unaware his wife is upset with him really had no right to keep her. Nick was flabbergasted Huntleigh didn't realize they had been having a disagreement all evening, perhaps longer.

"I must apologize for requiring so much of Lord Huntleigh's time. I had no idea you might not find other partners, or I would never have spirited him away."

"It is of no concern. My husband only ever attends parties to advance his business, and I keep myself entertained. The Estermore's picture gallery rivals any I've seen outside a royal residence or museum."

"I shall make a point of viewing it, so we might have a topic of conversation next time we meet." He paused, uncertain if his usual gambit would produce a positive result, but more impatient than usual in his pursuit. "Unless you should like to adjourn there to guide me through the collection."

She took two blatant steps away, but couldn't help her body turning toward him, eyes dropping. "I entertain myself, Sir, not gentlemen of my husband's acquaintance."

He immediately withdrew his impropriety, but not entirely the intent. "Such a shame you should have to entertain yourself in the absence of admiring company."

She looked around at the crowds either staring pointedly away from her or talking about her behind their hands, and shrugged one shoulder. "I prefer my own society to the entertainments of the Season."

"Do you?" He had seen the momentary longing on her face as she watched the couples dancing by, ladies' dresses shimmering like precious jewels under the candlelight, but not half as magnificent as her hair. A few loose strands fell from her upswept coiffure, draping like antique gold down the side of her face, her eyes set like sapphires on a diadem.

She glanced toward him to gauge his sincerity, collecting her conversation. He saw the lonely young lady she must have been as a debutante, and prepared himself to carry the conversation, if he managed to make her nervous enough to lose her head.

"Surely you have heard I am the biggest wallflower on Earth, well familiar with the edges of a dance floor."

"I have only heard you charmed your husband's associates and the king's ambassadors all over the globe," he half-lied, "and you are as responsible as Huntleigh for his many successes."

Her face turned away as a wall sconce flickered as though it would burn out. He could only be so lucky as to suddenly have a dimmer corner in which to carry out his quest.

"You will gain no advantage trying to please me. My husband will only take into account you tried and hold it against you."

"Surely I am at an advantage among friends, and it behooves me to cultivate such relationships."

"You are more likely to make me a friend, Wellbridge," Huntleigh interjected as he limped toward them, not a moment or two before the lamp sputtered out, "by cultivating relationships with everyone else's wife." He turned to her. "Have we kept you waiting too long, my dear?"

She slipped her hand into her husband's. "Of course not, darling, but I do so want to dance."

Huntleigh looked like she'd suggested he take his shoes off to be filleted for his supper. "Did you not already—? I mean, people are dancing. Is there no one—? Er—?" He looked hopefully back at the card room. "Surely we agreed on—"

Her head dropped, "You did ask I only speak with Lord Anson, nothing more, but the Pinnesters are now in attendance so perhaps Lord Enstrom might—Just one set?"

She stopped before the gossip ran *pêle-mêle* across the room. "No one knows me anymore. I suppose I should be grateful." All three of them knew the problem was too many people knew her. "Charlotte cannot be expected to entertain me all evening and Alexander—" She looked over at Nick. "I mean, Lord Firthley—"

"—is in the card room," Nick finished. He looked over at her husband, pointedly taking in the cane and Huntleigh's bad leg. "By the Knight's Creed, man, I swear I have no sinful designs on your wife, but she has been waiting like a saint to dance, and her suffering is all down to me. I think it only right I partner her for the next figure, since I am a very good dancer, and she is tapping her toe. The music is winding down; a new set will start in just a few minutes. What say you, Huntleigh?"

Huntleigh's delight at avoiding even the question of dancing warred with concern about Nick's prurient interests. In the end, he waved away any worry with a misplaced sense of confidence.

"Dearest, if you would like to indulge Wellbridge in a dance, you may, but you needn't entertain his addresses if you prefer not. He is entirely too brazen, but you have always proven quite capable of keeping a nobleman in his place."

Lady Huntleigh's fear of anyone observing her notice of the Duke of Wellbridge, especially the duke himself, crossed her face faster than gossip through the ladies of the *ton*. She couldn't hide a bit of what she was thinking. Nick was charmed again, though he felt a twinge of guilt finding himself pleased by the pained expression. And he was well aware her husband had seen her flashes of interest and was now rethinking his permission.

Before he had the chance, Lady Huntleigh said, "You must not be so familiar with the duke, husband," looking back and forth between them, "but if you would like me to dance with your *business associate*, of course, I will make no objection."

As the orchestra took up the next selection, Nick held his hand out for her. "What luck for me. A waltz." She placed her gloved hand in his, and he felt a trembling she couldn't control.

"Behave yourself, Wellbridge," Huntleigh admonished as Nick settled his hand at Lady Huntleigh's waist, and they swept into the current of the ballroom.

Of the many activities he shared with women, dancing was high on the list, though his reputation said otherwise. Because he avoided debutantes, and they often surrounded him to the exclusion of all others, it was thought he disliked the pastime, but in truth, the music always teased his senses, particularly when it was slow and intimate, as this set would be, allowing him and his partner to also tease each other. If only Lady Huntleigh would.

"I think you are making a mockery of me, Sir. You are flirting shamelessly at every party, and now right in front of my husband. You must desist."

"Nick, please—Wellbridge, if you prefer—and you are entirely correct. I would much rather flirt with you behind his back." He leaned in closer to her ear, "When we are in front of him, I am afraid your sweet blushes will give us away." The scent of flowers rose from her hair. Lavender. Maybe lilacs. Maybe both. He breathed deeply. Definitely both. "I cannot allow you to expose our secret, Lady Huntleigh, for I have sinful designs on you."

Bella's slipper caught on the waxed floor. Taking advantage of her instability, he held her waist more firmly, drawing her close to encourage her shivers and gooseflesh.

"You said you had no designs on me! You swore by the Knight's Creed!"

He leaned in to murmur, "I am not a knight, my sweet."

With less wallflower and more worldly woman, she laughed, "Sir Satyr, I'm sure, charter member of the Order of Rakehells, pledged to lead me down the path to depravity."

"You've caught me." He stared down at her ripe mouth. "Would that we were not in a crowded ballroom."

She bit her lip as they danced right past her husband, but by the time the music worked its way through a crescendo, she seemed to regain herself.

"I am not the type of woman one takes as a mistress."

Her frown meant to put paid to his indecorous intentions, but he had seen such glowering before, always from women he eventually took as mistresses.

"What type of woman is that, my lady?"

She stumbled again, muttering a reply; if he wasn't mistaken, "Deuced gentlemen and their accursed flirting." He asked her to repeat herself, just to see if the forbidding look would appear genuine. Oh, yes, it was certainly authentic.

"Would you rather," he asked quietly, a whisper across her earlobe, "a lifetime of only Humdrum Huntleigh?"

Her face momentarily softened, with the same brief look of longing he had seen as she watched the dancing, but just as he almost missed it, her expression grew as stony as gravel shore.

"*Lord* Huntleigh is a wonderful man who has just made me a countess... And I know perfectly well no man like you could possibly be interested in me."

How delightful she has considered it, he silently preened.

"On the contrary, a woman who *doesn't give a tuppenny damn* about Almack's is of enormous interest. And what do you mean by 'a man like me'?" He winked at her. "An incorrigible rogue?"

Bella blushed and turned her head away. She stuttered, "I just meant... a man of your... stature..." She gulped, "Your rank, I mean."

"Is that what you meant? I am quite devastated you weren't referring to my manly physique." Nick grinned at her, and she dropped her eyes, so he wouldn't see her taking in his handsome face, instead resting her gaze on the stature in question. He involuntarily puffed out his chest to prove himself decidedly manly, no trace of youthful lankiness, but neither fleshy like Firthley, nor frail like her aged husband.

She let out the tiniest of instinctive whimpers and, satisfied he had made his point, he turned the conversation. "What has Huntleigh done to upset you? A disagreement?"

She spoke without thinking: "In the carriage. He said—" She stopped short. "No, it is disloyal to speak of my marital concerns with anyone but my husband."

"Come now, you have been dying to have it out all night. What did he say?"

She huffed, "How do you know we had words?"

"The argument is all over your face, darling. And anyone with eyes can see he neglects you."

"He is not neglectful, just not roman—" Her eyes dropped, but then her chin raised and she set her jaw. "Lord Huntleigh is a good husband and the very kindest of men. I will not have you disparage him."

"I would never think of it. I just wonder how a man who is 'not romantic' manages to keep the interest of such a vivacious young lady. I mean, at home he can't just fob you off on the nearest man in dancing pumps. As you are so quick to defend, he must have hidden charms only on view in your sitting room."

Her giggle went past the point of politesse, bordering on an outright snort. However, she followed the minor calumny with, "Myron—Lord Huntleigh—and I spend more time in intellectual conversation than any two people I've ever known. We play backgammon and discuss politics and business, and he appreciates my intellect."

"As I say, you are being neglected." He ran his thumb across her wrist, and she almost choked. "You beautiful girl, poorly romanced by Humdrum Huntleigh in your very own drawing room." His voice lost volume and an octave. "Bedroom, too, I wager. The worst sort of crime."

She tried for dispassion, but her voice cracked. "I suppose being romanced by you in a ballroom is better?"

His smile was predatory. "How lovely of you to say."

"I made no such—" She harrumphed, "You will turn around every word, I assume?"

"In recompense, if one appreciates a turn of phrase, I do write truly passionate love poetry." She shook her head, loosening, but not losing, the unfocused gleam in her eye. He hoped quite sincerely she was envisioning him in a state of passion. Better yet, herself. In seconds, her jaw clenched and brows turned down.

"That is almost a good-quality judgmental look," he teased. "It will convince at least a few people you spurn my advances, although not quite as forceful as it might be if you were not so curious. Perhaps if you turn your brows down just a bit more… there! That's it." He leaned over and said, almost silently, "Although, if you purse your pretty lips like that much longer, I shall be forced to kiss you, and all of our subterfuge will be for naught."

Her mouth dropped open, astonished at the unabashed advance. "Your audacity knows no bounds!"

"No, none. Any man with a wife will tell you so."

She couldn't help laughing, but looked around to make certain no one was listening, and he could see her concerted effort to blank her expression.

"You have a very bad face for cards, my darling. Clearly, we must speak of nothing but the weather until the dance is over, or you will give away our lascivious intentions with your charming giggles. Your husband must believe you find me the most tedious man imaginable."

She tossed her head and lied, "That will present no difficulty at all." A few more strands of hair fell to her shoulders, drawing his attention. How he wished he could pull out the pins and run his hands through it.

"No?" he asked, one corner of his lips turned up.

"I find you deadly dull."

His voice took on a rasp as he remarked, "You would find me much less so had you taken me to the gallery."

"The gallery?! As if I would—you are indecent!" She almost pulled away but must have thought better of the scene she would create, instead merely stepping back, clearing her throat and calming her voice, if not her tone. "I can only think you have some plot to make my husband jealous to advance your business."

"If I make your husband jealous, I stand to lose twenty thousand pounds. I am plotting to advance myself with you, business be hanged. In no time at all, Huntleigh will think nothing of us using given names. Soon enough, I will be able to invite you to my home alone with your husband none the wiser."

"I think that unlikely."

"I have no doubt you do."

"You need not bother conniving. You are not half as fascinating as you seem to think."

"When my hands move beyond your waist…" One thumb brushed lightly along the edge of her corset under her arm, "or your wrist…" The other moved against her gloved palm. "When I do not have to restrain my kisses to your hand," he leaned close enough to leave the heat of his breath on her ear, "I think you will find me very interesting indeed."

Now he could see the attraction of the bright red blush. He made himself nearly drunk on the color rising, the white of her teeth against her lower lip.

"You have quite a high opinion of yourself. My husband would shoot you dead if he heard how you speak to me."

"Then you must be sure to tell him, so I'll stop."

He pulled himself a half-step back from her, still in perfect tempo. "The music is nearly over now, and you mustn't look sad to see it end."

She made a good show of hiding her disappointment, and when the music stopped, they weren't but a few steps away from her husband, so Nick delivered her without delay. She tried to give the impression Nick was tiresome, annoying, insignificant. She didn't entirely succeed, but Nick was pleased she made the attempt. He was also thankful her false disregard seemed to fool her husband, too gullible for his own good.

Nick's public behavior with her was immaculate outside the dance they shared, even while he engaged in speculation with her husband about the new cargo ship he had just agreed to buy outright. He left so little room for suspicion that he could see her wondering the rest of the night if she had dreamed his outrageous proposals. He didn't touch her arm or shoulder, didn't bring her ratafia, didn't try to find himself alone with her in a corner or on the terrace, and he spent no more time with the Huntleighs than his other acquaintances in attendance. She might as well have been a hundred-year-old dowager for all the notice he took while in public.

But when she sought him out at the end of the evening, with no reason but to say she and Lord Huntleigh would be leaving soon, he blocked her husband's view, then everyone else's, half-hidden behind a pillar, just on the right side of proper. While she kept her eyes from his face to make sure no one was watching, he gently tugged the glove from her left hand.

"I shall return this to you one day soon," he said, placing it in the pocket of his tailcoat, "and until I do," he ran his fingertip over the back of her hand, then dragged his fingernails across her palm, "you might consider what skin you next want to bare to me." She gasped. "I have ideas of my own, of course, but I would hate to disappoint if you were longing for me to touch you elsewhere."

Her face lost both its color and its objections, so he pushed his luck, moving his light contact from wrist to forearm to elbow. "How I wish it were your stocking I had just removed, and the back of your knee inviting my kiss, not the crook of your elbow." She looked as though the breath caught in her throat might keep her from speaking the rest of her life.

Nick turned then, feeling Huntleigh's eyes on them from across the room, and whispered, "Be careful, my dear. Everything you are imagining is all over your face." He bowed properly above her gloved fingers, arranged her shawl to cover the hand he had denuded, then walked her calmly to her husband, speaking of nothing more volatile than the price of tea as they strolled across the room.

Nick's speech to Huntleigh was designed to give Bella every reason to remain wordless and mortified from the tips of her toes to the top of her head; her husband would be suspicious had she not.

"I know how protective you are, Huntleigh, so I will put it to rest. I have done my very best to convince Lady Huntleigh to run away with me: offered her every shilling of my fortune, my undying devotion, the very cockles of my heart, and she would have none of it. My rotten luck she loves her husband. I shall have to muddle along a poor old bachelor another decade or two, I suppose, before anyone comes up to the mark again."

Nick placed Lady Huntleigh's gloved hand on her husband's arm, and she shyly tucked her face into Huntleigh's shoulder. Her bare hand hidden in her gathered skirts and scarf, her eyes roamed Nick's body, even as he kept his face open and friendly, no more or less formal than he had been with anyone else.

"You have been most indulgent this evening, Lady Huntleigh, allowing me to monopolize your husband with business, then listening to us go on all night. I am sure we are both deadly dull."

Nick was assured *entrée* with Bella as long as he had *entrée* with her husband, which was really only a question of money.

I have to stop thinking of her as Bella before I say it aloud, Nick thought, followed by, I wonder how Nick will sound when she whispers it in my ear. Better yet, moaning. Screaming. He couldn't remember the last time he had so wanted to render a woman mindless with pleasure.

He invoked the kings of England to keep his thoughts about the back of her knee from becoming obvious in his trousers: *Willie, Willie, Harry, Stee, Harry, Dick, John, Harry three,* he recited to himself until he managed to bring his physical reactions back under control. He hadn't been embarrassed by his own body since Eton, and wasn't planning to begin anew in the ballrooms of London. He was an Englishman, for heaven's sake, not a hot-blooded Latin.

The superiority wafting off her husband relaxed Nick to a certain extent; the man thought his wife had proved immune to the infamous Duke of Wellbridge, preferring Humdrum Huntleigh to the globe-trotting Lothario who stole a new man's wife every Season. Nick knew Bella—Lady Huntleigh—would be more appreciated at home in days to come, and might even receive an apology from her husband for whatever it was he'd said in the carriage to make her angry.

If nothing else, one dance with a duke would ensure too much interest from other men, including her husband. Nick would wait to send flowers until she had other admirers—most likely of her prospects, not her person—when her husband would be less likely to notice among other bouquets. He planned sonnets and sestinas in her name, delivered with orchids and gardenias to demonstrate in floriology his rising passion for her. If Lord Huntleigh knew a language of flowers even existed, Nick would eat Old Rowley's hat.

When Bella reached up on tiptoe to give her elderly husband a sweet kiss on his cheek, Huntleigh puffed up with satisfaction, outright smug when she whispered it was getting late and she would prefer to be safe and warm at home than out gallivanting all hours with rapscallions and rogues. Huntleigh won the battle, since he would take Bella home in his carriage. He didn't understand he'd lost the war as soon as he agreed to let Nick dance with her.

Read more of <u>Royal Regard</u>

The Duchess of Wellbridge's Start in Diplomacy

(Excerpt from Shipmate, *by Mariana Gabrielle, wherein the future Duchess of Wellbridge is introduced to her first ship by her first husband. The Amelia, named for and decorated by Prinny's sister, is the model for four "family frigates" the duchess has kept since, on which Toad spent a goodly portion of his childhood.)*

Chapter Eleven

May 27, 1805
On Board the Amelia

Watching the pier grow smaller by the league, the Effingales, Firthleys, and Amberlys almost too small to see, waving, Bella stared over the side of the Amelia, the ship that was now her home, fingers curved tightly around the railing, grasping at any last semblance of balance. Beside her, Lord Holsworthy—no, Myron—placed his hand over hers, squeezing the fingers gently. Neither said a word, but when a tear rolled down her cheek, he brushed it away with his thumb, and curled a comforting arm around her shoulders. They had never stood so close together, but she hid her face in his shoulder, sobbing, "I'll never see them again. They are my only family."

And truly, they must be, as no Smithson had made an appearance at the wedding. Bella could blame her sudden dizziness on the rocking of the ship, but it might as easily be her sense of giddy relief. She had escaped her father, her brothers, and the mess they were about to make of things. Bella thought she had caught a glimpse of John at the docks, from the height of the bo'sun's chair being brought up the side of the ship, but by the time she could steady herself for a good look, the man was gone.

No one had appeared to take her to Newgate, nor had her own family's downfall played out before her eyes. The reprieve inherent in watching the coastline be swallowed up in the horizon, when crossed with the despair of leaving so many people she loved in so much danger, left her in tears.

"Ah, ah, my dear. Now, that is not true." He chucked her under the chin, looking into her watery eyes. "As you now have me to call family, and soon a babe, should the Lord be willing." He kissed her forehead when she nodded, quickly hiding against his sleeve once more, letting him stroke her hair the same way John had when they were both younger, before their father had pitted his children against one other as best he could.

Just as she wiped the tears away, determined to meet her future head-on, a throat was cleared behind them.

"Sir, if you would…" Captain Rafe Johnson trailed off, foot turned to run the other direction rather than interrupt feminine distress. Placing himself between the captain of the vessel and his new bride, Myron answered, "Yes, Captain?"

"Sir, I… I only meant… I mean, I wondered…"

Bella sniffled, but stepped out from behind her husband, taking up Captain Johnson's hand, shaking it like a man might. "You must be Captain Johnson. I am so sorry we haven't had the chance to meet until now. Lord Holsworthy has spoken most highly of you."

Blushing beet-red in a way Bella would never have expected from a sailor, the captain bowed awkwardly over her hand, as though he were entirely unaccustomed to a lady being anywhere nearby. "My lady, I am pleased to welcome you to the Amelia. I was hoping I might show you the arrangements we've made for your quarters…" He looked at Myron. "But if this is an inconvenient time…"

"No, no, of course, I am delighted to see where I will be living." Belatedly, she looked up at her husband. "I mean, if it is acceptable to you, my lord."

He smiled down at her. "Entirely acceptable, my dear. Lead on, Captain."

Only a few steps from their position, the half-boots she had worn, among the most practical footwear she owned, proved her first mistake. On the first step up to the quarter-deck, her heel caught and she pitched forward. Had Myron not been holding her elbow, she might have broken the fall with her face.

"You may find, my lady," the captain said gently, after she was set aright on her feet again, "a pair of slippers will serve you better aboard ship."

She nodded silently, humiliation locked in her throat, vowing to dig a pair of walking shoes out of her trunk and drop the boots overboard at the earliest opportunity. Until then, she merely held on, like a barnacle, to her new husband's arm.

In a series of brief glances, he assessed the rest of her attire, the brand-new coffee-colored velveteen traveling gown Aunt Minerva had insisted she wear, already soiled with sea spray and tar. The skirt had already been rent by proximity to whatever sharp things had existed between the carriage block and the railing of the upper deck, and a length of torn lace trailed from the sleeve. "You might find all the…" he flicked his fingers at her, "ruffles and bows a nuisance…" He trailed off. "But Your Ladyship must wear whatever suits you…"

"I assure you, I have always found ruffles and bows a nuisance, and my attire shall be rectified as soon as I find my trunks. Clearly, I must learn the way of things, and I will be grateful if you gentlemen will make it your business to correct me, should I err." Myron smiled and squeezed the hand she had wrapped around his elbow. "I may wish to shorten my skirts a few inches to ensure I do not fall to my doom." Sudden nerves overtook her. "I mean… I would not wish to cause you any…"

"You must do as you will to avoid your doom, my dear," Myron assured her, kissing her hand and making her blush. "Though I will ask you keep the sensibilities of sailors in mind."

She nodded and stifled a giggle at the sudden redness of Captain Johnson's ears.

"On the subject of sailors, might be we should teach your wife to use a cutlass, Holsworthy."

"Oh!" Bella exclaimed. "I could never…" Turning to Myron, she whispered, "He wouldn't really…? I mean, he doesn't expect…?"

The captain answered, as though he had been meant to hear, "Only should you wish it, Lady Holsworthy, though I daresay you will find a surfeit of men who would like you to be able to protect yourself, since they will be held responsible should you be placed in danger."

"Oh! But… I'm sure I… I could never use a weapon."

Myron chided gently, "Pray, do not decide today how you will live the rest of your life aboard ship, my lady. There is much to understand before you can decide what you will wish to learn."

"Yes, my lord."

Following the captain across the deck, she was directed toward a series of closed doorways with glass insets, curtained to shut out prying eyes.

"On the starboard side—"

"That is to your right, my dear," Myron explained.

"On the starboard side," Captain Johnson stressed, "is Lord Holsworthy's cabin."

He opened the set of doors to a fair-sized room, far larger than she had expected, paneled in dark wood, containing a writing desk and a bunk built into the wall, less than half the width of her bed at Brittlestep Manor. The room also contained a large cannon, taking up no less than a quarter of the space.

"Must we live with guns in our quarters?" She swallowed hard. "And such large ones."

Myron nodded with a grim look. "This is a sixty-gun ship. There are no cabins that do not also house cannon, my dear, and I beg you recall it is for your own protection."

"Yes, my lord. Of course."

She stepped over to an interior door and said, "What is behind here?"

"Here, my lady," the captain continued, opening it for her, "we have carved out an ordnance-free sitting room for you, and office for Lord Holsworthy."

Painted in a delicate green, with an amber-hued Persian carpet reaching from wall to wall, this area had been designed to accommodate their family life. An escritoire sat to one side, a larger partner's desk to the other, and a clutch of armchairs and a loveseat in the center. A drop-leaf table hugged the back wall, providing a place to take a meal, beside a door leading to a small balcony that could only be accessed through their quarters.

"What a lovely balcony! What a wonderful place to have tea and think."

Even the jaded-looking captain smiled at that. "The stern gallery, my lady. Balconies exist only on land."

"Oh, of course. I suppose eventually, I will learn the language?"

"I think it inevitable," Myron said with a smile.

Another interior door, this time between two floor-to-ceiling gated shelves, according to the captain, led to "Her Ladyship's cabin." At her nervous grin, he unlocked the door, handed her the key, and pushed the door open. "Lord Holsworthy asked that—" The poor man's ears were burning again.

"I wished you to have a place on board that you could call your own, my sweet, and I asked the princess' advice in the decoration. I hope you find it pleasing."

"Oh, yes!"

Bella felt the smile reach from ear to ear when she took in the room, decorated as lavishly as any in Charlotte's parents' home, the same narrow bunk as Myron's, draped in gold muslin and not designed for two. Oil lamps lit the space, which might be illuminated further were she to open the curtains, but then anyone walking across the deck could see into her rooms. The gun so evident in

Myron's chamber was hidden by a dressing screen in hers.

The chamber was carpeted with a thick oriental rug, the walls painted a deep shade of blue. Her books were aligned on shelves that took up half a wall, kept safely in place behind gold chains that ran across each shelf from side to side. The comfortable chair covered in gold brocade turned from side to side, but was attached firmly to the floor, and the top of the candle stand next to it—which made it a reading nook, as far as Bella was concerned—was ringed with delicate brass to keep anything from falling off. An armoire and trunk stood open, her dresses neatly hanging on sprung hooks, boots and belts and bags neatly folded and secured, so her clothing wouldn't fly around the cabin if the ship were tossed about in a storm.

"How very clever it all is! I would never have thought to make certain everything was kept in its place."

The two bedchambers and sitting room conjoined a very large dining room that would serve to feed everyone in turns daily, and in between times, men might meet to plot out their duties. Without much trouble, though, Bella could see, it could be transformed to serve as a venue for a formal dinner or party.

Their quarters were extremely generous in terms of space, much larger than the prince had implied when he had told her about the accommodations, but no inch of space went unused, and every area served more than one function.

Stumbling against the rocking of the ship, she observed, "I'm not accustomed to the world always shifting under my feet. Not in a literal sense, at any rate."

"You'll have your sea legs in no time, my lady," Captain Johnson said with a smile. "Though I caution, you may find yourself feeling quite ill within an hour or two. Most people do."

"Yes, Lord Holsworthy has warned me."

Bella balked at the ladder she was asked to descend to view the royal and ambassadorial quarters directly below theirs, so Myron climbed halfway down first, apparently intending to protect her from falling, but finally, she shook her head.

"No, my lord. If I will live on this ship, I must learn my way around it under my own power." Myron stepped back at the end of the steps and smiled as she gathered up her skirts and climbed down. "I am now certain I must shorten my skirts a bit, however."

The three rooms below had been designed to the taste of the Prince of Wales and his sister, as had a dozen smaller cabins, not quite as sumptuous, for lesser aristocrats and their staff, but which would quarter various officers until their official use was required. Bella felt both the weight and exhilaration of being mistress of this small portion of the large ship, much as she had the first time her aunt had taken the Effingale family to London and left Bella *chatelaine* of

Brittlestep Manor in their absence. The weight of it began to tug at her stomach.

In fact, her stomach was starting to feel a bit out of sorts. She wrapped an arm around her middle.

Myron took one look at her face and said, "You look suspiciously green, my dear. Into bed with you, Lady Holsworthy." He motioned her to the ladder to her cabin. Bella and Captain Johnson both flushed bright red before Myron realized his double entendre. "I mean—as I should think you know, Captain—that Lady Holsworthy is about to be very ill for an undetermined interval, and will be far more comfortable in her nightrail, in her cabin, in her bed, with ginger tea and hardtack at hand. There is nothing salacious in that, surely."

The idea that her new husband was about to watch her casting up her accounts made her that much queasier, and she scrambled up the ladder. By the time she reached her quarters, she was swaying on her feet a bit more than the ship's movement warranted. Myron, right behind her, put a bucket underneath her retching mouth just in time to save the lovely carpet.

"Oh, no, my Lord," she moaned, once she had cleared enough of her stomach contents to find her voice again. "I will give you a disgust of me. You cannot be—"

His hand stroked the back of the head. "Where else should I be on my wedding night, but with my bride, for better or worse? I have been a sailor since the age of fourteen and seen many a case of *mal de mer*. You will survive it, though I daresay you will doubt me before it is done."

At that, her stomach lurched again, and he steadied the bucket and her shoulder. As the episode shuddered to a close, his gentle fingertips brushed the hair out of her face that had fallen from its pins, pulled it back, and tucked it into the back of her dress. As she caught her breath, he produced a box of ginger pastilles from his waistcoat pocket.

"Ginger tea in a matter of minutes, if I know Captain Johnson, and our ship's doctor, Charles Anders, will likely make an appearance, though there will be nothing particular he can do. For the moment…" He held out the tin and she took one. "Unfortunately, my dear, we cannot know how severe your ailment will be, nor how long-lasting, but I am of good faith that our Lord will see you well in short order. And I will be here to act as your…" His eyes twinkled, and he touched her chalky cheek, "I suppose 'lady's maid' is the role I am asked to fill, is it not?"

She stared at him bleakly, sucking on the candy, as her stomach rolled with the motion of every disparate wave within ten leagues.

Read more of <u>Shipmate</u>, always free at all retailers.

<u>The Son of Privilege Meets the Son of Shame</u>

(Excerpt from Revealed in Mist, *by Jude Knight, wherein the Marquis of Aldridge, future Duke of Haverford, born to the purple, meets his base-born half-brother after a long estrangement engineered by their father.)*

Chapter Three

Exasperating woman. Three days after the *soirée*, David Wakefield, the Shadow, was still trying to extract more meaning from his encounter with the woman he could not forget. He had seen her as soon as she entered the banquet hall, drifting along the wall. She'd vanished among the companions, but he'd seen Tolliver and guessed she was there to meet him.

After his own meeting with the daughter of the house, interrupted to expel the Earl of Selby, he'd gone upstairs more eagerly than he wished to examine, hoping their time apart might have affected her as it did him. The guarded look on her face, the stiff way she held herself, stopped him in his tracks.

And her voice. Calm. Devoid of emotion. As if that passionate night had never existed. Or as if it meant nothing to her. It didn't escape him that he had given her his real name on that night, but he knew only her code name, Mist, and a few of the invented names she changed job by job.

Perhaps, while David had spent five months yearning for her, she had moved on, and his presence was an embarrassment. Surely his own cravings created the longing he imagined in her eyes when she first saw him.

He should be thinking about the coming meeting instead of mooning over a woman who had decisively rejected him. Lady Georgiana had hired him to find out who was blackmailing her friend, the courtesan Lily Diamond, and had given him the names of her most persistent admirers. And one name on the list was very familiar.

He frowned at the fire in the small hearth. The private parlour he had hired was small and shabby, but at least its size made it easy to heat. And it was neutral ground, which mattered. David hadn't had a prolonged conversation with his expected guest in a decade and a half.

He must have been seventeen or eighteen on the last occasion, staying at Haverford Castle in Kent between the end of the school term and his first term at university. The Duke of Haverford's son and heir, the Marquis of Aldridge, would have been twelve. The day had begun happily enough with the boy tagging along while David went out after small game with a gun. It had ended with David beaten and driven from the property.

Aldridge had tripped and knocked himself out, and Haverford, finding David leaning over his unconscious heir, had not waited for explanations.

Once the young marquis left school and entered Society, they met from time to time, usually when the Duchess of Haverford insisted on David coming to one of her entertainments. Her husband, the duke, was almost always engaged elsewhere, but her sons often attended. They paid their mother the courtesy of not being rude to her *protégé*, and he responded with the same polite reserve.

He was expecting Aldridge now. Older brother to one of the courtesan's lovers. David's despised father's oldest legitimate son. His half-brother.

A knock on the door heralded Aldridge's arrival. A maid showed him into the private parlour. He'd clearly been treating her to a display of his facile charm: she was dimpling, blushing, and preening.

David examined him as he gave the girl a coin "and a kiss for your trouble, my darling." The beautiful child had grown into a handsome man. David had heard him described as 'well-put together, and all over, if you know what I mean.' The white-blonde hair of childhood had darkened to a guinea gold, and he had his mother's hazel eyes under a thick arch of brow he and David had both inherited from their father.

Aldridge navigated the shoals of the marriage market with practised ease, holding the mothers and their daughters off but still not offending them, and carrying out a gentleman's role in the ballroom with every evidence of enjoyment.

But his real success, by all accounts, was with bored widows and wives, where he performed in the bedroom with equal charm, and perhaps more pleasure. Society was littered with former lovers of the Merry Marquis, though he had the enviable ability to end an affair and retain the friendship.

Aldridge ushered the laughing maid out of the room and closed the door behind her, acknowledging David's appraisal with a wry nod.

"Wakefield. You summoned me. I am here."

David ignored the thread of irritation in the young aristocrat's voice, and took a shot in the dark. Lord Jonathan was unlikely to be the blackmailer, Lady Georgiana thought, but was probably also being blackmailed. Would he have confided in Aldridge?

"I have some questions I wish to ask about the blackmail."

Aldridge arched a brow, a trick they had both picked up from the duke. "Tolliver has engaged you?"

David hid his surprise at the spymaster's name. "What is your brother paying blackmail for?"

Uninvited, Aldridge grabbed a chair and straddled it, resting his chin on his forearms. "Our brother," he said, flatly.

"That won't prevent me from turning him in if he is a traitor," David said.

"He isn't. He's young. He's an idiot. But he isn't a traitor." Aldridge met David's eyes with an uncompromising glare of his own.

"Then you have nothing to lose by answering my questions."

Aldridge held the glare for a long moment, then let his breath out with a huff and unfurled himself from the seat. David watched him pace, content to let silence do the job of convincing Aldridge to talk.

It worked.

"You have to understand, Wakefield. If he hears what Jon has done, His Grace will… I don't know what precisely, but it won't be pretty. You don't know what he is like. When he loses his temper, anything can happen. And once he's said something, he won't go back, no matter what."

"Oh, I know," David said. "I do know." For a moment, he was seventeen again, the duke screaming at him, the walking stick crashing on his shoulders and arms as he tried to protect his head. "But you haven't explained to me why I should care what His Grace does to your brother."

"Your brother, too," Aldridge said again. "I don't suppose you do care. Not about Jon, and not about me. And I daresay you'd do His Grace an ill turn if you could, and I would not lift a finger to stop you."

David shook his head. Yes, he had resented the duke for years. But he refused to waste the energy any longer. "No. Though I wouldn't cross the road to help him, either," he said honestly.

"But you care about Mama," Aldridge insisted. "You do. You would not tolerate her *soirées* otherwise."

David said nothing. He was not going to discuss Her Grace with Aldridge. The son of privilege could never understand what David owed the woman who had rescued her husband's bastard after his own mother died, saving him from the workhouse, if not from death. She had his lifelong devotion just for that, but she'd done so much more. She'd paid for his education and keep, found him his first job, protected him from her husband, and never ceased believing in him.

"Mama would be heartbroken if His Grace disowns Jon, or sends him away, or worse. And, truly, Wakefield, he hasn't done what they will tell His Grace. He hasn't. He's just been a fool, and any normal father would cut his allowance and give him a job to do."

"If what you say is true, he has nothing to fear. I'm only interested in finding the blackmailer, not in causing trouble for your brother."

"Our brother," Aldridge insisted. "If you find that Jon is a blackmailer, or a traitor, I'll stand aside while you do whatever you have to do. But you won't."

"So you'll answer my questions." David brought them back to the main point.

"You promise that this will stay between us unless you find something you need for your case?"

"I promise." David didn't want to be impressed by the man's devotion to his brother. Far better for David's peace of mind if Aldridge were the useless, self-centred fribble he appeared.

Aldridge said, hesitantly, "I've heard you are a man of your word. I'll trust you."

David waited, but Aldridge took his time.

"He went to The Diamond because she is fashionable, of course," he began, after a while.

"Of course."

"She favoured him. Well. He's a pretty boy, and will be rich when he comes into his own, for all he's a second son."

David nodded to show that he understood. Miss Diamond had welcomed young Jon to her bed in return for lavish gifts.

Aldridge continued. "Do you know Selby and that ghastly pack he runs with?"

"By reputation."

"They were at school with me and Jon, but he has had nothing to do with them since he came up to town. Given how they hounded him at school, I have no idea why he... he met them again at The Diamond's, and they are in this mess up to their necks. Whatever is happening, they are part of it, you can be sure."

"He started playing with the card sharp, I take it?"

"That was part of it, yes."

"He lost a lot of money." David sighed. Such a predictable story.

But Aldridge was shaking his head. "If that were all... If it was just money, His Grace would blow him up, Mama would make him feel about two inches tall, I'd dress him down and then pay the bare minimum to keep him out of prison, and he'd go with pockets to let until the next quarter day. No. They set him up, Davey. They set him up well and truly."

It was a measure of Aldridge's concern that he slipped back into his boyhood name for his half-brother.

"What happened?"

"Drink. Drugs. Women. But one morning, when he woke up, he was with a man. Well, a boy really: a naked boy."

"Is he in the habit of...?" How could David delicately ask if his younger half-brother had such inclinations?

"No, not at all." Aldridge shook his head. "He adores women. All kinds. Put him in a brothel and he's like a child in a sweet shop. He'll try the whole range. He was horrified. He's…" Aldridge shook his head.

"I take it there were witnesses."

"A number," Aldridge confirmed. "Selby and his pack among them. They all swore they'd keep it quiet. It's a hanging offence, and you can be sure His Grace wouldn't lift a finger. Even if we could keep him from the gallows, he'd never be able to stay in England."

David knew what happened next. "But then the demands began to arrive. Money?"

"At first. He paid. He stole some of Mama's jewellery and pawned it. Silly fool told me he only took the stuff she didn't like, as if that made it better! Then the letters asked for papers from His Grace's office. It was something to do with a land deal. He thought it wouldn't matter."

"Idiot. Couldn't he see they were sucking him in deeper and deeper?" David shook his head at the sheer stupidity of the boy.

"I know. Even if His Grace could overlook the embarrassment of the first escapade, even if he forgave the theft from Mama, he isn't going to let a theft of his ducal papers pass. He'd regard it as betrayal of the worst kind. More than *lèse majesté*. Blasphemy, really."

They both contemplated the duke's likely reaction. No wonder Aldridge wanted to keep this information between themselves. "So what happened next?" David asked.

"That's when they overstepped. They asked for more papers, but when he checked the paper they wanted, he realised that it was… well, he didn't tell me what it was. Just that it was information Napoleon would give his eyeteeth for. So, he came to me and told me the whole, and I made him tell Uncle Tolly. He has put a servant in the house. And hired you, apparently."

Uncle Tolly? The Marquis of Aldridge called the aloof and secretive Tolliver 'Uncle Tolly'? And a servant in the house. Mist, perhaps? It could be someone else, but if it were Mist… Would they be allies or opponents?

"So, now you have it," Aldridge said, oblivious to David's sudden stillness. "I've paid the gambling debt, of course. And redeemed Mama's jewellery. Uncle Tolly thinks that will help to draw their fangs." David shook off the red herring of the relationship between Tolliver and the Grenford family, and got back to the point.

"But they still have the duke's papers, and the witnesses to the catamite incident." What was he thinking? Saving his half-brother wasn't his job, nor his inclination. He was here to catch the blackmailer. Still, if saving Lord Jonathan was a by-product, he would do so. For Her Grace's sake, if nothing else.

As if following David's thoughts, Aldridge said, "My mother knows nothing of this. For her sake, won't you see what you can do?"

David nodded, shortly. "I'll catch the blackmailer, and if I can, I'll clear your br…" Aldridge opened his mouth to object and David conceded, "…our brother.

Now, we go back to the beginning and you tell me everything you know. Who Lord Jonathan met at Miss Diamond's; his card-playing friends; Selby's cronies; who was there the night they trapped him. Everything."

Their pasts could bring them together or separate them forever

Prue's job is to uncover secrets, but she hides a few of her own. When she is framed for murder and cast into Newgate, her one-time lover comes to her rescue. Will revealing what she knows help in their hunt for blackmailers, traitors, and murderers? Or threaten all she holds dear?

Enquiry agent David solves problems for the ton, but will never be one of them. When his latest case includes his legitimate half-brothers as well as the woman who left him months ago, he finds the past and the circumstances of his birth difficult to ignore. Danger to Prue makes it impossible.

David and Prudence continue their story in *Concealed in Shadow* (coming in 2018). When Prue disappears, David goes after her. But finding her again may mean choosing between his country and his woman.

Read more of <u>Revealed in Mist</u>

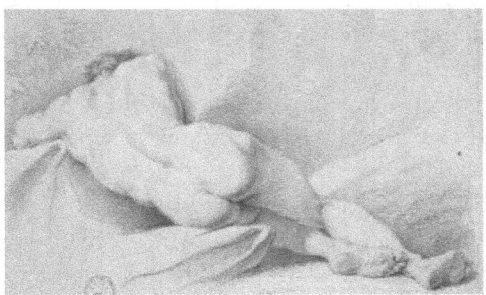

A Gentleman is Never at a Loss

(Excerpt from A Baron for Becky, *by Jude Knight. After what he did to his half-brother and his former lover in Concealed in Shadow [still to come], Aldridge, the future Duke of Haverford, took refuge in alcohol, until the day he awoke in a country garden.)*

Chapter One

1807, West Gloucestershire

Aldridge never did find out how he came to be naked, alone, and sleeping in the small summerhouse in the garden of a country cottage. His last memory of the night before had him twenty miles away, and—although not dressed—in a comfortable bed, and in company.

The first time he woke, he had no idea how far he'd come, but the moonlight was bright enough to show him half-trellised window openings, and an archway leading down a short flight of steps into a garden. A house loomed a few hundred feet distant, a dark shape against the star-bright sky. But getting up was too much trouble, particularly with a headache that hung inches above him, threatening to split his head if he moved. The cushioned bench on which he lay invited him to shut his eyes and go back to sleep. Time enough to find out where he was in the morning.

When he woke again, he was facing away from the archway entrance, and someone was behind him. Silence now, but in his memory, the sound of light footsteps shifting the stones on the path outside, followed by twin intakes of breath as the walkers saw him.

One of them spoke; a woman's voice, but low—almost husky. "Sarah, go back to the first rosebush and watch the house."

"Yes, Mama." High and light. A child's voice.

Aldridge waited until he heard the child dance lightly down the steps and away along the path, then shifted his weight slightly letting his body roll over till he was lying on his back.

He waited for the exclamation of shock, but none came. Carefully—he wanted to observe her before he let her know he was awake, and anyway, any sudden movement might start up the hammers above his eye sockets—he cracked open his lids, masking his eyes with his lashes.

He could see more than he expected. The woman was using a shuttered lantern to examine him, starting at his feet. She paused for a long time when she reached his morning salute and it grew even prouder. Then she swept her light up his torso so quickly he barely had time to slam his lids shut before the light reached and lingered over his face.

She was just a vague shadow behind the light. He held himself still while she completed her examination, which she did with a snort of disgust. Not the reaction to which he was accustomed.

"Now what do we do?" she muttered. "Perhaps if Sarah and I...? I will have to cover him. What on earth is he doing here? And like that? Not that it matters. Unless he has something to do with Perry? Or the men he said would come?" Incipient panic showed in the rising pitch and volume, until she rebuked herself. "Stop it." She took a deep breath and let it out slowly. "Stay calm. You must think."

Aldridge risked opening his eyes a mere slit, and was rewarded by a better look at the woman as she paced up and down the summerhouse, in the light of the lantern she'd placed on one of the window ledges.

Spectacular. That was the only appropriate word. Hair that looked black in the poor light, but was probably dark brown, porcelain skin currently flushed with agitation, a heart-shaped face and a perfect cupid's bow of a mouth, the lower lip—which she was currently chewing—larger than the upper.

The redingote she wore fit closely to a shape of amazing promise, obscured, then disclosed, as the shawl over her shoulders swung with her movements. Even more blood surged to his ever-hopeful member. "Down, boy," he told it, silently.

"Mama?" That was the little girl, returning down the path. "Mama, I can hear horses."

The woman froze, every line of her screaming alarm.

Aldridge could hear them too, coming closer through the rustling noises of the night. The quiet clop of walking horses, the riders exchanging a word or two, then nothing. They must have stopped on the other side of the house.

"Sarah." The woman's voice, pitched to carry only as far as her daughter's ears, retreated as she crossed the summerhouse. "Sarah, we must go quickly."

"But, Mama! The escape baskets!" the girl protested.

"I dare not wake the man, my love. He might stop us."

Aldridge responded to the fear in her voice. "I won't stop you. I am not a danger to you." The woman turned to a statue at his voice, her hand on the framework of the arched entrance, as if she would fall without support. He swung himself upright, wincing as the headache closed its vice around his skull. Though he slitted his eyes against the pain, he kept them open just enough.

"Mama?" The girl's fearful voice released the woman from her freeze, and she moved to block the child's sight of him. "Sarah. Watch the house. Do not turn around until I say."

Eyes open, he could confirm his initial assessment as she spun to face him. Spectacular. Then she shone the lantern straight on him, and he flinched from the light. "Not in my eyes, please. I have such a head."

She made that same disgusted sound again, then stripped the shawl from her shoulders and tossed it to him, taking care to stay out of arms' reach.

"Please cover yourself, Sir."

Aldridge stood warily, and made a kilt of the shawl—a long rectangle that wrapped his waist several times and covered him from waist to thigh. "I beg your pardon for my attire, Mrs..." he invited.

But she was ignoring him. While he'd been tucking in the soft wool of the shawl, so it would hold securely, she'd crossed the summerhouse again and lifted the lid of the bench, tipping the cushions onto the floor, pulling various bundles, baskets, and packages from the recess.

"Mama!" The child sounded panicked. "They are in the house."

Aldridge, headache forgotten, moved to a better vantage. Yes. Lights moving through the darkened house. And the men were not bothering to be silent, either, calling to one another as they searched swiftly and methodically: the ground floor, then the next, then the attics.

A rustle and chink came from the other end of the garden, then an eldritch groan that cut through his head like a knife.

"The gate!" The woman's eyes were wide and fearful. Yes, complaining hinges would make that noise, and clearly frightened her more than any unnatural denizen of the night.

"Sarah, come to me."

At the woman's soft command, the child brushed past Aldridge and rushed right into the woman's arms, wrapping herself around her mother's waist. She was a small thing, not quite short enough to fit under the curve of her mother's breasts. The delicate features, a miniature of her mother's, showed fear and a quite adult determination. Aldridge had little experience of children but she was much the size of his cousin's stepdaughter, who was six or seven.

The woman was holding something against the child's temple. In a swift movement, he was almost on her, but he held himself apart, afraid of frightening her into pulling the trigger of the small pistol.

Outside, a rough voice spoke in the kind of argot he'd learned when slumming in St Giles. "Keep by t'prads, I'll see 'tis all bob. I'll crash the culls if uns've banged that Rose." "Wait with the horses," he understood the man to say. "I'll see that all is well at the house. I'll kill the men if they've raped that Rose." Heavy footsteps retreating down the path. If they were quiet, they could talk.

"What the hell are you doing?" he demanded, keeping his voice low enough to carry no further than her ears.

Her whisper was even lower, and he had to strain to hear. "Praying they will pass us by. For the love of all you hold holy, don't give us away!"

"You cannot mean to hurt your child."

"Better death at my hands than what they have planned for her," the woman hissed. Her free hand, the one around the girl's shoulders, returned the frantic hug, patting and soothing even as the other hand held the little pistol firmly in place.

"Better we all live," he retorted. "Who are they?" He needed information. Damn his current state of undress. A fat billfold solved most problems.

"My... Mr Perringworth owes their employer money. He owns... he *used to own* the cottage. He came down this morning, said he had given them the cottage and everything in it, and it wasn't enough. He has fled the country. He said..." She fell silent, her face bleak, but the little girl piped up. "They are very bad men, sir. You should hide until they are gone."

"Why did you not run with this Perry person? Or after he left?" Aldridge was glad he had been woken by the woman rather than the bullies—the heavies of a criminal loan shark, unless he missed his guess.

"He locked us up," the woman said. "We were to be part of the 'everything' he gave this man. It has taken us the whole day to break through the wall into the next room."

Before she had finished, Aldridge was calculating his next move. The pistol was next to useless. Good enough to execute the child, but against at least four men, maybe more?

"I don't suppose you have a sword or another gun in that seat of yours?"

She shook her head.

It would have to be his tongue, then. Well, many a woman had called it his finest weapon.

"Help me drop your bundles out into the garden," he ordered. "I have a plan."

She watched him warily, not moving, as he suited action to words and dropped a covered basket, then a hatbox, then a tied bundle, one from each of the arched sides so they would be hidden in the low shrubbery around the summerhouse.

"Now, let's see how much room there is."

The space inside the bench seat was big enough for a slender woman and a small child. He began clearing out the clutter that accumulates in such places. The woman suddenly seemed to realise what he intended, and bent to whisper in her daughter's ear. Together, they silently moved around the small room, collecting the bits and pieces he found and dropping them out into the garden.

Aldridge put one of the cushions into the space for their heads, and offered his hand to help the woman in. She ignored it, lifting her skirt with her free hand to show one shapely leg, and then the other, as she climbed inside the space and lay down.

"Here, Sarah," she whispered. "On top of me."

It crossed Aldridge's mind that he would welcome the self-same invitation. Perhaps the woman might be inclined to reward his act of knight errantry in what he had always suspected was the time-honoured manner. "Focus," he told himself.

"Whatever you hear," he told the woman and child, "don't make a sound. Trust me. I'll get you out of this." He closed the seat lid and retrieved the scattered cushions, then opened the woman's lantern to blow out the candle, and lay back down.

Just in time. Multiple boots on the path; voices talking, complaining, or so he understood, that furniture was all well and good, but the real treasure had flown.

He hoped the child couldn't understand what they said. He could, all too well, and the woman—Rose? Was that really her name? It seemed too appropriate to be true. Rose was right to be frightened.

They might get away free and clear, if the thugs believed she was long since gone. One of them suggested the cove had taken the two with him. The cove, this Perringworth, presumably.

But Aldridge's momentary hope was immediately dashed. Another laughed. He and his mate had Perringworth safe and sound, his legs broken so he couldn't run again. And the cull swore he'd left this Rose and her get safely locked up, tied for good measure.

"Swore afore ya bruk 'is munch bones. Won't do no yammerin' now," grumbled one. A broken jaw? Good to know Perringworth couldn't deny whatever lies Aldridge spoke.

The group stopped on the path and argued about what to do next.

The boss was expecting to sell the woman and her child to recover the money he was owed, and more. And breaking Perringworth an inch at a time might act as a lesson to others, but it wouldn't replace the money.

The London bullies were anxious to get back to the safety of their verminous slums. This wide-open countryside made them nervous. But they were more frightened of their master than the strange environment, and when one of them mentioned a name, Aldridge understood why.

Smite. Whether the single syllable was a given name, a surname, or a nickname that described the terrible power of his fist, nobody knew. But Smite was the uncrowned king of large swaths of the underbelly of London.

And, in some sort, Aldridge's debtor, since the night Aldridge had waded into a fight for the sheer joy of battle, foiling an assassination attempt on Smite by a rival gang. If he could convince these men of his identity, he might pull off the rescue.

But they'd never believe him if they found him hiding. "Shut your noise," he shouted. "I'm trying to sleep in here." Instant silence on the path, then the moonlit entrance was blocked as several large men tried to enter at once.

"Don't shine that lantern in my face," Aldridge ordered, with all the hauteur of his generations of ducal ancestors, and the men—like the curs they were—responded to the voice of command and turned the lantern away. In the returning shadows, six large male shapes loomed over him.

"Who the hell are you, and what are you doing here?" Aldridge demanded. "Do you know where Perry's gone?"

"It be the Merry Marquis," said one of the men, pushing his way through from the back. Now there was a stroke of luck! Smite had sent one of his chief lieutenants. What did they call the man? Tiny. That was it. A typically laconic comment on his enormous size.

"Hello, Tiny," Aldridge said. "You're a step away from your usual haunts."

Big Tiny might be, but he hadn't come unscathed through a life of violence. His nose had been broken several times, was flattened and twisted towards his right cheek, which bore a livid knife scar from the outer edge of the eye to the corner of his thick, misshapen lips. He'd been beaten around the ears, too, many times, leaving them swollen and deformed.

Aldridge knew, though, that the rough appearance hid an incisive mind. Smite looked for intelligence in his lieutenants, and Tiny's presence here, who knew how many days from London, and Smite's control, was evidence of how much Smite trusted him. In this instance, intelligence was all to the good, if Aldridge played his game well.

One of the other men grunted a question. 'Shall I take his head off?' Aldridge translated. Thankfully, Tiny shook his head. "Smite likes 'im." Useful to know, but not something to count on. Rumour had it, Smite's rise to the top had been aided by a childhood friend, killed by his own hand when the friend dared to disagree with him.

The crime lord's lieutenant turned back to Aldridge. "Whacha doin' here, m'lord?" he demanded. "And whassat ya got on?"

Aldridge looked down at his improvised shawl kilt as if he'd never seen it before.

"This? The piece of perfection in the garden was most insistent. Didn't want her daughter seeing my…" he waggled his eyebrows and made a graphic gesture with one hand, prompting a guffaw from the man who wanted to decapitate him.

"A skirt wiv a little un? Where is she?" Tiny wanted to know.

"Gone. She was in a hurry, said she and the little girl had a ship to catch. She couldn't tell me where Perry was, either. Bastard. He'll be sorry when I find him. Drugged me, the lowlife, treacherous cur. Stole my horse and my clothes. Swine. Exquisite female, though. Worth the trip, if she'd have had me. Pity she wouldn't stop to… chat."

Another guffaw from Decapitator, and a pungent comment about a better use for a female than chatting.

"'ow long?" Tiny was not to be distracted.

Enough friendliness. Time to remind them of their place again. He trotted out the ducal manner. Nostrils flared, chin lifted, a glare infused with scorn and disdain.

Tiny flinched, but persisted. "I needs to ask, m'lord; 'ow long since ya seen the skirt? She belongs to Smite. 'Er and the little un."

"Really?" said Aldridge. "Dammit, that's the last straw. I was promised first chance. Perry, damn his cowardly, lying eyes, said he was leaving the country, and she needed a new protector. And all the time… Smite? Really? I say! Do you think he'd consider an offer?"

"We 'ave to find 'er first, m'lord. 'Ow long since ya seen her?"

Aldridge sighed. "Really, I don't know. It was around dusk. How long ago was that? After she left, I… I suppose I passed out again."

Tiny let out a string of profanities, some Aldridge had never heard, and several that sounded painful, if not impossible. "Doxy's got ten hours on us, but we 'ave to search," he told the others, and began organising his men to search the garden, the house, the nearby village of Niddberrow, and the surrounding countryside.

He was near Niddberrow? The last Aldridge remembered, he had been just outside of Bath, half a day's ride away. "If you're off to search the countryside, perhaps one of you would take a message to my cousin in Longford, the Earl of Chirbury at Longford Court."

"No time," Tiny told him.

Aldridge sighed. "So much for Smite's promises," he said. "Ah well. I daresay I can walk to Longford, though it might alarm the local populace. When I get to London, though, I'll be having a little talk with our mutual friend. 'Anything you need, any time,' he said." Aldridge made shooing motions with his hands. "Go on, then. Go, if you're going. I might as well get some more sleep."

Tiny looked a little hunted. He'd witnessed Smite's first meeting with Aldridge. Clearly, Tiny knew no better than Aldridge what the crime lord would expect of him now.

Aldridge let him stew for a minute, then offered him a way out. "I suppose whoever rides over to Longford could just give my note to a villager. That would do."

Tiny agreed, and found a scrap of paper in one pocket and a pencil in the other. Pity. Aldridge had hoped to move the entire meeting up to the house, so Rose and Sarah could release themselves from their prison.

He wrote quickly and handed the message to Tiny, who read it before giving it to the searcher heading for Longford. Would Rede recognise his writing? He had no idea if his cousin had even seen a letter from him. Well, if no carriage came, Aldridge would have to think of something else.

Read more of A Baron for Becky

<u>Three Names in a Day</u>

(Excerpt from The Bluestocking and the Barbarian, *by Jude Knight, coming in 2018. Charlotte [Cherry], the future Duchess of Haverford, is one of the Winderfield twins from Jude's new series* Children of the Mountain King. *In the following scene, she helps Sophia get ready for her wedding to Charlotte's cousin James, heir to the Winshire dukedom. James is the oldest brother of Bey's mother, and he and Sophia will be the parents of Sally's cousin, Elf.)*

Chapter Fourteen

When she woke, Sophia was disoriented, dazedly wondering where she was. The room was richly but heavily furnished in dark depressing colors that did not much improve when she sat up and lit the candle beside her bed with the tinder and flint left ready.

The fire was burning merrily, and hot water steamed in a jug on the washstand. Someone had clearly already been in the room. Sophia slipped out of bed and wrapped herself in the shawl from the foot of the bed.

The door opened, and a maid entered with a tray containing a teapot from which a luxurious aroma rose. "There you are, my lady. Feeling better, I'll be bound."

"Yes, thank you." She was aching and bruised from the travel, even in the well-sprung and luxurious Haverford coach. "The maid who came with me? How is she?"

"Still asleep, my lady. Lady Sutton said as how we was not to disturb her, such a day she had. So I am to do for you, my lady. Shall I lay out your clothes?

Do you wish for me to bring breakfast?"

Lady Sutton was the dowager countess, widow of the dead heir, and mother to James's twin cousins Charlotte and Sarah Winderfield, whom Sophia knew slightly from London's ballrooms.

Sophia could see through a chink in the curtain that it was light outside, so it must be after eight o'clock. "Perhaps I should go down," she said.

"The family has had theirs, my lady," the maid explained.

Sophia sent the maid for breakfast while she washed and dressed as much as she could without someone to do her buttons.

The next knock at the door was not the maid, but Charlotte, Sarah, and a dark slender girl of around the same age whom the twins introduced as James's sister Ruth. "Rosemary would be here, but she is sitting with Grandfather," Ruth told Sophia. "She is most anxious to meet her new sister."

"James left at first light to visit the Archbishop," Charlotte said, "and swears he is not coming home until he has a license."

"Charlotte, I hope you do not mind..." Sophia trailed off. What did one say to the woman whose potential husband one had stolen?

"Mind? You marrying James, you mean?" Charlotte enveloped her in an enthusiastic hug. "I could just kiss you. I was never going to agree to Grandfather's plan, of course, but now Grandfather will stop suggesting it. And Mama and James's father, too."

Another knock at the door brought the twins' mother, who asked to be called Aunt Grace, and James's other aunt, the duke's only daughter.

"Call me Aunt Georgie, Sophia," that lady said, "as the other girls do."

"What do you have to wear for your wedding, Sophia?" Charlotte asked.

Sophia had packed the dress she had chosen for the charity ball, but when she showed it to the ladies, they were at one accord in rejecting it.

"It is the wrong color for you, Sophia," Sarah said decisively. "What do you call it? Brown? Cream? We can do better than that."

In short order, Sophia found herself in the middle of preparations for her wedding, as the ladies brought one dress after another for her to try on until Aunt Georgie and Aunt Grace whispered together and left the room, returning a short while later with an elegantly dressed lady of a similar age to the two aunts. She was carrying a gown in a light silk the soft blue-gray of the sea at dusk, figured with shapes woven so that they gleamed in the light against the muted background. White lace trimmed the low curve of the bodice and the high waist, and finished the cuffs and the flounce below the multiple pleats in the skirt.

They held it up in front of her, and she smiled at her reflection in the mirror. Yes. This one.

"And we will not need to alter it," the other lady said with a satisfied nod. "You and I are much of a size and height."

"I cannot wear your dress, my lady!" Sophia faltered. "I do not think we have been introduced?"

"Dash it." Aunt Georgie sighed. "I left my manners in Somerset, Letty. Lady Sophia Belvoir, Miss Letitia Matthewes, my dear friend. You had better call her Aunt Letty."

"The dress is quite new, Lady Sophia," said its owner. "And it looks better on you by far than it did on me. I liked the color when we saw it at the store, but Georgie should have had it made up for her, not for me."

"Wrong blue for my eyes, Letty. I said that at the shop. But I quite agree; it is just the thing for our new niece. You will be kind enough to let us give it to you, will you not, Sophia?"

What could she say? She managed to stammer her thanks, and Ruth said, "Now all we need is James and a license."

James was a long time returning home.

Washed, perfumed, and with her hair elegantly dressed, but still in her own gown rather than the one chosen for her wedding, Sophia was taken upstairs to meet Rosemary and the two schoolroom boys and to pay her respects to the duke.

"For we do not know how much he can hear, though he is unconscious," Ruth told her.

Everyone welcomed her, even the servants smiling as they passed her in a hallway or entered the duke's sitting room where she sat with her new family, sharing in their vigil.

Lunch was served, and still no James, but as the food was cleared, he appeared, a small rotund cleric trotting at his heels. He crossed directly to Sophia. "I have it, my heart, and the Archbishop's own chaplain to perform the ceremony."

After that, things moved very quickly. James proposed marrying in the grand salon downstairs, but Sophia suggested the duke's bedroom. "For Ruth says he may be able to hear us, and surely it will give him comfort to know that you are safely married, James."

"And to an English girl of impeccable heritage," the Earl of Sutton—Papa—said, grinning. He winked at Sophia. "Even if she is more than half French."

The ladies carried Sophia off to prepare her, producing fine clocked stockings and delicate slippers in white silk, and a corset richly trimmed with lace and ribbon plus a fine lawn petticoat intricately tucked and embroidered white on white.

Sophia had never worn anything so delicate and feminine. "I cannot," she protested, even as she stroked the offerings.

"You don't want Elfingham taking off your gown to see the plain things you have with you," said Aunt Georgie bluntly. "Give the boy a thrill."

"Georgie!" Aunt Letty scolded.

At the same time as Aunt Grace warned, "Remember the girls!"

Sophia consented to the shocking garments, blushing at the thought of James seeing them. Perhaps touching them? Her color rose higher as her imagination considered what might come next, with little to go on but the occasional careless comment from matrons who considered her too old to protect from their more salacious discussions.

Aunt Georgie said shrewdly, "I imagine young James knows what he's about, Sophia. Leave it to him."

In the gloom of the room, the old man lying still on the bed, James's bride shone like the star over the nativity, and everything faded except for her.

James hoped she heard the joy in his voice as he said his vows. She repeated hers with firm assurance. The ring he placed on her finger was a Winderfield ring, worn by one of the duchesses of his line. Would she have preferred a new one? He would shower her with as many as she wished, he vowed to himself as he bent to kiss her, keeping the salute light and brief so he did not embarrass her in front of their interested audience.

Ruth crossed to the bed and peered at the duke's face. "He is breathing more easily and... is he smiling?"

James saw no change, but the chaplain was impressed. "My Lord Archbishop shall be pleased to hear that Lord and Lady Elfingham have received His Grace's blessing. I shall pray for an easy passing for the poor man, you may be sure."

His sisters and cousins swept Sophia off into the next room, Rosemary exclaiming over the ways this wedding differed from the ones at home in the mountains. The chaplain, after a torturously long exchange of courtesies, announced that he could not stop for a meal and must get back to Lambeth Palace, and Andrew volunteered to take him.

At last! James started through to the sitting room, with every intention of extracting his new wife and taking her off to their room, but the duke coughed and then fought to take another breath, setting off a flurry of activity. Was this the end? He cast an anguished glance at Sophia and joined the group praying in the sitting room.

The crisis passed, the duke sinking back into the slowed breathing that had been his state for days. James examined Sophia hopefully but hesitated at the dark smudges under her eyes. "You are exhausted, my heart. Go to sleep, and I will send a servant if there is any change."

In the duke's bedroom, James had greeted her with such joy that her doubts seemed foolish, but they came back to her that night after he had sent her to bed alone, while he kept vigil with his brothers and sisters.

A servant came for her in the early hours of the morning. As soon as she was called, she knew.

"Lady Sutton, Lord Sutton asked me to fetch you."

The old man had gone out with the year, and she—who had woken less than twenty-four hours ago as Sophia Belvoir—had been Lady Elfingham for fewer than ten hours.

He won't settle for less than true love; she doesn't believe in it

James must marry to please his grandfather, the duke, and to win social acceptance for himself and his father's other foreign-born children. But only Lady Sophia Belvoir makes his heart sing, and to win her, he must invite himself to spend Christmas at the home of his father's greatest enemy.

Sophia keeps secret her tendre for James, Lord Elfingham. After all, the whole of Society knows he is pursuing the younger Belvoir sister, not the older one left on the shelf after two failed betrothals.

The Bluestocking and the Barbarian **will be released as a novel in 2018.**

Haverford's Courtship of His Cherry
Followed a Bumpy Road

(Excerpt from The Reformer and the Rake, *still to come from Jude Knight, wherein the Marquis of Aldridge has his first run-in with Charlotte Winderfield [Cherry], who will, in due course, become his bride and future duchess, making Sally's eventual birth possible.)*

He could not sense the presence of Lady Charlotte Winderfield in his room. The idea was ridiculous.

For a start, the bluestocking social reformer they called the West Wind would rather die than enter the bedchamber of any man, let alone the notorious Marquess of Aldridge.

For another, he was not in a position to sense anything outside of the plump white thighs of Baroness Thirby, unless it was the expert ministrations of her close friend, Mrs Meesham. Lady Thirby's thighs blocked both his ears and his line of sight, and—in any case—no-one in the room could hear a thing over the yapping sounds she made as he drove her closer to her release. And he could not possibly smell the delicate mix of herbs and flowers that drove him crazy every time he was in Lady Charlotte's vicinity; not over the musk of Lady Thirby's arousal.

Damn it. The thought of the chit was putting Aldridge off his own release, despite Mrs Meesham's best efforts. It was no use pining after her. With his reputation, her family would not even consider him. And if they could be persuaded, she couldn't. She had made her opinion perfectly clear.

Above him, Lady Thirby stiffened and let out the keening wail with which she celebrated her arrival at that most delicious of destinations. At any moment, she would collapse bonelessly beside him, and he could maybe bury himself in her or her friend and forget all about the unattainable Saint Charlotte.

Instead, Lady Thirby stiffened still further. "What is she doing here?" She scooted backwards so that she could look him in the eye, still crouched, thank the stars. He didn't fancy the weight of her sitting on his chest. "It's one thing to do this with Milly. But you didn't say you were inviting someone else."

Standing in his doorway, her lips pressed into a tight line and her face white except for two spots of high colour on her cheekbones, was the woman of his fondest dreams. And she didn't look happy to be there.

The cold air on his damp member told him that Mrs Meesham had likewise abandoned what she'd been doing to stare at the doorway. "She's never here for a romp, Margaret. She's one of the Winderfield twins."

Aldridge sighed. He couldn't imagine what sort of a crisis had brought Saint Charlotte here, but clearly he was going to have to deal with it.

"My lady," he said, "if you would be kind enough to wait in the next room, I'll find a robe and join you."

She pulled her fascinated gaze from what had been revealed by Mrs Meecham's movement, and glared at him. "More than a robe. Your son has been kidnapped. You have to come with me and we have no time to waste."

"He can't go out," Mrs Meecham objected. "Aldridge," (when Lady Charlotte said nothing but just retreated into the next room), "you can't go. You haven't done me, yet."

Aldridge had already left the bed, and was pulling on his pantaloons. "I am sorry to cut our entertainments short. Sadly, the messenger—who, by the way, neither of you saw…" He gave them the ducal look learned from his father. "…brings me word of an appointment I cannot miss. My heartiest regrets. Please, feel free to carry on without me." He bowed with all the elegance at his command. He could shrug into his waistcoat and coat and pull on his boots while she told him what the problem was. It was a little late to worry about appearing in front of her improperly dressed.

The Reformer and the Rake will be the third book in the Children of the Mountain King series.

Stories about Other Characters

A Mother is Always Right

(Excerpt from A Baron for Becky, *by Jude Knight, wherein Eleanor Haverford demonstrates, once again, how ruthless she can be in pursuit of happiness for her progeny.)*

Chapter Four

The entire next day, Rede and Anne must have been conspiring to keep them apart. Anne took Mrs Darling to the village in the morning. Since she wasn't about, Aldridge accepted Rede's invitation to go riding after he'd dealt with the day's mail, and regretted it when the two men on horseback passed the carriage returning through the gate.

He and Mrs Darling met over lunch in the company of the Chirburys, and he found her alone four times during the afternoon, only to have Rede, Anne, or both enter before they could exchange more than one or two moves in their game.

Had he ever desired a woman this much? Perhaps it was the chase; mostly, they fell into his bed with little effort. Or they didn't, and he looked elsewhere. And she wanted him, too. She might manufacture the shiver of desire when he breathed on her ear, the way she moulded herself to him when they managed a stolen kiss. But the flush of colour on that perfect skin? That was genuine. And he saw no artifice, no calculation, in the lovely eyes.

When Aldridge joined Rede for a drink after dinner, he asked, "Rede, are you and Anne deliberately trying to stop me from talking to Mrs Darling?"

Rede laughed. "Whatever makes you think that, cousin?"

"Please desist? I promised I wouldn't bed her under your roof, but I am trying to negotiate a contract. And it is damned difficult when I can't even talk to the lady."

"Why not leave it till you get to London?"

"First," Aldridge explained, "Mrs Darling has no place to live in London, nor the money to rent anything, until I have the right to provide for her. Second, I am not letting those wolves in London get a glimpse of her until she is under my protection."

"Anne thinks I should protect her from you. She wants to find her a job here in Longford. Or, at the very least, she wants me to ensure you give the woman a fair contract."

"I don't mind a contract. A contract is a good idea. But a job? A jewel like that? She's a courtesan, Rede. It's not as if I'm seducing a virgin."

Rede grinned and slid the port along the table. "Pour yourself another, Aldridge. Mrs Darling has the right to make her own choices. I've told Anne that Mrs Darling can stay in Longford if that is what the lady wants, but I won't stand in your way, either."

"Then please stop trying to keep us apart."

"Very well, cousin," Rede agreed, and conceded, "I'll take Anne out visiting tomorrow with the girls and leave you with Mrs Darling. Good enough? But I will tell her if she wants advice on the contract, I am happy to be at her service."

Aldridge went to find Mrs Darling, but she had already retired for the night.

Rose bundled Sarah well against the cold, blustery day before sending the girl off to the market in Chipping Niddwick with the earl and his family, hopping up and down and chattering like a starling. When Rose turned back to the house, after waving farewell, Aldridge was waiting.

"Mrs Darling, I've asked the housekeeper to set out tea in the library. Will you join me?"

She brushed against him as she moved through the doorway, which clearly set him off-balance, but she gained no advantage because it affected her as much. They had to end this negotiation soon. It was killing her.

Last night, Lady Chirbury had followed her to her room and offered to help her find 'honest work.' She could be a seamstress or serve in a shop, and Lord Chirbury would lease her and Sarah a cottage at favourable terms. "I would suggest teaching, Mrs Darling, since you are obviously well educated, but if your past were to come out… The Longford villagers are good people, but they can be very hard on those they don't understand."

Rose's sewing was mediocre, and neither occupation would earn her more than a pittance. "Forgive me," she told Anne. "I need to make more than that, if

I am to give Sarah a chance at a better life than mine…" She could not meet Lady Chirbury's eyes, fearing the scorn and rejection. But the countess surprised her. "I understand better than you might think, Mrs Darling. Make sure he gives you a favourable contract, then. My husband will read it for you, if you wish."

In the library, several closely-written pages were lying on a table under the window. "You suggested a contract, Mrs Darling," he said. "Here is a start. Everything is negotiable. I want you to be happy." He looked nervous. Did he really think she had a choice?

She took the chair in front of the table and began reading.

Two years? He wanted *two years*? An upfront payment, hers to keep plus an allowance. Was two hundred and fifty guineas a quarter low? But wait; he would pay all her costs: the wages for servants, unlimited accounts at the grocer, the butcher, and the candlemaker, as well as her choice of milliner, *modiste*, bootmaker, and any other makers of clothing and adornments.

Dear Heavens. Her eyes must be out on stalks!

He would pay for, and keep, a carriage and horses for her use, including grooms and stabling. He would pay for a nurse for Sarah, and teachers for Rose in dance and pianoforte.

She read on. She couldn't help the grin, though she managed not to dance in her seat.

Aldridge would purchase and staff a town-house within easy distance of Haverford House. At the end of two years, the house would be hers, free and clear.

Two years. She could do anything for two years.

Surely between the value of the town-house and what she could save, she would be able to start again in the country? Be free? Give Sarah a decent life?

He wanted a key to the house. He wanted her to be available whenever he wished, and travel if he wanted her company. He wanted the right of renewal after two years, should he wish to continue to keep her.

He would expect her to host and accompany him to entertainments and activities. She frowned a little.

He was watching closely. "Something wrong?" he asked.

"Would you… would you expect me to 'entertain' other men?" She hated that. Her third protector had used a night with her to reward his friends or bribe his allies.

"I'm not good at sharing what is mine," Aldridge said. "Mrs Darling, I won't insist on you doing anything that makes you feel diminished. Though I hope you'll try new things, even if they seem a bit odd or uncomfortable at first."

She considered him carefully. Even in Bristol, even in her circles, Aldridge's parties were discussed in scandalised whispers. But rumours were seldom accurate.

His usual twinkle deserted him, and his eyes were level and serious as he said,

"Mrs Darling, I ask one thing of my lovers, and I ask it of you. Tell me what pleases you. Tell what does not please you. Never pretend pleasure you do not feel."

"My lord," she protested, "this arrangement is about your pleasure, not mine."

He rejected that with a swift shake of the head. "My pleasure is enhanced by your pleasure. Women know this; that is why they pretend. But I will know if you pretend, Mrs Darling, and that will destroy my pleasure. If you wish to please me in intimate matters, then you must first allow me to please you."

Rose's mouth was hanging open. She closed it, gathering her scattered thoughts.

"I want Sarah to have her own apartments, and not to…" she blushed again, not sure quite how to say she was ashamed to let her daughter to see her being the harlot she was. And afraid those attending Aldridge's entertainments might be a danger to Sarah.

Aldridge nodded. "A town-house with a top floor that has its own entrance."

She studied the papers some more. She was sure she must be missing something. At her age, this might be her last chance. And Sarah was growing older, too, and better able to understand what she observed. Rose had to be careful. "My lord, Lady Chirbury said… I wish to discuss the contract with the earl."

Aldridge nodded again, smiling. "Good idea. He's not a solicitor, but he is a good businessman and has read many hundreds of contracts. Not this sort, precisely, or not that I've heard. But he will give you good advice."

"You have no objection?" The man was a miracle.

No. A miracle would save her without expecting the use of her body as a reward. But he was kind and generous, and that was miracle enough.

"I want you to be happy," Aldridge said again.

To give her hands something to do, besides trembling and shaking pages of parchment, Rose prepared a cup of tea for Aldridge the way he liked it—black and strong with lemon. Then she sliced into the cake.

Aldridge put out a hand to stop her. "That's not what I'm hungry for, Rose." She glanced at his fall. The fashion for tight knit pantaloons left a man with nowhere to hide his lust. Her mouth suddenly dry at the size of what she saw, she met his eyes. For once, he was not smiling.

"I promised Rede I'd not bed you under his roof," he told her. "So perhaps we could think of something quenching to discuss?"

Rose reached out and ran a fingernail along the object of her fascination. "Did he specify bed?" she asked.

Aldridge had to make two attempts to speak, which she counted a success. "Bed or otherwise tup," he told her. "Have you another suggestion?"

Her voice dropped into another register. "I wouldn't encourage you to break your word to your cousin. Nor will I—complete the act with you until I decide whether or not to accept your contract. But can we not find a way to enjoy one another short of…?" She slipped her sleeve down her arm as she spoke, revealing more and more of her breast.

He swallowed again, and croaked, "Several ways. Give me one moment to lock the door."

But before he could, it opened. Rose just had time to pull her dress to decency before an imperious little woman sailed into the room, talking over her shoulder as she entered the room.

"No, indeed, my dear Cole, no need to announce me. I know my own nephew's home. Not that it ever was my sister's, of course, but we often visited. Do you not remember, Aldridge, my dear? Hello, darling, do you not have a kiss for your Mama?"

Her Grace of Haverford, for it must be she, presented one perfumed cheek to her son, then glanced around the room.

Rose attempted to gather up the pages on the table before the duchess saw them.

The duchess frowned, clearly taking in Rose's dishevelled state and perhaps the rampant erection Aldridge was valiantly trying to hide behind an occasional table, too low to do a good job. "Oh, but I have interrupted. Cole tried to tell me… Oh dear. Shall I go out and come in again, my love?"

Aldridge, in a tone equidistant between exasperation, amusement, and despair, said, "No need, Mama. May I beg your permission to present Mrs Rose Darling, a guest of the earl and countess? Mrs Darling, this, as you may have guessed, is Her Grace, the Duchess of Haverford. My mother."

Rose performed her best curtsey, grateful for the training that allowed her to perform the manoeuvre while shrinking inside, and then made her escape while the Marquis was interrogating his mother on her unexpected appearance.

She had no idea how she felt. Elated, undoubtedly. She had never imagined such a contract. Shamed, embarrassed… Aldridge's mother clearly thought… And she was right. And she was a duchess! If she had arrived two minutes later… no, Aldridge was going to lock the door.

Rose giggled nervously at the thought of the Duchess of Haverford knocking on the door, demanding her son's attention while he attempted to put himself back into his pants. Not that the actual scene was much better. A bucket of cold water could have separated them no more quickly.

The duchess's arrival would not change Aldridge's mind, would it?

The entrance hall was full of people—no doubt ducal servants and attendants. Rose took the contract papers up to her guest room and sat studying them until the earl and countess returned and she had to go down to be sociable.

The Duchess of Haverford had been visiting friends in Cirencester and was on her way to call on a goddaughter in Bath. "You will remember Polly, Anne, dear. She married the Viscount Sudding. And she has been delivered of a son, which is such a relief for the family. Three daughters, you know, and the cousin a very odd man. One would not want him to inherit. And she is still young, so there may be more."

The thought clearly reminded her of her own offspring. "Rede, I had such a comfortable coze with Aldridge today." Aldridge was seated on the floor at her feet, and she patted his cheek lovingly. "I had no idea you were here, darling. So pleased. I thought you and your friend, Lord Overton, had gone off to a party somewhere."

"Overton returned home, Mama," Aldridge told her. They had separated in London two months ago, after Overton read Aldridge a lecture on his drinking, refusing to 'follow him to perdition.' Overton headed back north to his estate, his wife, and his stepdaughters, and Aldridge rambled from house party to house party. "His wife is in expectation of a happy event."

"How lovely! Lord Overton was at school with Aldridge, my dears. You remember, Rede. Such a nice boy. Injured in the war, you know, then came home to inherit the barony."

She patted her son's cheek again. "He has settled down nicely since he wed. Aldridge quite misses him, do you not, my love?"

"He is staid and boring."

"And a new baby," the Duchess continued, taking no notice. "How lovely."

Aldridge shifted from under his mother's hand, and got to his feet. "Perhaps Mrs Darling would play for us. Would you be so kind?"

Rose nodded, taking the message from the abrupt change of subject. His Lordship's friend was not a topic to be discussed in front of a mistress, however expensive.

Her Grace watched her son thoughtfully as he arranged music for Rose, then turned pages for her. "You play beautifully, my dear," she said, when Rose returned to her seat.

"Simple things, Your Grace," Rose said. "I fear anything difficult is beyond me."

"You do well, my dear, to know your limits and stay within them," the duchess replied, her grave look giving the words another layer of meaning.

By the time dinner was called, Rose knew where Aldridge came by his conversational dexterity. The duchess swooped, with butterfly ease, from family to family, throughout the *ton*, and up and down society. Her Grace, it seemed, knew everybody in England, was related to half of them, and was godmother to the other half.

The addition of a duchess to the table did not change the informality with which they dined, and the conversation ranged freely around the table. Her Grace had news of Lady Chirbury's sister, Kitty, who had been staying with her in London. "Dear Kitty; she is meant to be refreshing her winter wardrobe, but she and Mia will be spending their pin money on music and books, I dare say." And she had spent half an hour with the nursery party. "Your Sarah is such a pretty child, Mrs Darling. And lovely manners."

After dinner, the ladies withdrew to the great parlour, leaving the two men to the port.

"I am travelling in the morning, so will go up to bed," the duchess announced. "Mrs Darling, perhaps you would give me a few moments of your time?"

"Be nice, aunt," warned Lady Chirbury, making Rose even more nervous. The duchess gave an enigmatic smile and led the way upstairs.

"Leave us, dear," she said to the maid who was standing ready by the bed. "I shall ring when I want you." She took a chair by the fire and waved Rose to the other.

"Do not look so nervous, Mrs Darling. I do not intend to bite you."

Rose blushed scarlet. Aldridge had promised to bite her, and had explained exactly where. No. She must not think of that. She sat, as commanded.

"Mrs Darling, you were raised gentry, were you not?"

Rose nodded, cautiously. Where was the duchess going with this?

"The manners, the speech, the accomplishments—they can all be taught, of course. But one who has learned them from the cradle..." Her Grace waved a hand as if to flick away counterfeits.

"The usual story, I imagine? Seduction or rape? And no father to defend your honour?"

"My father..." Rose swallowed hard to remove the lump that closed her throat at the memories. "My father was a librarian. He took the part of his employer."

"Ah." Her Grace nodded. "And the employer was the cause of your downfall. Or his son, perhaps?"

"His son," Rose confirmed. His sons, in fact, but she would not say that.

"And Sarah was the...?"

"No, Your Grace. Sarah... came later."

"Mr. Darling?"

"There was no Mr. Darling," Rose admitted.

The maid must have added a fresh log to the fire just before they arrived. The top was still uncharred, but flames licked up from the bed of hot embers. A twig that jutted from one side suddenly flared, turned black, and shrivelled. The bottom of the log began to glow red.

The duchess spoke again, startling Rose out of her flame-induced trance.

"What do you want for your daughter, Mrs Darling?"

"A better life," Rose said immediately, suddenly fierce. "A chance to be respectable. A life that does not depend on the whims of a man."

"The first two may be achievable," the duchess said, dryly. "The third is highly unlikely for any woman of any station. You expect my son to help you to these goals, I take it."

Rose was suddenly tired of polite circling. "I was saving so that I could leave this life, start again in another place under another name. But my last protector cheated me and stole from me.

"I do what I must, Your Grace. Should I have killed myself when I was disgraced? I had no skills anyone wanted to buy. I could play the piano, a little; sew, but others were faster and better; paint, but indifferently; parse a Latin sentence, but of what use was that in my circumstances? Should I have starved in the gutter where they threw me?

"Well, I was not given that choice. Those who took me from the gutter knew precisely what I had that others would pay for. As soon as I could, I began selling it for myself, and I. Will. Not. Be. Ashamed."

Her vehemence did not ruffle the duchess's calm. "We all do what we must, my dear. I am not judging you. Men have the power in this world, and women of the gentry are raised to depend on them for our survival. But you must know that Aldridge cannot offer marriage to a woman with your history."

The mere thought startled a laugh out of Rose. Marriage had never crossed Aldridge's mind. Of that she was certain. "His Lordship has offered me a two-year contract as his mistress," she said, "with very favourable terms. If I accept, and if I save carefully, I will never need to take a protector again."

"Two years!" The duchess arched a delicate eyebrow. "Aldridge seldom keeps a mistress beyond six months. He must be utterly besotted."

"He has no thought of marriage," Rose found herself reassuring the duchess. "And neither do I. I like him, but do not love him, and I think only love could make marriage tolerable."

It was only partly true. She could easily fall in love with Aldridge... was, perhaps, beginning to do so already. That way, she knew, led to heartache, for the duchess was right. Aldridge would never offer her marriage, or even permanence.

The duchess nodded, decisively. "You are wise. I think you will be good for him, Mrs Darling—which is a ridiculous name. May I call you 'Rose'?" Her Grace's smile was a wonderful thing, another feature her son had inherited.

"Would you..." Rose had never imagined having such a conversation, but there was something about this woman. Nothing shocked her, and she listened. "Would you call me Becky? It is my real name."

"Becky, then. Becky, as long as you remember that you will never be accepted as a fit mate for the future Duke of Haverford—which is a great shame, for you seem to be a fine young woman, but we must live in the world as it is—you and I shall be friends, and I shall support you and little Sarah to find the new life you seek when Aldridge is finished with you. He needs someone like you. He is not happy, poor boy."

That squashed the nascent hope that the duchess's sponsorship might mean she could avoid accepting Aldridge's protection. Still, it was a good offer. Becky accepted the duchess's outstretched hands. "Thank you, Your Grace. I will do my best to make him happy."

Read more of A Baron for Becky

<u>Old Scandal Comes Home to Roost—</u>
<u>and Inherit the Firthley Marquisate</u>

(Firthley's first days in England, and his last unfinished business.)

December 15, 1803

The last time the Earl of Herrendon's voice was heard in the confines of England, the Watch was called to the London residence of the Marquess of Firthley, where it was feared the marquess would kill his firstborn son, rather than allow him to marry the woman of his choosing. That circumstance, however, is of ancient vintage, and who can remember back more than a quarter-century?

Luckily for you, dear Readers, this reporter can.

During the 1775 Season, the featured soprano at the Royal Opera, Miss Lourdes Andreadis, was a dark-eyed, Grecian beauty who had traveled the Continent, performed for the Crowned Heads of Europe, and reportedly taken more than one royal son, in more than one principality, as lover. Inevitably, every British nobleman with the purse to finance a mistress wanted a contract, but she was not a woman for hire. No, she was heiress to a shipping fortune and had made her own money and fame. She chose her paramours for the enjoyment and had no need of a husband, even one with a title.

When the Earl of Herrendon, heir to the Marquess of Firthley, fell in love with her, no one thought there was any question of marriage. Not only was he only one of dozens of men offering her their sincere devotion (by way of worldly goods), but Preston Marloughe was a dutiful son, not given to fancies like love at first sight and midnight elopements. Older, wiser men than he had been ensorcelled by Miss Andreadis, however, and Herrendon was caught up like all the others. Before the end of the Season, they were publicly acknowledged lovers, and she announced she would retire.

Speculation was rife she was increasing with his by-blow, but still, no hint of a marriage until one morning, in the small hours, the Watch was called to Belgrave Square by the screaming of the marquess' housekeeper, who ran from the house, shouting about the master killing his only son. News of the earl's marriage arrived back in London within a fortnight, and announcement of a birth no fewer than three years later, but the Earl of Herrendon was never seen in England again.

Until now.

Readers, I can confirm that the Earl of Herrendon has returned to English soil. The son of Firthley's prodigal heir and his scandalous opera singer has taken up residence in Belgravia as heir presumptive to his grandfather, the Marquess of Firthley.

So, who is Alexander Marloughe, the new Earl of Herrendon? If the ladies of London are lucky, he is his father's son, for anyone who remembers Preston Marloughe, does so fondly. He was a kind, funny, honorable young man, and this writer admits to shedding a tear on news of his death by fever some dozen years ago. The noblewomen of England were done a great disservice when Miss Andreadis took him out of the marriage mart, and no less a personage than Lady Sefton has said so.

But will the same be true for the son? For surely, the first order of business for this young bachelor must be securing a bride.

He is handsome, it is reported, and a noted businessman in Greece, but after a lifetime in trade in Crete, raised to manage a shipping operation rather than take his seat in the Lords, one wonders if the new earl will have even a loose grasp of the social graces, to say nothing of understanding the social, political, and economic realities of our nation. It is sure he will have but a slim purse, as his mother's fame and fortune have long since dimmed, his English property has been lying fallow since his father's desertion, and his mother's family's fleet of ships has been requisitioned at gunpoint by Napoleon's forces, which is presumably why he has chosen now to make his return and take possession of Herrendon (both the Hall and the courtesy title).

But does any of that matter at all?

Even were he a bricklayer, he will yet become Firthley and take a seat in the House of Lords upon his grandfather's passing. The marquessate is wealthy and strategically significant, the current Lord Firthley is a hinge vote in his bloc in

Parliament, and no one has the least notion of the character or temperament of England's latest peer. The question uppermost must not be whether Alexander Marloughe will fit in with the *beau monde*—for his bloodline is irrefutable—but rather, how?

What kind of nobleman will he be, and perhaps more important (certainly more entertaining to contemplate), which of our noble daughters will redeem Preston Marloughe's betrayal of his class and welcome Herrendon back home?

Read more of 'Tis Her Season

<u>The First Public Appearance of Lord Firthley and Toad's Aunt Charlotte.</u>

(Excerpt from 'Tis Her Season, by Mariana Gabrielle)

Chapter Twelve

January 29, 1804
London, England

"Mother!" Charlotte's brows drew together as she threw yet another argument at Lady Effingale's reflection in the looking glass. "Why must I marry at all? No one knows anything, and there are months of parties left in the Season."

Lady Effingale stopped combing her daughter's hair, looking as though she would speak, but Bella's soft voice started first. From the chair near the dressing screen, where she was brushing Charlotte's slippers, she said, "Because my brother will ruin you if you do not."

"Quite right, Isabella, dear. Is that a tear in the sole of that shoe?" Lady Effingale snatched the left slipper from Bella's hand, and the two girls performed twin eye rolls in the mirror. "You will marry in two days' time, as your father has arranged, and we will say nothing more about it."

"But I don't want to!"

"And I care not at all what you want, Charlotte Amberly. You have had 'what you want' for nearly a month, and the only thing to come of it is an offer to destroy the reputation of this entire family. You have made a mockery of everything I ever taught you, and ruined yourself into the bargain. Let this be your punishment."

"To be married to a man I hate for the rest of my life?"

"Yes."

"But—"

"Not another word, Charlotte. You might have stopped this before it started by exercising the slightest bit of restraint. Isabella, please check that the lace has been properly tacked onto the green gown. There wasn't time to see to it before I left."

Bella took the dress in question to the corner, where she settled herself on a shepherdess chair almost the same green as the bodice. Once the lace was reattached, she tightened a seam.

"Must I really attend a party and pretend to be happy about marrying in haste and repenting in leisure?"

Lady Effingale let out an exasperated huff and wrenched the brush through Charlotte's hair, inspiring a yelp. When Charlotte reached up to discover whether she now had a bald spot, her mother slapped her hand away.

"You will attend the party. You will stand up for every dance with your new betrothed and make enough lovesick calves' eyes to put a herd of beeves to shame. And you will marry in two days' time, whether you like it or not!" The boar-bristle brush caught on a tangle and brushed through it with no concern for Charlotte's wincing.

"But—"

Lady Effingale grasped Charlotte's hair and pulled her head back to glare upside-down. "You will do exactly what I say, Charlotte, or I will turn you out with nothing. Do you understand me? No dowry, no money, not even a pelisse to keep you warm. You wish to run away from your family? Very well. I will let you go, but you will not use Amberly or Effingale money to do it. We will see how long you last on the streets of London."

Shoving Charlotte's head forward, she used the brush to turn a curl around her hand, tipping her head to gauge whether it was too wide to frame her daughter's face. Apparently, she decided it was, as she separated it into strands, using a pin to secure one ringlet to the crown of Charlotte's head. Charlotte's mutinous expression in the looking glass finally resolved itself to resignation and despair.

"Perhaps it will not be so bad, Charlotte," Bella offered. "You will be living close by. You can visit any time you like."

"Easy enough for you to say!" Charlotte shouted as she turned, locks of hair flying about her face like driving rain. "You'll be living in my room, in my house, with no unspeakable husband to tell you what to do!" At that, her screeching turned to sobs, and she put her head down on the dressing table and cried.

Bella sat quietly with her needlework, waiting for the storm to pass. Charlotte's fits of temper, while fiery, had no lasting heat.

Lady Effingale, on the other hand, would have none of it.

"That is the outside of enough, girl. I will have no truck with this unseemly behavior. Stop that sniveling, sit up straight, and act like the lady you were raised to be."

Finally, after several long minutes of her mother's toe tapping in an angry rhythm, Charlotte sat up and glared at Bella in the mirror.

Two hours later, Charlotte was handed down first from the carriage, holding her emerald green silk skirt and black velvet cloak just slightly higher than her slipper, to avoid the muddy street. Throwing her shoulders back, head high, she marched to the front door of the Popham's town house, not stopping until her father snapped sharply, "Charlotte, you will wait for the rest of us."

Once Lady Effingale, and finally Bella, were on the walk, straightening their clothes from the carriage ride, Lord and Lady Effingale joined arms and led the two girls to the door. Immediately upon entering, before she had even removed her cloak, a familiar voice spoke in her ear as a set of large hands helped her off with her outerwear. She shuddered at the contact.

"You look charming, my dear, and so lovely in green. I believe this shade perfectly matches your eyes."

Tossing his hands off her shoulders, spinning on her heel, she narrowed the eyes that matched her outfit and her jewels and snarled, as quietly as she could manage, "You do not have permission to touch me, Sir, and I do not appreciate your forward behavior."

"But, dearest…" Lord Firthley smiled in that infernally appealing way, one side of his lips turned up, and his eyes sparkling the way they did when he laughed. "Surely you cannot object to your betrothed merely touching your arm."

She turned away from his low bow with a harrumph. When he offered his elbow to lead her to the ballroom, she stared at it like he was hiding a snake in his sleeve, until her mother grasped her hand and placed it under Lord Firthley's arm, hissing in her ear, "You. Will. Not. Make. A. Scene. Smile, Charlotte Amberly, or I will make you wish you had."

With a beleaguered sigh, she allowed herself to be led away by the horrible man who had offered for her without once mentioning his intentions.

When they entered the ballroom, the buzz of conversation stopped, then restarted, all eyes trained on her. Jeremy had clearly begun his campaign to see her ruined, but Lord Firthley merely patted her hand, smiled down at her with genuine pleasure, and said, "If nothing else, we will be amused all evening by the assembled lords and ladies who cannot decide whether to vilify you or fawn over me."

Charlotte hardened her face into the sharp smile she had perfected years ago, and said, "Perhaps the rest of the assemblage will toady to you, my lord, but if I am to be your wife, you should not come to expect it from me."

With a chuckle, he brushed his gloved hand across her cheek and whispered in her ear, "I will expect many things from you as my wife, my sweet; toadying is not one of them."

At her gasp, watching the blush fill her cheeks, he nodded in satisfaction and led her to the dance floor.

Read more of <u>'Tis Her Season</u>

The Scandal Keeping Gills Unmarriageable

(excerpt from La Déesse Noire: The Black Goddess, *by Mariana Gabrielle, wherein Lord Joseph Gildeforte's father, the Viscount Fitzmarten, future Marquess of Coventon, ruins his children's chances before they are even born.)*

Chapter Seven

God in Heaven, how could he ever manage this?

The sun streamed through the diamond-paned windows of Kali's bedroom—their bedroom—warmth belying the unqualified mess Fitz was making of things. Not purposely, of course, but unavoidable. The rays of incongruous sunlight shone on the tasteful, pale-green, silk-covered walls in the room she had redecorated, once comfortable enough in their arrangement to tell him his idea of a mistress' home far too easily called to mind a brothel.

Perhaps he should have demanded she keep the red and gold.

He had never intended for her to fall in love, had told her again and again she must not. Hell's eternal fire, she had told him again and again she had not. Would not. Could not! But she had.

In truth, he had, too. Not so far he couldn't do his duty, but enough to wish to keep her safe from Birchbright's blackmail, with which Fitz had no intention of complying.

After the earl's first demand three months ago, he had begun curtailing talk of his black mistress, then spread a rumor of the end of his dalliance with the help of a few close friends. He had ceased his attendance at the theatre, begun visiting her only after dark, and stopped staying the night. He had allowed himself to be seen periodically at brothels catering to white noblemen by serving up white women.

Then his father had finally died, which gave him a window of time during which he could reasonably withdraw into grief and familial duties. His father now buried, the title passed, Lord Fitzmarten's affairs must be set in order so Lord Coventon could begin the plodding life that had been plotted for him.

The only way to minimize the scandal now—for a scandal there would assuredly be—was to walk away from his mistress, honor his betrothal, and find a way to make Birchbright's accusations appear ludicrous, or better yet, the meanderings of an unhinged mind incapable of further service in government.

He dragged a hand through his hair, knowing that, by now, he looked like a hedgehog, including the new white hair showing among the dark curls. The fine linen of his shirt and the worsted wool waistcoat did nothing to keep out the cold seeping through the window sash; he should not have left off his jacket. Perhaps then he would feel less like he had come to visit and more like he planned to go.

The gold-and-ruby necklace he had brought was suited for a queen and priced as such. But fittingly, it clashed with the blue-and-silver ensemble—his favorite of her many dresses—and sat abandoned on a console table near the door, tossed there carelessly as soon as she discerned its purpose. Which took less than five seconds and no words.

At least she could be counted on to never, ever cry. Though this fake smile was not much better.

"Of course you must do your duty, Fitz. Lord Coventon must have an heir." Even through the ever-broader smile, she wasn't able to entirely keep the snappishness at bay. "A lily-white heir with no taint of the exotic."

At his narrowed eyes, she moderated her tone, almost apologetic, amending, "It is not as though we had no warning."

Tugging at his waistcoat, he reminded himself they had been preparing for this day for weeks, ever since his father fell ill again. Nor had it been the first time. They had been through the exercise thrice before. Only this time, the marquess had finally died, taking with him all the freedom Fitz imagined he had. And forcing his hand on a topic he had been resisting for years, especially since his betrothal had been announced.

Very quietly, almost under her breath, she said, "Many married gentlemen keep a mistress. I've no objection."

Shoulders twitching under his linen shirt, fingers worrying a waistcoat button, he replied, in as kindly a manner as he could muster, "You know I will not, sweeting." Fitz finally wrapped his arms around her shoulders, pulling her tight, but she only stiffened. "We've spoken of this."

She nodded, but the motion was sharp, jerking her out of his arms. With a suspicious rasp, she retorted, "If you must marry that woman, so be it. As I've said, it is folly—you'll not be happy one moment the rest of your life—but far be it from me to advise you about women, a topic on which I am expert." For the first time today, the first time in months, she snarled: "And you, clearly, are not."

"My sweet, it is only she—"

"She comes with ten thousand a year and her father will ease your way in Parliament. Yes, you've said. She is also—"

"A harridan, and ugly besides. 'No joy to bed on my wedding night.' You've made yourself known on that score." His voice began to take on volume, and he pulled away from her, straightening his cuffs to keep his anger in check. Right away, he discovered the sleeves could be torn from the shoulders before that would happen. "As though I haven't eyes or ears of my own! I don't *want* to marry her, Kali! You act as if I have a *choice*!"

Kali began screeching, so out of character he took a step back. After almost three years of spending most twilights at her dining table, most evenings in her sitting room, and most nights in her bed, he was entirely accustomed to an unflappable countenance. The part of him that wished to ease her pain had been warring all day with the part that hoped she would revert to her *tawaif* training and show no emotion at all. Good fortune was not with him on either count.

"Will she hold a dagger to your throat on the way into St. George's? Of course you have a choice, you wretched man! You horrible, vile, despicable man!" She stomped her foot hard enough to set the floor shaking and formed fists at her sides, probably forcing herself not to box his ears. "You needn't marry some miserable woman who will torment you and your children to her dying day!"

"Well, I can't marry *you*, if that is what you suggest!"

"Of course that is not what—"

"Heaven help me if I married a half-caste whore who sells tickets to look at her body!"

The words fell like a boulder into the center of the bedroom, and Kali's face paled unnaturally as she lurched backward and turned toward the cheerful, snapping fire in the hearth.

Now he had done it. The first time he would ever see her cry, if she permitted it, and he had been the reason. Unreasonable anger that should have been directed inward had forced him to say things he would never have allowed another man to speak.

"Kali, I—"

"Get out!"

One last shout, apparently, before her voice fell strangely quiet, scratching in her throat, leaving scrapes across his heart. "Go to your perfect bitch of a bride and may she be a stone under your heel the rest of your days. I will remove myself inside a sennight and leave the keys with your solicitor."

"I never meant—"

"Get out." The gravelly tone made him want equally to run away and never let her go.

"If ever you should need—"

She turned her tear-streaked face on him; the unimaginable anger and terror and sorrow had wiped away everything familiar. She looked like an entirely different—more formidable—woman. The sight stole his breath, nearly knocking him off his feet.

"Out! *Out!* You have said this is *my house*, that I am mistress here. So, get out before I... before..." She dissolved into wrenching sobs, dropping onto the floor into a sea of blue and silver ruffles, and he did the only thing he could to ease her.

He left, closing the door gently behind him.

Read more of La Déesse Noire: The Black Goddess

<u>Lord Coventon is Provided a Second Son</u>

(Excerpt from Lord Coventon's Concubines, *by Mariana Gabrielle, wherein Lord Coventon is provided a second son, Lord Joseph Gildeforte, otherwise known as Gills.)*

Chapter One

Mayuri Falodiya rose to her feet as the Marquess of Coventon crossed her drawing room for the first time in almost a decade. His frame was still tall and lean, but slightly stooped now, as though he had carried too heavy a weight for too long, and the laugh lines she remembered so clearly were outnumbered by creases dragging his mouth into a weary frown. Her butler trailed behind, trying to relieve Lord Coventon of his coat, hat, and cane, but stepped back as she allowed the marquess to kiss her hand.

"I am pleasantly surprised to see you, my lord. It has been a good many years."

"Yes."

There was no need for a reminder of the last time he had been in this room: the night he asked her advice on breaking his contract of protection with Kali Matai, the Black Goddess, who was, then, only beginning her rise to fame and fortune as a dancer. To him, she had been, first and foremost, his beloved paramour. Her presence was palpable in the room.

"It is difficult to think of you as Lord Coventon now, after knowing you for so many years as Fitz. Of course, I follow your actions in Parliament in the papers with the rest of England, but I admit great curiosity about the type of man you have become since your marriage and elevation."

She took his hat and cane and handed them to the butler, then ran her hand up the collar of his coat, allowing her fingertips to drift underneath, then guide him to shrug it off his shoulders. When she gave it to the servant, she told him, under her voice, to bring tea and an extra decanter of cashew *feni*.

Coventon had always been a restless man, but now he seemed touchy, nervous, bouncing from one foot to another, his eyes shifting back and forth, not meeting hers for more than a few moments at a time. She reached out to touch the greying hair at his temple, but he shied away. Mayuri smoothly turned the truncated motion into the offer of a seat before her fireplace.

"Your age suits you well, Your Lordship. You are as handsome as ever."

"Flattery is a young man's flaw."

He hesitated to sit, and she chivvied him to the chair, clucking her tongue. "Did I not think your looks worthy of notice, I could have flattered the cut of your coat or your wealth or position or wisdom in matters of politics. You may be sure I can always find a genuine compliment to pay a gentleman. Will you have dinner tonight?" She smirked slightly. "My girls will surely wish to compete for your attentions."

With his fundament halfway to a resting spot, he startled and stopped himself, hands on his knees, before slowly lowering himself into the armchair. "I do not wish—that is… no girls, if you please. I'd just like to make myself quietly drunk, perhaps play a game of cards with whomever is about. Some food later, but to start: *feni*. Perhaps to finish as well, should the night progress as expected, and a bed, though I will prefer to sleep alone. Can you accommodate?"

"There are few noblemen I will not accommodate, and you are not listed among their number." Crossing to her liquor cabinet, she poured his first glass of *feni*, which she expected he would take quickly, like medicine.

She was not the least surprised when he held the glass out for a second ration. Once it had been poured, he settled back slightly in the chair, relaxing his shoulders just enough to signal he wouldn't bolt.

They sat in silence for long minutes, he twisting his glass in his hands, she watching him fight with himself. Finally, she said, "Do you still smoke seegars, my lord?"

He laughed, with an edge that brushed against her heart. "By all means. Kali would say it is an evening to celebrate!" He downed the spirits and held out the glass again, so she poured. If he must be removed, dead drunk, to a solitary bed in a quarter-hour, so be it.

"There is little celebration in your eyes, my lord, and as you bring up Kali, she would beg I provide whatever succor you might wish, if only you will tell me how I can best soothe."

She opened a drawer in the side table between their chairs and offered a seegar, which he accepted. "Genevieve hates tobacco."

"Then it is well your wife is not here to be bothered by the smoke. I rather enjoy it, myself." She cut and lit it. "We are not unknown to each other, you and I, though it has been so many years. I hope you remember I will keep your confidence."

He had been very young the night he spent in Mayuri's bed and bared parts of his soul no other woman had seen before or since, even Kali. And she had been wise enough to never take him to bed again, rather providing him his choice of all her other girls until he learned the difference between being in love, being infatuated, and being in bed with a whore, years before Kali had even come to London. "How may I be of help to my old friend this eve?"

After a few draws and puffs in her generous silence, he said, "By God's grace, I am granted a second son today."

Without being so bold as to express an opinion by her tone, she said, "Congratulations, my lord. He is healthy?"

"Yes. Oh, yes. A strapping thing, with a fine set of lungs and a strong kick. Lord Joseph Henry Gildeforte. I could not be happier with His Little Lordship. As beautiful a baby as his brother and sister before him."

His frame straightened when he spoke of his new son, and his eyes lit from within. She had never doubted he would be a loving father, as he had always been a kind, fair, even-tempered man, but it was good to see proof of the promise, years later.

She sat quietly, her hands draped motionless across her lap. He would only come to the point in his own good time. Kali had shared as much with Mayuri out of sheer frustration, while she had been contracted to him.

He looked away, his face flushed, one hand running through his hair. "He's the spare, you see. With the heir and spare delivered, my wife has asked I keep myself away from her bedchamber, and has suggested I take a mistress."

Mayuri raised a brow. By nearly all moral codes, and by law, Lady Coventon had been bought as much as any courtesan, though for more money and with greater security. She had no right to bar the door to her bedchamber, though Lord Coventon was not the type of man to force himself on anyone, least of all, his wife.

"It has been a miserable decade, Mayuri. I find myself inclined to agree; the sound of her voice withers me. I would gladly banish her to the countryside, but I cannot deprive myself of my children, nor my children of their mother." He finished the glass again and held it out.

She took her time pouring. "My lord, will you allow me to order you supper from the kitchen?"

He smiled. "I have missed your kitchen, Mayuri. One hates to always eat like an Englishman. Is Pranjal still your chef?"

"He is, and I believe he will give his all if he hears you have returned, for no other Englishman has ever ordered native foods delivered to his bachelor quarters. He remembers you with great fondness, I am sure, my lord, as do any of the girls you might still know in the *kotha*. I am sure there are a few left who will tell legends of your prowess to the younger dancers."

"I am immune to your blandishments, vixen. You will do better to feed me and send me six sheets to the wind tonight. Perhaps I will think of mistresses another day." He cleared his throat. "Perhaps."

She walked across the room to find an ashtray. When she brought it back, she placed a hand on his shoulder and bent over him to set it in arm's reach on the side table, draping her body gracefully, like an ell of silk, across his torso.

"I have known you since you were a very young man, surely too young to be in a house of ill repute, and have no trouble believing you honor your promises to Lady Coventon. You never wished to dishonor your wife, my lord. You said so to me nine years ago, sitting in exactly that chair, when we spoke of breaking your contract with Kali so you might marry, and you have never come back until you were given explicit leave."

His entire being stilled, and she removed herself. "Kali."

With no attempt to cushion the blow, she said, "She is contracted to another man, and it will be best for all concerned if you leave her alone."

"Yes, Binningham. Poor sod is painfully besotted. But he is such a… is she… is she happy?"

She took her seat again. "She is not mistreated. Kali is a *tawaif*; she has no right to expect happiness. And she is not under your protection. Her wellbeing is another man's concern, not yours. He has paid handsomely to own the privilege."

He winced as though she had raised her hand to hit him. She reached between their chairs and touched his wrist in a small apology, and he didn't pull away. Mayuri did not believe in allowing false hope, but there was no need to be cruel about it. He took the opportunity to give her his empty glass.

As she poured again, she said, not meeting his eye, "I hope you do not think I, of any person you know, would judge a decision you make about your wife or family. That would not be my place at all, nor any person on the premises."

His voice was low and gruff. "I know that. I know it." He choked a bit. "I just find… I am not prepared to make any such decision."

"Of course, my lord. Might I…"

He looked up. "Yes?"

"Might I make you comfortable in a private sitting room and send Nan in to see to your needs?" At the narrowing of his eyes, she said, "Perhaps you do not recall, my lord, that any girl I place at your disposal will accommodate anything you ask, and only what you ask. Should you wish her to sit invisibly in a corner, you have only to say so. But her presence will ensure there is no delay should you have need of food or drink... or anything else."

Letting out a breath she hadn't realized he was holding, leaning back and crossing his legs, he said, "Yes. Yes, of course." He stopped, his eyes roaming the room again. "I found myself... tonight... I found myself walking here, not to White's. I never intended... but there is a feeling of... coming home, an instinct that brought me here. I am glad the Masala Rajah is still here, and that you are willing to accommodate an old fool."

"Not so old, my lord, and we are all fools about the people we invite to our beds."

"I should never have given her up, Mayuri. She was perfectly right. I should have Kali under contract yet. God help me, some days I think I should have had children with her."

"I can't think that would be a good idea."

"No, of course not, but still... to raise children with a woman I loved? It would have been... incomparable. A day like today would have been...well...no need to be maudlin." He cleared his throat and uncrossed his legs.

"Noblemen," she said, rising and straightening her skirt, "more than any others, make their decisions about love for all the wrong reasons." She held out her hand. Without taking it, he also stood and bowed slightly, stumbling. She took his empty glass and set it aside, then wrapped her hand around his elbow, as though he were facilitating her balance, rather than the other way around. "I am certain, my lord, I can arrange to take your mind off Kali."

She guided him out of the receiving room and down the hall.

"Cease your bleating about the newest crop of *tawaif* girls before you even begin, Mayuri. I will not hear it this night."

"The blue room, my lord? It has been updated since last you saw it, but still blue, and still the third door on the right in the lower hall. There is a day bed, should you wish to rest, it is close to the kitchen, and the card room is only steps away." She pointed out the card room, and three doors down, she stopped and opened a door with a key, then handed it to him as she ushered him inside.

Read more of <u>Lord Coventon's Concubines</u>**, free at Wattpad**

Can Money and Wealthy Connections Buy a Respectable Groom?

(A letter concerning the marriage of Antonia Wakefield to Sir Alfred St James, a captain in His Majesty's Navy. The St Jameses will become the parents of Michael St James and his sister Henrietta.)

Dear Agnes,

I was never more shocked than to see the announcement about poor St James's betrothal. I know you had hopes of him for your Gloria, who must be deeply disappointed. Such a handsome and charming young man, and well-connected, too, with an earl not too far away on the family tree.

But console Gloria with the thought that her lost suitor's character must be wanting to marry into such a family. The Wakefields, my dear! They are received, I know, for who does not fear what they know, that family? But one cannot deny they are in trade, and such a trade! Enquiry agents, indeed. When I was a girl, we called them thief takers. Not a respectable occupation, and hardly what one would wish for in a marriage. St James's noble relative must be hanging his head in shame.

You know, of course, about Mr and Mrs Wakefield's children. A Miscellany, Agnes, I assure you. Riffraff and flotsam gathered from who knows where, and thrust into Society as if they have a right to be there. It is an open secret that the oldest boy, Anthony Wakefield, is the natural son of Lord Jonathan Grenford, the one who married a foreign princess. One can understand Mr David Wakefield's sympathy for his adopted son's dubious origins, since he himself is the outcome of his mother's sins with the Duke of Haverford. The previous one, you understand.

I know you will not whisper a word about what I am next to tell you, but given Gloria's expectations, I thought you should know. While the world has been told that Antonia is Mrs Wakefield's daughter from an earlier marriage, a friend told me in strictest confidence the chit is very likely as base born as her brother. Mrs Wakefield's daughter? Perhaps, though in that collection of misbegottens who can tell? But an offspring of one of the Haverford rakes? Certainly.

One has only to look at the eyes, Agnes, to see the truth. The old Duke of Haverford has them, and so do all three of his sons. Antonia Wakefield, or I suppose we must call her Antonia St James, has the Haverford eyes.

One might have guessed at the Haverford connection from seeing the guests at the wedding today. Yes, Agnes, I thought it my duty to you to observe at St Georges. I ask you! St Georges! Just as if the bride's family were fit to associate with decent people. But who is to say them nay? Not only are they improperly well informed on all sorts of matters that should remain hidden, but the connections, my dear!

They were out in force. The current Duke and Duchess of Haverford, of course, and Lord Jonathan Grenford, splendid in some foreign uniform. Such a handsome man. I had quite a tendre for him in my youth. Who knows what might have been had he not been exiled by his father? A lucky escape, I now realise, for he must have committed a truly awful crime for a man like the former duke to send him away.

The church was filled with all the Haverford connections. Earls, viscounts, barons, even the Duke and Duchess of Winshire and many of their children. I suppose they had to come, though I can hardly think they approve. They at least pretend to be Christian, even the foreign ones.

And no expense was spared. Wakefield is known as a warm man, and Haverford is fabulously wealthy. Money, my dear Agnes. Money and influence, that's what St James married today. Yes, take it from me. Gloria had a lucky escape.

Ever your friend,
Marjorie

<u>Lady Athol Soddenfeld was Once a Darling Child</u>

(Excerpt from Royal Regard, *by Mariana Gabrielle, wherein the Duke of Wellbridge is first introduced to Lady Julia Marloughe, Jewel, who will grow up to be Toad's detested cousin and Sally's nemesis, Lady Athol Soddenfeld.)*

From Chapter Twelve

An hour later, against Bella's silent, but somehow still vociferous, objections, Charlotte's wish was granted. Bella, Charlotte, the two children and the nurse were seated across the square from Gunter's in the Firthley's open landau. Standing alone nearby, the Duke held a dish of lemon ice in his hand, condensation dripping onto his glove. He made no attempt at contact, but for the occasional look their way, nodding at others in the crowd, but engaging in no conversations.

It couldn't last long, however. The speculative looks of the ladies nearby presaged an imminent mob of gently-bred females. He was starting to look a bit chary.

"Duke," Charlotte called out just as a very brave young woman and her mother began to cross the square directly toward him. Charlotte made a bit of a scene, rising slightly from her seat and motioning for him to join them, Bella trying unsuccessfully to stay her hand. When he walked over, avoiding the gaze of the disappointed debutante, he removed his hat and bowed, but didn't even suggest joining them in the carriage.

Bella sighed, "I vow you are following me."

He laughed, "Of course not, Lady Huntleigh. It is just my great good luck to come upon you twice in one day. Please, do keep your seat, Lady Firthley." Wellbridge held his free hand out to forestall any deference from anyone, though Bella had already decided she would nail her slippers to the carriage floor before ever curtseying to him again.

Charlotte offered, "Would you care to join us?"

"I would love to sit, Lady Firthley. I'm afraid it has been a trying afternoon of fruitless shopping for my nephew's birthday. I'm sure I've walked at least fifty furlongs."

As the Firthley's tiger pulled down the stairs and opened the door, Charlotte poked Jewel. "Your Grace, my daughter, Lady Julia Marloughe." The six-year-old carefully, reluctantly, set her coconut ice on the seat so she could stand, her knees and the carriage wobbling as she curtsied, lisping, "Pleathed to make your acquaintanthe, Your Grathe."

"Lady Julia, I am honored beyond measure," he said with a deep, formal bow. As he entered, he gave her his hand to help her scramble back onto her seat and removed his top hat. Jewel giggled madly at being called Lady by a stranger, but quickly went back to the important business of the treat in the glass dish on her lap. Wellbridge turned to Nurse and chucked baby Alex under the chin. "And this must be the young Earl of Herrendon."

"Hare-din," Alex agreed, chewing on the melted chocolate all over his fingers.

Wellbridge smiled at Charlotte. "Keep him this age as long as you can, Lady Firthley. Seventeen-year-old boys are miserable beasts. I had promised to buy my nephew a curricle and team for his birthday, but his mother forbade it, which provoked the most appalling fit of temper. He called my sister names for which I might have killed any other man."

Charlotte nodded sagely, as though she had raised hundreds of young men. "Lord Firthley says if our son resembles him in temperament, Baby's adolescent years will be better served away at school, but I can't believe my sweet boy will cause me even a moment of wretchedness."

She pinched Alex's cheek and spoke to him in baby talk: "Mummy's boy doesn't want to go away to school, does he?"

Alex dragged his face away, yelling, "No touch Hare-din! No, Mama! No!" Wellbridge managed to keep from snorting, but Bella did not.

"The point of boarding school, Charlotte," she said, caustically, "is that other people will manage his wretchedness, and you may take credit for manners someone else will enforce with a stick."

Wellbridge pursued a policy of appeasement. "I'm sure Herrendon will grow up a fine chap who adores his mother." Then he took the even wiser course of changing the topic. "Unruly though my nephew may be, it is his birthday, and he has achieved top marks in his examinations, so I must find a gift as excellent as a curricle, but which will not incur my sister's wrath."

"Have you any other ideas?" Charlotte asked, looking at him the same way she looked at baby Alex when he tried to learn a new word.

"A skiff received the same reception as a carriage. He is too young for an estate where he might hide from his mother in a fit of pique, or an account he might use to run away to some half-heathen British colony, which would be laid entirely at my feet. Neither White's nor Brooks's will entertain him yet for membership, and I've been banned from giving him brandy or snuff, my gifts from a favored uncle at eighteen. And Allie will lock Henry in a box before she allows him out in the evening with me, afraid I'll take him on a tour of disreputable London, which my father did for both me and my brother, and which Thad will do if we can find a way between us to sneak it past her."

The nurse gasped, reflexively covering the baby's ears before she remembered herself, rapidly ducking her head to clean the sugar off Alex's clothes.

Wellbridge shrugged, "One afternoon with Henry at Gentleman Jackson's, a few unfortunate bruises that made him the envy of all his friends, and suddenly I am the worst influence imaginable. But I assure you, I have never been so bad as my sister makes out."

"Are you certain?" Bella asked sweetly, drumming her fingertips on the carriage door.

Wellbridge's lips turned up in much the same fashion as when she had cut him at the linen draper's shop.

"I simply think a boy should know how to fight and play cards before he is old enough to lose his money to Captain Sharp."

Before Bella could draw enough breath to give her palpable opinion, Charlotte changed the subject faster than a two-year-old dashing across a room. Her lips looked like they were trying to outrun the words on the tip of her tongue.

"So what will you do for his birthday?"

"I'm afraid all I am left with is ordering him a wardrobe, but no matter how elegant the tailoring, I am sure it will be deemed far too boring from such a brilliant uncle as I. Cravats and gloves are so pedestrian."

"A riding horse?" Charlotte suggested.

"That was my first thought, Lady Firthley, but I met his father at Tattersall's with the same idea, and Nockham claimed it as a father's privilege before I could offer a fencing match to decide the matter. In truth, I had to concede, in recompense for the puppy I gave Henry without consulting his parents when he was ten."

Bella's countenance softened for half a second, and Charlotte turned almost treacly, saved from fawning over his kindness only when she exclaimed, "Ah! I have it! A pocket watch! He is old enough to mark the occasion formally, your sister can't possibly object, and I'm sure you can think of something terribly clever for the inscription. We just saw the most interesting timepieces at Rundell's."

"That is a capital idea, Lady Firthley! I wish I had told you my troubles when we spoke earlier. I might be home by now."

"Pity," Bella said, looking for a reaction sideways.

Wellbridge ignored Bella's insult entirely, holding his gloved finger out to Alex, who grasped it with both of his grubby hands. "You have a very smart Mama, Herrendon. I hope she is not so strict as my sister and lets you play cards and fight with the other boys."

"Knowing my husband, I'm sure the lessons have already begun. And of course, there is no way to know what bad habits he might pick up at school."

Nick agreed, "As an Eton man myself, I can confirm such scurrilous tutorial, though it won't do at all to discuss the hallowed halls with you ladies." As he spooned the last of the lemon ice from his bowl, he asked, "Is everyone quite sated? I would be pleased to buy Lady Julia another, if she so wishes."

Jewel piped up, "Pleathe, Mama? I want the goothberry, too."

"Heavens, no. That is very kind of you, Sir, but Jewel has had more than enough. Bella has been spoiling her with treats all day long. It will be a wonder if she eats any dinner at all."

"Well, Lady Julia, I cannot disregard your mother's wishes, but perhaps she will allow me the pleasure of a gift that will not spoil your appetite?" He arched a brow at Charlotte and she nodded with a sly smile. Bella looked back and forth between them, sensing a devious plan that neither could have arranged.

Wellbridge reached into his pocket and took out the bag from the linen draper. Without even a glance at Bella, he turned over the ribbon with a flourish of his hat. Jewel took it with wide eyes and started begging Nurse to replace the blue ribbons in her messy ringlets.

"What do you say to the duke, Jewel?" Charlotte reproved.

Jewel stood up and curtsied again. "Thank you, Your Grathe, for your kindneth?" As Charlotte nodded, Jewel turned back to Nurse, shoving the ribbons at her and demanding attention to her hair.

Nurse responded with, "Seen and not heard, Miss," but she took the ribbons anyway, finally smiling at Wellbridge, untying the blue ribbon, uncurling the purple, and taking embroidery scissors from her reticule.

"And you, Lady Huntleigh? Have you had enough?"

"I have had more than my fill," she said, not referring to ice cream. "We cannot stay long, in any case. I've promised the children a Punch-and-Judy show at Covent Garden before we return home."

His eyes gleamed as he observed, "By Jove, it has been years since I took in a puppet show. My sister's youngest is just past twelve, and informs me she is far too old now for such childish pursuits, but I have always enjoyed the marionettes. Lady Julia," he said, replacing and tipping his hat, "might you allow me the honor of accompanying you to the theatre this afternoon?"

Bella rolled her eyes, Charlotte stifled a laugh, and Jewel just stared around the carriage at all of the adults, unnerved by the continued attention of a man she'd never met.

Charlotte prompted, "What does a young lady say when a gentleman asks to escort her?"

Screwing up her forehead, tongue between her teeth, Jewel said, "Yeth, Your Grathe, I would be pleathed for you to join uth?" She looked up at her mother for approval, and Charlotte nodded.

"It will be my privilege, Lady Julia."

Read more of <u>Royal Regard</u>

<u>The Parents of Longford and Stocke Meet</u>

(Excerpt from Farewell to Kindness*)*

Chapter Six

Rede passed through the lychgate on his way to church, and the bell tower of St Martin's Under the Edge didn't fall on his disbelieving sinful head. He smiled at his own fancy. If there was a God, He'd shown a complete lack of interest in Rede's actions.

Rede was only here because John insisted that the people expected the Earl to attend services. When he commented that his uncle and cousin never did, John answered dryly, "Just so."

Rede had not yet met the Rector. He was waiting at the door, welcoming his parishioners as they moved through into the church. As tall as Rede, he was a well-formed man in his forties or fifties, silver touching the edges of his hair around his ears. He greeted Rede with a smile and a warm handshake.

"Lord Chirbury. Welcome back to St Martin's."

"Reverend Ashbrook, I presume. It's good to be back."

It was true, Rede realised, not just a meaningless politeness. It was good to walk through the old oak doors into the tiled vestibule where he'd played as a little boy while his father practised a homily. Up the centre aisle between the carved pews to the Redepenning box at the front of the nave.

He pulled out the keys and let himself in. He'd spent many Sunday services in this box with his aunt and cousins—and with other Redepennings when they visited.

Of course, when his father and mother came down from Town, he'd moved across the nave to the Rector's box, currently occupied by a mature woman, a lovely young girl on the cusp of adulthood, and two smaller children—a girl with black ringlets and a boy still young enough to be in skirts.

The free pews further down the church were rapidly filling as the last comers took their seats. In the west gallery, the village musicians were tuning their instruments. John would be with the Redepenning servants in the north gallery, out of sight above his head.

The Redwood box was beside him—Rede nodded to the Squire, whom he'd visited as his first duty the day after he arrived. The two young men and the girl with him had a strong family resemblance; all three shared Sir Thomas's Saxon colouring and square, handsome features.

As the service began—with a rousing hymn led by the psalm singers up in the gallery—Rede focused his attention on the Rector and his curate.

The words of the rite wrapped around him like a familiar blanket. Once, he'd heard them every Sunday, though he'd not been in a church for over three years and seldom attended even before that. Once—long ago when he was a boy—he'd believed in a just and loving God. The familiar prayers and songs made him nostalgic for the young Stephen Redepenning.

Ashbrook gave a passionate homily about patience in the face of adversity, building on the words of the day's epistle to demand that the congregation treated one another fairly and with respect, giving a helping hand in need, not taking offence at slights but offering forgiveness.

There must be a story behind this homily. Nervous shifting near the rear of the church hinted that certain people took the words personally.

The Rector went on to explain that he was administering Holy Communion on the Feast of Whitsunday, the following week. "Examine your conscience," he told the congregation. "Forgive others who have offended you, as you would have forgiveness of your offences at God's hand."

Those words struck close to the bone. But Rede expected no forgiveness. And, by all he no longer believed in, he would give none. Forgive those responsible for his losses? No. By every clod of earth he laid over their broken bodies, no.

"Repent of your sins, or else come not to that holy Table."

His quest for vengeance wasn't a sin. It was a solemn vow. It was a war, undeclared on both sides, but a war nonetheless.

Ashbrook struck him as the sort of man who wouldn't see it that way.

He occupied himself for the rest of the service with picking out faces. This week, he'd met a number of the tenant farmers and their wives, and some of the senior gentry of the district. Others were familiar from many years ago, surprisingly unchanged.

The service wound to its final blessing, and the congregation followed the Rector from the church as the bells pealed.

He moved towards the door, through a rippling sea of bows, curtseys, touched foreheads, murmured 'My Lords'. Out in the churchyard, the villagers and gentry stood in groups, exchanging greetings and enjoying the warm spring sunshine. Children ran in and out of the shrubbery in the adjacent Rectory garden, in a game of chase. Some had the look of the Rector, who introduced Rede to his wife. Mrs Ashbrook had a no-nonsense manner, direct light-blue eyes, and the well-padded shape of a matron with a growing family and a healthy appetite.

A trio of prettily dressed young ladies—the dark-haired girl from the Ashbrook pew, the Saxon-blonde Redwood and a remarkably attractive girl whose face was framed in brown curls—strolled arm in arm up and down the path to the church gate, as bright as butterflies in their light dresses and their charming bonnets, chattering away like starlings.

Rede stayed for a while, shaking hands with those who came for an introduction, catching up with those he'd met during the week, and generally making himself pleasant.

Several times, he met eyes as blue as his own, fringed like his with dark lashes. His predecessors had certainly left a mark on the population. Many of the poorer members of the community bore the certain sign that a female ancestor had caught a Redepenning's fickle attention.

Mrs Forsythe, the rent-free tenant, wasn't introduced. He had been hearing her name all week. His tenants spoke of her warmly, and with respect, listing her good deeds, and praising her kindness. From what they said, she was a linchpin of village life. Listening to their stories, he'd formed a picture of a mature widow; a gentlewoman of private—if straitened—means: a bustling matron with a finger in all the charitable activity of the parish.

The trio of young ladies on the path broke up, two coming over to be introduced as the daughters of the Rector and the Squire. The third young lady collected a child and another young woman from the Rectory garden.

The child was a little older than his Rita would have been: perhaps the age Joseph would have been, had he lived. She studied him curiously as she passed, meeting his blue gaze with her own. Indeed, he could have been looking at one of his own childhood portraits, cast in a more feminine mould.

She didn't take her colouring from the two young ladies with her. And a quick glance after her showed that bonnets masked the faces of the two ladies they joined.

"Once my cousins arrive, we'll invite the local gentry to dinner," he told Mrs Ashbrook. "I've met some of them. Could you perhaps introduce me to others?"

As he'd hoped, she launched into a list of all the gentlemen and ladies in the neighbourhood, starting with those present. He listened impatiently as the objects of his interest moved further and further towards the gate.

At last, just as they passed under the arch, Mrs Ashbrook said, "And Mrs Forsythe and her sisters, the Miss Haverstocks. They were standing right there by the church... oh dear, you've missed them. They've just left."

The slender figure hurrying away down the road with her sisters and daughter did not fit the picture he'd formed of the busy Mrs Forsythe. Not at all.

He continued listening to Mrs Ashbrook, commenting when appropriate, murmuring pleasantries to the people she took him to around the churchyard. And with another part of his mind he planned a change in the order of his tenant visits.

Meeting Mrs Forsythe, owner of the trimmest pair of ankles he had ever noticed and mother of a Redepenning by-blow, was suddenly a priority.

Spring in the garden was a delight, especially as more and more vegetables ripened. Even in the first years, before Anne learned how to make the most of her small patch of land, her family had eaten well in May, though she, Hannah and Ruth had often gone hungry in winter to ensure that the younger ones ate.

These days, as long as they kept the pernicious Mr Peep out of the young seedlings, the garden supplied most of their vegetables year round.

Picking young pea pods in the sunshine was a foretaste of heaven. Not far away, on the other side of the garden path, Daisy and Meg were holding a dolls' tea party, using leaf plates and acorn cups. They were sitting on the broad top of the stone wall between her garden and the lane, having as much fun with their impromptu place settings and rag dolls as she remembered in the nursery of her childhood. In fact, the breakable porcelain of her tea set and dolls may have meant less fun!

Next year, after her twenty-fifth birthday, things would change again—all going well, she'd be able to give Kitty the chances her birth and beauty deserved. She sat back on her heels, her head full of dreams and plans. A Season for Kitty, that was certain, if she could figure out a way to reintroduce them into society without attracting the attention of her cousin. Perhaps their Godmama would help? More than one Season, if Kitty wanted.

For Ruth, an independence so she never had to work again. Help for Hannah, to do the heavy work of caring for Daisy and Meg, and other servants to take up all the household duties they currently shared. Perhaps drawing lessons for Daisy, whose pictures, Ruth said, were remarkable for a five-year-old.

They'd buy a comfortable country home—not too large, but big enough to give them all their own rooms, and to have space for guests. They'd have a bit of land so that Daisy could have a pony and Anne could have a garden. And they'd rent a place in London for the Season, and go to the museums, and the Tower of London, and all the other places she'd read about in the social columns of the papers that the Squire let her borrow after he and his family had finished with them.

In some ways, she would miss the simple life they had built in Longford, and she would certainly miss the friends she'd made here, but undoubtedly money would make their lives easier.

All going well. The path to giving her family the life of her dream was narrow, with many possible obstacles in the way. So much that could go wrong.

The Earl hadn't yet proved the danger she feared, though the longer he stayed the harder it would be to avoid him. Yesterday in the churchyard, she had peeked at him from under her bonnet. She didn't dare go close, but from a distance he was far better-looking than his cousin.

She'd had a nasty moment when Daisy walked right past him, but they didn't speak and he didn't seem to pay them any attention after that.

Perhaps he would not be a danger. The villagers were still reserving judgement, but he was earning their cautious approval. The people who had met him spoke well of him. They were thrilled that he visited them, listened to him. After decades of neglect by one Earl after another, they'd have liked him for that alone. His willingness to spend money on long-overdue maintenance won him more points. They were not yet convinced, of course. But the general opinion was that he was more like his Uncle Henry, whom they'd respected, than the previous three Earls.

Her reverie was broken by the clopping of hooves in the lane beyond the wall. Daisy called out, "Good day, Mr Baxter!"

Meg rolled off the wall, her eyes wide in fear, and huddled down into the shadow at its base, whimpering a little.

"Miss Daisy," the rider beyond the wall replied, cheerfully. Young Will, from the sound of it. The land steward's son, who'd come six weeks ago to take care of the estate when Matthew the elder was injured. Meg was always nervous around men she didn't know, but young Will had visited before, and had spoken to them several times during this visit. Anne had just concluded that he must have company when another voice spoke.

"Please, Baxter, will you not present me to this beautiful young lady?" The voice was deep and compelling, with a slight rasp that somehow added to its appeal.

"My lord," Will began.

"No, no," the Earl—it must be he—insisted. "Fairy queens take precedence, and surely she must be one?"

Daisy giggled, but straightened her back proudly. So much for keeping her daughter from his sight.

"Miss Daisy, may I present Lord Chirbury? My Lord, Miss Daisy Forsythe, queen of Lilac Cottage."

"An honour, your Highness," the Earl said.

Anne snorted at the easy charm. She stopped on the path to pat Meg soothingly, before straightening so she could see over the wall.

The ground dropped on the other side, putting the heads of the two horsemen on a level with Daisy's. Anne met eyes the image of her daughter's. His hair was like hers, too—a golden blonde. It was trimmed tightly to his nape, but she knew from seeing him outside the inn and in church that the elegant hat disguised curls.

It was the eyes and general colouring that gave the impression he looked like his cousin. The shape of his face, his generous mouth, his broad shoulders—in all these ways he was somehow more than the former Earl. He had, in some ways, a hard face—even grim. But it didn't look unkind. If he was not such a threat to her family, she would find him attractive, which had certainly not been the case with George.

"My Lord, Mrs Anne Forsythe. Mrs Forsythe, Stephen Redepenning, Earl of Chirbury." Will did the honours, adding unnecessarily, "Mrs Forsythe is young Daisy's mama."

"A pleasure to meet you, Mrs Forsythe."

She bobbed a curtsey. "Lord Chirbury."

"I hope the other charming young lady I saw is not hurt, Mrs Forsythe?"

"Aunt Meg does not like strange men," Daisy volunteered.

Meg was still crouched at the foot of the wall, hugging herself. At least she'd stopped whimpering. A pleasant conversation between Anne and the gentlemen might be the best way to calm her down.

"She is very shy," Anne added. Which was not exactly true, but worked well enough as an explanation. "I apologise, my Lord."

He smiled, drawing her attention back to that generous mouth. "Not at all. I apologise for startling her. Have your dolls been enjoying their picnic, Queen Daisy?"

Daisy lifted her little chin imperiously. "They are at an assembly, sir. Not at a picnic."

"You say 'my lord,' not sir," Anne whispered.

"Of course they are," Lord Chirbury agreed, amusement warming the deep voice that seemed to set her skin vibrating as if it was stroked. "And a fine assembly it is, I'm sure."

"It would be better if the kittens had not run off," Daisy confided. "They was going to be the gentlemen, and now the dolls have to dance with each other, and they are both ladies. Aunt Kitty and Miss Ashbrook dance with each other, but only to practise. When they go to an assembly, they will dance with gentlemen."

Lord Chirbury's eyes danced, but his voice remained grave as he agreed with the little girl that ladies preferred to dance with gentlemen when they were at an assembly.

As they continued to talk, Meg slowly uncurled, stretching up until she could peep over the wall. She dropped down again, tugging on Anne's skirt.

"It is the bad Earl," she whispered, when Anne bent down to her.

"No darling. It is a different Earl. The bad Earl is dead, remember?"

Meg rose again, burrowing into her sister's side as she did so. This time, she took a long look. Anne could tell the Earl was aware of her sister's examination, but—apart from a single flick of his eyes—he kept his attention on Daisy and continued talking to her.

After several long moments, Meg nodded and relaxed a little, though she didn't let go of Anne.

"It is a diff'ent Earl," she agreed.

Now Lord Chirbury looked at Meg, then at Anne, with a question in his eyes.

"Lord Chirbury, may I present my sister Meg, Margaret Haverstock?"

"How do you do, Miss Haverstock? I am sorry I startled you." How had she thought him grim? He smiled at Meg with the same kindness he'd shown to Daisy.

Meg, however, was anxious again. "Chirbee?" She clutched harder to Anne. "A different Chirbury," Anne reassured her.

The Earl excused himself graciously, claiming that he and Will were expected elsewhere. Did he leave so that Meg would be comfortable? Surely not. An Earl couldn't be expected to show such sensitivity. Though the Earl wasn't at all what Anne expected. She'd never imagined that a *ton* gentlemen would talk about dolls with a little girl, especially a *ton* gentleman with such a disturbing physical appeal.

Charm and kindness did not make him trustworty, of course, but it certainly made him very disarming.

Read more of Farewell to Kindness

The Birth of Twins Brings Joy During a Difficult Time

(Excerpt from A Raging Madness, *by Jude Knight. When Anne gives birth to twins, the Redepenning cousins are delighted. The older twin was Viscount Longford from his birth. The younger was declared Viscount Stocke, for reasons that will be clear to those who have read* Farewell to Kindness.)

Chapter Twenty-Five

The sun was barely above the horizon. "Will he even be up, Alex? And we are dressed to explore old buildings," Ella gestured to her plain gown, one of the few from Henbury Susan had allowed her to keep, "not to go visiting." Dodd might not notice, but Mrs Dodd, if he had a wife, and the other woman of the village would feel affronted if the lady of the village's great house turned up without warning and took no care of her appearance.

Alex looked so disappointed, she would have caught the words back, but Mr Morris said, "Bless you, Dodd was undoubtedly up with the dawn and off to Louth. He is building cottages there, and he will not miss a minute of a fine day like this. But come down after dusk, and you shall catch him in, I am sure. I can let Abbie know you are coming. Abigail Dodd is his wife, Lady Renshaw, and a fine woman."

Ella made up her mind. "Mr Morris, can we invite you to join us for a cup of tea? The house is as you see it, but Mrs Broadley was setting the kettle to fire when we left the house, and Lord Renshaw and I would value your knowledge of the local people. We have much to learn and much to do if we are to carry out our responsibilities here."

Before she had finished speaking, she was second-guessing the invitation. Was there a room fit to have a cup of tea in? Would Mr Morris be offended at their casual manners and informal dress? But Alex was smiling.

It was too late to change her mind. "Thank you, Lady Renshaw," the rector said, and he showed no shock at being ushered into the old-fashioned kitchen, where he took off his large overcoat and muffler, disclosing a powerful frame still well-muscled and only slightly bent with age.

Mrs Broadley apologised that no other room in the house was fit to entertain guests, but Mr Morris took a seat at the kitchen table and declared himself well satisfied when she offered them all drop scones and jam to go with their tea, "For I have this minute made up the batter, Lady Renshaw, and the griddle is hot, so you shall have scones to break your fast."

They were deep in conversation over tea and scones when Miller arrived, stopping uncertainly at the door of the kitchen. Jonno looked over her shoulder, grinning at his master, and Oscar leapt from his warm spot by the fire to bark at the invaders.

Miller backed away, her eyes wide, and Mr Morris called the dog to his side and scooped it up. "Do come in, my dear. Oscar is not at all a gentleman to frighten you so, but there is no harm in him."

"Yes, Miller," Ella agreed. "Come in. Mr Morris, this is my maid, Miller, and Jonno Price, my lord's man."

After a token protest, Miller and Jonno joined them at the table and listened as Mr Morris continued his exposition on the topic of the villagers and tenant farmers. Everyone, according to Mr Morris, was delighted to have the new viscount in residence and was looking forward to meeting the viscountess, although his beatific vision was slightly at odds with his warning about the suspicion and resentment they might face.

It was not personal, he assured them, but based on the character of the last incumbent followed by nearly two decades of neglect, where the only contact with any kind of authority had been rent collection. The villagers and tenants were cautious but willing to be won over, and when they saw that Lord and Lady Renshaw meant to make their home here and bring back employment to the village, all would soon be well.

Certainly, if his stories about the families were to be taken at face value, Renbridge was as peaceful and as happy a village as could be found in all of England.

This far from the main routes, the mail was delivered three times a week, fetched from the nearest posting house and sorted at the inn, to be held until collected, or delivered for an extra fee. Alex paid for the innkeeper's son to bring the Grange mail as soon as it arrived, and a few days into their new occupancy, he had a letter from Atkins, confirming he accepted the commission, outlining his fee, and asking a few more questions.

A letter had also come for Ella from Susan, writing from Longford, and a package for Alex, which proved to be the London papers and a brief note from his father that suggested ruralising was no excuse for falling behind in the news. "I shall send you a package each week, dear boy, and will include *The Ladies' Gazette* for my new daughter. When your sister suggested it, I assured her that Ella was as informed on the issues of the day as any gentleman, but Susan insists that she will enjoy stories about fashion and society as much as the war, business, and political news."

When Alex read her his father's letter, Ella coloured a little at Lord Henry's claim to parenthood but agreed with his choice of paper. "It will be nice to know by how far I am out of the *mode*," she told him. "And I am much more interested in the comings and goings of the *Beau Monde* now I have met some of them."

She waved her own letter. "But I have much more exciting news than anything in those papers, Alex. Anne has presented Lord Chirbury with not one but two sons!" She smiled, but her eyes were wistful.

Within a couple of weeks, the repairs were underway. Dodd inspected the house, planned the work, and set up the work crews, assigning the village carpenter to supervise the project while Dodd finished up in Louth. In late winter, with little to be done on the farms, the local labour force was pleased for some extra coin, and—as word spread—the house, stable block, and outbuildings filled with cheerful men carrying out the most urgent tasks to secure the structures against further damage.

Meanwhile, Mrs Broadley and Ella set an army of local women to work clearing and cleaning the rooms inside of the house, leaving those that required new plastering to fix fallen ceilings or walls, but swiftly making enough of the house habitable for daily living.

First, they moved Jonno and Miller each to their own sleeping quarters. A bed chamber each for Alex and Ella came next, the study in their suite being restored to its former purpose. Soon, the new viscount and viscountess were able to eat their meals in the dining room, entertain the occasional neighbour who braved the weather to ride over and to greet them, and contemplate accommodating guests.

Miller disapproved of Ella cleaning and mending with her own hands, though she said nothing after their first exchange on the subject. "It isn't fit work for a lady, ma'am," she had insisted. "Making a home is fit work for any woman," Ella replied, but Miller argued until Ella insisted they would not again discuss the topic.

The grooms remained at the inn until the stable buildings could receive the carriage team, and Mrs Broadley still went home to her own cottage each night, but was at the house all hours of the day, taking on the roles of both housekeeper and cook. "I could not do your fancy dinner parties," she had confided, "but I can manage plain food, Lady Renshaw, and not too proud to do it until you have a house fit for a proper staff and time to hire them."

Plain food and plenty of it was all they needed at the moment. For the rest, Ella had written to Susan asking advice about finding a cook and a butler who might be willing to settle in a tiny village in the Lincolnshire Wolds, with an unconventional viscount and viscountess who would rather breed horses than waltz around London.

Much of the old-fashioned furniture was found to be so riddled with woodworm that it needed to be discarded, but the remaining pieces—polished to high shine—were sufficient to furnish the several bed chambers, private sitting rooms, and public reception rooms Ella was able to bring back into use.

Alex thrived on the hard physical labour of the rebuilding, his injured thighs gaining strength and flexibility as he used them. And being out of the house most of the day and tired to the point of exhaustion each night, helped him to cope with the constant urge to make love to the woman everyone believed to be his wife. He would not take her choices from her. He had promised. But he was not strong enough to spend all day with her and not attempt to seduce her.

By evening, he could spend half an hour after dinner talking with her in their private rooms. She even let him into her bedchamber, as long as she was still fully dressed. The intimacy soothed his heart, if it did nothing for his body.

Ella was brushing her hair at her mirror while Alex lounged nearby watching her over the brim of his brandy glass. He had sent Jonno off to bed, but Miller was still in the dressing room.

"I will just lay out your things for tomorrow, m'lady," she'd said when dismissed. "Save time in the morning."

Now she came out into Ella's bedchamber, her face troubled.

"M'lord, can I show you something?" she asked, keeping her voice low, as if she did not want Ella to hear.

Alex followed her and Ella, watching in the mirror, saw Alex's shoulders stiffen as Miller showed him—whatever it was. Ella put down her brush and went to see.

It was a gown, one of those she'd had made up in London. It was ruined, torn dozens of times from waist to hem so the skirt hung in ribbons. She pressed up against Alex's side and he put his arm around her.

"How could this have happened?"

"Ask rather 'who could have done this?' It has been cut, Ella." He pulled her closer and kissed her forehead. "If one of the workmen has done this…"

"One of them, or a villager or the like," Miller groused. "The house is always open all day, with anyone who wants wandering through."

"Take the gown and put it in one of the unused bed chambers, Miller," Alex ordered. "Then go to bed if your lady is finished with you. The miscreant is undoubtedly lying snug in his."

Ella nodded, and Miller took the gown away. Ella was pleased to have it gone; its tattered shreds too graphic a reminder of an unfathomable hatred.

"Or hers," she said. The vandalism would not have taken great strength, and an attack on clothes seemed subtly female in its nature.

"We'll find the perpetrator, Ella," Alex promised. "Never you doubt it."

But they did not. No one had seen anyone out of place, and after several days of widening their circles of enquiry, they had to let it drop.

Miller was following him around again. Jonno didn't want to be rude, but she wouldn't leave him alone.

"You'll have to excuse me, Miss Miller. I need to finish here and then go help my lord." They had finished the demolition of rotting and broken walls in the stable and were now rebuilding, which Jonno was enjoying as much as Mister Alex.

"He shouldn't make you work outside like that," Miller complained. "It isn't decent. You're a valet, not a labourer."

"I am my lord's man, Miss Miller," Jonno told her.

"You could be my man," she offered, with a coy look from under her lashes.

Did she think he hadn't heard about the others on whom she bestowed her favours? One of the grooms and a farmer's son who was helping with the rebuilding? And he'd seen her himself with the gentleman scholar who lived in the village and studied with the Rector. Not that it was any of Jonno's business.

"I must be about my work, Miss Miller," he said again.

"Purchase whatever you want, Ella," Alex told Ella on the first evening they ate in the dining room, a month after their arrival. Highly polished silver and gleaming china made a brave show against a mended tablecloth, mismatched chairs, and faded wallpaper.

It was a misstep, and he caught it as soon as he caught her slight frown, swiftly smoothed away. "If you wish to. You have worked miracles to make me comfortable, and if you do nothing more, I shall be happy. But I am wealthy, Ella, and if you want the latest *Egyptoise* furniture, silk curtains, and hand painted murals on all the walls, then you shall have them."

Was that the right thing to say? Yes; the tension went from her shoulders, bravely displayed in one of her London gowns. They had dressed for dinner tonight, for the first time since their arrival at Renwater Grange. How was a man to watch his words for fear of dismaying the woman he loved when his eyes were feasting on the soft skin of her breasts, the tops of which were framed in the lush red of the gown?

But she was so anxious to please him, and so prone to believe she had offended. Just this afternoon, he had caught her sitting on the refurbished window seat in the private sitting room of the master suite, looking dreamingly out the window, her mind clearly a thousand miles away.

"What? Not working?" he had said, startling her so that she jumped. She took a moment to return from whatever far place she had travelled, but her voice vibrated with indignation as she responded, "I have been working all day, Renshaw. I sat for only a minute." She blushed when she glanced at the little mantel clock Susan had given them, making him wonder how long she had been wool-gathering, but he didn't ask, just hastening to assure her he was teasing.

"You are turning our house into a home, Ella, and I've seen how hard you are working."

"As are you," she conceded. "I barely see you during the day, Alex, and especially not up here. Is something wrong?"

He was Alex again, and he just wished he had the right to take her to bed in the next room and make sure she shouted the name a few times to remind her of it. But he was bound by his promise and besides, duty called.

"Nothing major, but we dropped a beam we were removing in the carriage house, and one of men has a scrape I'd like you to look at." No need to tell Ella that the injured man was the one whose inattention had let the beam fall, and that only the quick reactions of the man on the other end of the beam had stopped it from swinging the other way, where Alex would have taken the full force of the blow.

It was more than a scrape; a deep graze down one leg, seeping blood. Ella cleaned the bits of trouser cloth from the wound and dressed it, and Alex sent to the inn for their carriage to take the man, a villager called Fox, home. In a day or two, they'd be able to stable their own horses. Alex smiled, imagining the stables completed and full.

"I'll be back up tomorrow, my lord," Fox insisted, but Ella scolded, "Not for a week, and I shall be down to your house tomorrow to make sure the wound is not inflamed."

He'd be worrying about money, of course, but perhaps he'd be more careful next time. Or maybe they would have to let him go, since this was not the first incident. Dodd had not wanted to employ the man, but Mr Morris had begged for him to be given a chance, for the sake of his wife and large family.

Ella was once again ahead of Alex. "Tell your wife that I will have work for her while you watch the children. You can do that with your injury." And Mrs

Fox would be paid directly, which meant she might actually see the money before it was spent at the inn or one of the countryside's hedge-taverns. She was a clever woman, his Ella.

Remembering, he smiled at her sitting beside him at their shabby table in her evening finery.

"You did a good thing for Mrs Fox, Ella," he told her, changing the subject from whatever chimera she had made out of his casual offer to empty his purse.

"Yes, perhaps."

"You can doubt it? She has—how many children to feed?"

"Seven. And the oldest growing out of her clothes and not yet large enough for her mother's. I cannot regret helping them, Alex, and I am sure Mr Morris will support me even if some of the women are not pleased."

Ella had obviously heard the same rumours as Alex. He frowned. The highly attractive and apparently very available woman could cause real trouble away from her husband's supervision and on his building site. "As long as she does not distract the men."

That put Ella's hackles up. "As long as the men leave her alone, I dare say she will be delighted to have some peace for a change and an honest coin that does not require her to pretend to be enjoying herself."

His own unfulfilled lust honed an edge on his voice. "How do you know she doesn't? After all, she has a husband of her own, but still chooses to 'entertain'."

"For a coin or two to feed and clothe her children after her husband has lost yet another job by turning up drunk or has gambled away his wages and beaten her to force her to give up anything she might have saved." Ella sighed. "He is her husband, Alex, and can do anything he pleases short of killing her. The law would take exception to that, but somewhat too late for Mrs Fox. Or the children."

The bitterness in Ella's voice left his dinner sitting heavy in his belly but retrieving the evening was beyond him, and when she said she wanted to finish a letter to Susan, he told her he'd take his brandy here at the table and read the paper Rede had sent from London.

She wasn't happy. In London, he had thought she might be softening to the idea of marriage. But once they arrived here, in this wreck he had offered her as a home, things had changed.

He never knew what to expect from her mood. Sometimes, like this afternoon, she was close to tears at the least sign of disapproval. Other times, she swung to irritability. And still others, she drifted off into her mind, recalling herself with a mighty effort when he or one of the servants spoke. Today wasn't the first time he had found her staring into space, doing nothing.

He had tried to convince himself he was imagining things. Surely, she was just tired, as he was. She worked as hard as he did, building this estate back into what it had once been, and he had thought they were building a future. But from tonight's outburst, clearly her views of marriage hadn't changed.

He went up to bed reluctantly, aware he was wrong to blame her. After all, what would she gain from the bargain? His wealth and his title, but Ella had never been swayed by money and status. And for the rest, a broken-down man and a broken-down house, neither of her choosing.

She was already in bed. She had transformed their rooms as she had the downstairs, cleaning and polishing; using a brief fine spell to wash the curtains and all the bedding and spreading them on racks in the attics to finish drying after the late Winter rains set in again.

He hesitated at the door of her room. It was partly open. In the bed, Ella lay tucked under the blankets so only her cap showed, her eyes shut.

Jonno and Miller had long since gone to their own freshly repaired rooms, accustomed to their master and mistress managing for themselves each night. Alex sighed and went off to bed himself.

The soft glow of the fire, the gleam of the furniture, the wash of colour in the deep wine red of the drapes, made the room seem welcoming, but it was all an illusion. There was no welcome for him here. He disrobed in silence and slipped under his covers.

But it was a long time before he fell asleep that night.

Read more of <u>A Raging Madness</u>

About the Authors

About Mariana Gabrielle

Mariana Gabrielle is a pen name for Mari Christie, who is not romantic—at all. Therefore, her starry-eyed alter ego lives vicariously through characters who believe in their own happy-ever-afters. And believe they must, as Mariana loves her heroes and heroines, but truly dotes on her villains, and almost all of her characters' hearts have been bruised, broken, and scarred long before they reach the pages of her books.

She is a professional writer, editor, and designer with almost twenty-five years' experience, and a member of the Speakeasy Scribes and the Historical Novel Society. She has written two Regency romances, *Royal Regard* and *La Déesse Noire: The Black Goddess*, and two *Royal Regard* prequel novellas (with two more yet to come), and a mainstream historical, *Blind Tribute*, released in 2017).

Website: www.MariAnneChristie.com
Facebook: https://www.facebook.com/MariChristieAuthor
Twitter: https://twitter.com/mchristieauthor
Pinterest: http://www.pinterest.com/marichristie/

Other Books by Mariana Gabrielle

Masala Rajah Series

La Déesse Noire: The Black Goddess
Sired by a British peer, born of a paramour to Indian royalty, Kali Matai was destined from birth to enthrall England's most powerful men. She hadn't counted on becoming their pawn.

Lord Coventon's Concubines
When Lord Coventon returns to the Masala Rajah Gentleman's Retreat, his marriage a shambles and dreams of reuniting with Kali Matai naught but ancient fantasy, Madame Mayuri Falodiya has a plan to take his mind off his troubles…

Sailing Home Series

Royal Regard
When Bella Holsworthy returns to London after fifteen years roaming the globe, she faces unwelcome attentions from two wicked noblemen, the ton's spiteful censure, and the bitter realities of a woman alone in England.

'Tis Her Season: A Royal Regard Prequel Novella
Charlotte Amberly gives back a Christmas gift from her intended—the ring—then hares off to London to take husband-hunting into her own hands. Will she let herself be caught?

Shipmate: A Royal Regard Prequel Novella
For shy Bella Smithson, landing a husband seems laughable, so when shipping magnate Myron Clewes offers to buy her from her unfeeling family, she is obligated to accept his suit—and a long list of demands she might never be able to meet.

Never Kiss a Toad
(with Jude Knight)
Caught together in her father's bed, Sally and Toad are wrenched apart, to endure years of separation. But neither distance nor malice can destroy true love. (Being published episode by episode on Wattpad)

Writing as Mari Anne Christie

Blind Tribute
(Historical Fiction)

As America marches toward the Civil War, Harry Wentworth, gentleman of distinction and journalist of renown, finds his calls for peaceful resolution have fallen on deaf—nay, hostile—ears. As such, he must finally resolve his own moral quandary: comment on the war from his influential—and safe—position in Northern Society, or make a news story and a target of himself South of the Mason-Dixon Line, in a city haunted by a life he has long since left behind?

The Press Wrestles with the President
(Historical fiction novelette; in the Speakeasy Scribes anthology,
Rejoice and Resist)

If the White House wishes to discuss meaningful restrictions on the seditious press, the Fourth Estate should surely be allowed to send a champion. In this backstory vignette from *Blind Tribute*, Harry Wentworth, one of the America's most influential journalists, meets another reasonable moderate—and a primary adversary in the Executive Branch—when President Abraham Lincoln and his cabinet convene a meeting in the back room of the Final Draft Tavern.

About Jude Knight

Jude Knight writes stories to transport you to another time, another place, where you can enjoy adventure and romance, thrill to trials and challenges, uncover secrets and solve mysteries, and delight in a happy ending. Meet strong determined heroines, heroes who can appreciate a clever capable woman, villains you'll love to loathe, and all with a leavening of humour.

Follow Jude on Twitter
Like Jude on Facebook
Subscribe to Jude's blog
Subscribe to Jude's newsletter
Follow Jude on Goodreads

Jude's books are available in print and as ebooks at all major e-retailers. Find links, blurbs, excerpts, and special features at her website.

Regency books

Gingerbread Bride
(A novella in The Golden Redepennings series)
Mary runs from an unwanted marriage and finds adventure, danger and her girlhood hero, coming once more to her rescue.

Candle's Christmas Chair
(A novella in The Golden Redepennings series)
They are separated by social standing and malicious lies. How can he convince her to give their love another chance?

Farewell to Kindness
(Book 1 in The Golden Redepennings series)
Love is not always convenient. Anne and Rede have different goals, but when their enemies join forces, so must they.

A Raging Madness
(Book 2 in The Golden Redepenning series)
Their marriage is a fiction. Their enemies are all too real. The truth will need all the trust Ella and Alex can find.

A Baron for Becky
She was a fallen woman. How could the men who loved her help set her back on her feet?

Revealed in Mist
As spy and enquiry agent, Prue and David worked to uncover secrets, while hiding a few of their own.

Lord Calne's Christmas Ruby
Lalamani prefers her aunt's quiet village to fashionable London, its vicious harpies, and its importunate fortune hunters. Philip wishes she wasn't so rich, or he wasn't so poor. (novella.)

A Suitable Husband
A chef from the slums, however talented, is no fit mate for the cousin of a duke, however distant. But Cedrica can dream. (novella)

The Bluestocking and the Barbarian
How can a viscount under a cloud win the proper English maiden who holds his heart? Why would a handsome barbarian want a bluestocking past her prayers? (Coming 2018.)

Lunch-length reads: story collections

Hand-Turned Tales and Lost in the Tale
A double handful of short stories and novellas. Hand-Turned is free from most eretailers. Try the range of Jude's imagination one bite at a time, in a lunch-length read.

If Mistletoe Could Tell Tales

Stories to warm your heart with holiday romance. A collection of four novellas and two short-stories, all previously published.

Victorian books

Never Kiss a Toad
(with Mariana Gabrielle)

Caught together in her father's bed, Sally and Toad are wrenched apart, to endure years of separation. But neither distance nor malice can destroy true love. (Being published episode by episode on Wattpad)

Forged in Fire
(novella in the collection Never Too Late)

Burned in their youth, neither Tad nor Lotte expected to feel the fires of love. Until the inferno of a volcanic eruption sears away the lies of the past and frees them to forge a new future.

Contemporary books

A Family Christmas
(novella in the Authors of Main Street collection, Christmas Babies on Mains Street)

She's hiding out. He's coming home. And there'll be storms for Christmas.

Post-apocalyptic fiction

A Midwinter's Tale
(novella in the Speakeasy Scribes collection, *Rejoice and Resist*)

Verity Marchand is an orphan of time, her family tavern under the ice that grips Boston. When Verity's dreams lead her into a nightmare, she'll need a miracle—or the family cat—to save her.